RIVER OF LUCK

A TORN WORLDS NOVEL

DONNA AUGUSTINE

CHAPTER 1

R*iver*

The door to the basement opened, and I shifted farther into the shadows of my cell. It was too early for mealtime, which meant they were coming for something or someone else. They'd stopped experimenting on me a while ago, but every now and then, they'd have a guest who'd want to check me out, like the one last week. He was called Heiko, and when he'd touched me, smelled my skin, it felt like someone had taken a metal grater to my intestines.

Multiple footsteps and a female crying. I sagged into my spot, guilt warring with relief. They weren't here for me. They were bringing in a new human. I'd lost count of how many had come and gone in my time here. None of them lasted long. A few feedings at most before the vampires would drain them. Expendable lives, meaningless to the creatures that kept us, no more important than a bug squashed under their heel.

The steps grew louder as she came into sight, with flushed, chubby cheeks, shiny hair, and all the hallmarks of health. She might make it a couple of weeks if she could pull it together, but right now her tears were wetting the floor as the vampire dragged her past my cell.

She caught sight of me, and her sobbing went from a pathetic whimpering to full-blown nose-running melt-down. She assumed I was the fate waiting for her. She didn't realize her situation would be much worse. The vampires didn't feed on me, an unknown curiosity they were afraid to sample. She wouldn't be so lucky. She'd be dead soon.

Or maybe she was the lucky one.

I closed my eyes, trying to forget about the crying as they threw her in one of the cells with the other humans. My mind took me somewhere else, away from the cold stone floor that puddled when it rained, away from the smell of mildew, sickness, and death.

This wasn't a dank basement anymore but a meadow with birds chirping and the wind rustling through trees, carrying the scent of flowers.

And dark clouds with obsidian specks of light...

My eyes snapped open again, seeking out the cracks in the window for a hint of what I'd seen in my mind. Something was about to happen, but what?

I didn't have to wait long before there was a loud bang overhead, followed by thumps and then screams. The vampire who'd brought the new girl slammed the cell shut and dashed back upstairs, the sounds of screaming and things thudding and crashing growing louder.

There were loud footsteps crisscrossing overhead, as if utter chaos was breaking out. A growl split the air, so loud it nearly shook the foundation. That noise wasn't a vampire.

Shifters?

There'd been rumors that the pact that held the shifter-vampire alliance together, the one that had enabled them to take over the U.S., had been growing tenuous. Even locked away down here, I'd heard snippets of gossip, talk of the inevitable war. Had it finally come?

Everyone in the basement had grown quiet, including the new hysterical girl. Something very bad was happening, and we didn't need it to spill over to us. The enemy of your enemy wasn't always your friend. The shifters had as large a part in suppressing humans as the vampires, and my kind hadn't fared any better.

The new girl let out another wail. One of the women in the same cell walked over, laying a soothing hand on her back. The girl kept crying loudly, as if she'd cracked.

One of the men loomed over her. "Shut the fuck up before you get us all killed." He spoke in a hushed voice, but it didn't strip away any of the violence he promised.

She quieted down and curled into the woman's arms.

Upstairs, the screams slowed as well, the running and thumping turning back into brisk walking and loud voices.

The door to the basement creaked open and the lights were flipped on.

I squinted, my eyes unaccustomed to the brightness.

"Jobo, put some pants on. There's a bunch of humans down there already freaked out, and I don't need them all screaming," a male by the top of the stairs said.

Definitely shifters.

A young man walked downstairs, his russet hair in disarray. He had jeans on, but his torso and feet were bare, and there were red droplets and splatters all over his flesh. Another young man followed behind him in sweatpants and similar remnants of blood.

The shifter's face skewed as he took in the scene of the

cells filled with humans. Or maybe it was the smell that disgusted him. After a while, you became nose-blind to the odor of mildew mixing with the latrine buckets, until you saw the horror on a newcomer's expression.

The sweatpants-clad shifter with raven hair made a gagging noise as he followed his friend.

"What the fuck, Frankie? I hate when they do this shit," Jobo said.

Frankie scanned the place, found a hook with several keys, and tossed them to Jobo.

"Start down that end. Let's get them out and get out of here before I gag," Frankie said. He made his way to the closest cell that was packed full of humans, including the new girl, who was still sobbing quietly. He tried several keys before finding the right one and pulling the door open.

"Come on, we're letting you out. You're all free." Frankie spoke like someone who had said his lines repeatedly.

No one moved. Typically if you left this cell, you had fifty-fifty odds of living to see the next morning.

"You can come out. We're not vampires. My name is Frankie. I'm a shifter, and I don't have all day for this. You can leave the cell or stay, but I've got other things to do." Frankie was either the best actor I'd ever seen or clearly didn't give a shit what these people did. My money was on the latter.

The others must've had a similar read. The wailing girl broke for the exit first, followed by a stampede from the rest.

"Go outside. There'll be someone there to direct you where to go next," Frankie said, sounding a little like an underpaid cruise director.

Another two cells opened, and with no cajoling needed, the humans fled outside.

They both finished up in front of my cell. I was on my feet, halfway back, trying to keep a buffer in between us.

Frankie toyed with the key in the lock for a minute or so. My cell was always jammed. Half of my meals had ended up thrown on the floor because of it.

"Why are you in one by yourself?" Jobo asked as Frankie kept trying to force the rusted metal to open.

"I don't know." My heart was thumping so hard that I was afraid it would give out before I was let out.

Frankie sighed, and Jobo tried, fidgeting with it. Just as my fear that they'd give up and leave me began to grow, the lock gave out and the cell door opened.

Frankie waved me forward. "Come on. You're free. Time to leave."

Frankie waited for me as Jobo began making his way out of the basement.

One part of me wanted to run past Frankie and the other didn't want to get too close, knowing what might happen. It was the same thing that had landed me here.

"Come on already," Frankie said, watching me.

His friend at the bottom of the stairs turned back around. "Do vampires bake?" Jobo asked Frankie, looking confounded.

"You smell apple pie too?" Frankie said.

"Yeah," Jobo said. "Smells so good I'm getting hungry."

Shit.

Shit, shit, shit.

With a deep breath and a leap of faith, I exited the cell, hoping they wouldn't catch on.

Frankie stepped in front of me, stopping me from getting to the stairs. Everything I'd feared showed in his expression. Even as dirty and grimy as I was, they knew the smell was coming from me. It had been my downfall last time, and would be again.

"Hang on a second. What are you?" Frankie moved closer, his nostrils flaring. Odds were he wouldn't recognize my race, just that it was different. This was a setback but not an absolute disaster.

"I'm River," I said.

"Not who. *What?*" Jobo asked, coming closer and smelling the air around me as well. His face scrunched up with a thousand questions.

Even as young and inexperienced as they might be, they knew something was off.

"I'm human," I said, pretending to be as confused as they were.

Frankie nodded and moved out of my way. There was still hope, but it was slim.

I walked up and through the mayhem of the main floor. Shifters, still in their beast form, were patrolling the house, probably looking for missed vampires. I'd seen shifters from afar, but not up close, like this. They were huge in their beast forms, tightly muscled and with fangs. Most had to be seven feet tall. They had so much going on that they'd forget about the odd girl and move on.

I kept heading toward the door. A shifter slowed down and moved closer, sniffing loud enough to be audible.

"Keep it moving, Charlie," Frankie said, stepping in between us and ushering me outside.

It was a crisp autumn evening with a huge harvest moon lighting the landscape. The smell of wet leaves and fresh dirt was the most beautiful perfume ever created. At least if I died tonight, I'd felt the fresh air on my skin one last time.

"Stay there," Frankie said, pointing to a spot off to the side.

The place was crawling with shifters, and all the human captives were being shuttled onto an old yellow school bus.

Frankie and Jobo walked a few steps away but didn't bother to keep their voices down.

"What do you think?" Jobo asked. They both kept looking at me.

"We can't put her on the bus with the others until we get Dante over here, just in case."

Dante. The name was familiar. He was the alpha of a nearby pack, and the vampires had spoken of him being a possible problem. Looked like they'd gotten part of that right but had underestimated how much of one he truly was. From the clear wreckage of this place, and the dead vampire parts I'd stepped over on the way out, he hadn't pulled his punches.

I crossed my arms in front of me as the chill seeped through my threadbare t-shirt, the same one I'd been wearing when I came to this place. I didn't care. The fresh air was better than any shelter I'd gotten in that hell.

"Stay with her," Frankie said right before he took off, probably in search of this Dante.

I tracked Frankie's passage through the crowd as he approached one of the scariest beasts in the clearing. He was one of the largest, all lean muscles with a smattering of fur, and the meanest looking of them all, which said something in this group.

He started to shift to his human form, which was almost as intimidating as the beast. He was still over six feet, with blood marring his tanned skin and something gooey in his black hair. His dark gaze met mine across the clearing, and a shiver shot through me, this one having nothing to do with the cold.

Even if the amount of blood on his skin hadn't warned me, there was something even more alarming in his eyes. He had the hard, cold stare of a killer, equipped with a body to execute his desires, and it was instantly obvious he was about to become a big problem for me.

CHAPTER 2

D*ante*

This particular hive of vampires had been causing issues for way too long, with humans disappearing from the nearby town—humans I hadn't hated. The pact between shifters and vampires, the one that held our two races together, decreed that humans were beneath contempt. That didn't mean it was smart. It was bad business, in my opinion. There were too many of them and not enough of us.

Frankie walked over to me as I shifted back into human form, blood splattered over my skin. He might be young to be my second, but he had a loyal streak a mile wide, plus brilliant instincts that seemed next to perfect.

Except right now he was looking stumped.

"What's wrong? Do we have a problem?" Everyone else was moving around, doing their job as if the attack had gone off without a hitch.

"The vampires are all dead, but when we let out the humans, we found an unexpected…" His gaze shot across the lawn. "We found something…*odd*."

"What's odd?" Everything about our life at this point was odd. We were out in the open as a species. We were supposed to be in a pact with vampires, our mortal enemies, except we were secretly at war. Odd was our day-to-day existence.

"Technically it's a female. I'm not sure what to do with her." Frankie was scratching his jaw.

A human female? That was the issue?

"I'm sure you'll figure it out." I began walking around the perimeter, having more important things to do.

Frankie jogged to keep up with me as I surveyed the building, making sure there had been nothing missed. This place had to be scoured for any potential information that could help us going forward before it was burned to the ground, the evidence destroyed.

"I don't know if I will. She's pretty weird," he said. "I don't know if I want to make a call on her without you checking her out."

"She's a human?" I asked, scanning the trees. Some of these places had surveillance rigged up and connected to the cloud. Every mission was inviting an open war we weren't ready for, but if I didn't try to keep the vampire numbers down, when the war did come, we'd have no way of winning. They were becoming the supernatural version of rabbits lately, except instead of fucking their way to numbers, they were biting.

"Well, she's definitely not a vampire." His gaze kept shooting back across the lawn.

"Then what's the issue? If she's a human, ask her if she wants to go to the sanctuary or scare the shit out of her about talking and let her go. I don't have to tell you all this.

You know the drill." This wasn't the first raid or the first stash of humans. At this point, I'd be more surprised if there *weren't* a few humans locked away somewhere. Vampires kept stashes of people in the basement the way humans kept chips in the cabinet.

"That's not quite clear either. She's not a vampire, but I'm not sure she's a human. That's the problem. I can't tell, and neither can Jobo. We found her in the basement in a cell by herself. She definitely wasn't here willingly, but she's not exactly looking at us like we're her saviors—not that it means that much." Frankie ruffled his hair.

At this point, it was becoming easier to check out the female than continue this conversation. Over on the other side of the property, recently freed humans were being loaded onto the bus. One female stood out immediately, like a jolt of color on a black-and-white canvas.

She was slender, overly so, as if she'd been in that base-ment a long time. Her long tawny hair hung in nappy locks, like it hadn't seen a brush in months. Her t-shirt might've once been white but was now a dingy gray with mottled stains, including blood, and hung from her shoul-ders like it was on a wire hanger. Her jeans weren't in any better shape, and her feet were bare and dirty. She looked like she'd break in a strong wind, but her back was ramrod straight.

I walked over as she watched me unflinchingly. She tilted her head back, meeting my stare with bright eyes the color of light beryl. They dominated a delicate face covered in grime. The shade wasn't impossible in the human race, but it wasn't common either, not with the way they nearly glimmered.

But beyond the fire in her eyes, her scent was what slammed the door shut on there being a remote chance of her being human. Even as filthy as she was, there was an overpowering sweetness to her scent, an aroma reminiscent of warm cinnamon apples baking in the oven. I'd smelled it the second I walked into the vampire's house, but had written it off. It wasn't a perfume or a chemical re-creation. I'd never picked up a scent like this from a human, or any other race, but it was something coming from who or *what* she was.

I tilted my head, signaling Jobo and Frankie to give us a little space.

Her narrowing eyes shot to Jobo's retreating back for a flicker, but that was all that was needed. By the looks of her, she hadn't been well treated by the vampires, but she didn't appear to be a fan of shifters either, or at least not us. Her attention shot back to me fast enough to signal who she thought was the bigger threat.

"What are you?" I asked.

"I'm River. Your man wouldn't let me get on the bus with everyone else, and I'd like to know why." Chin up, she stared at me as if she were the one in the position to ask questions.

She probably hadn't had a good meal in months, maybe years. She had one foot sitting on top of the other, as if her feet were frozen, and there was a smattering of goosebumps up and down her arms.

"He wouldn't let you on the bus because that's where the *humans* go." I moved closer. The moon was full, but seeing her wasn't the issue. I didn't need a bright light to know something was wrong, but damned if I could say what it was.

Not only was I a werewolf, a shifter, I was an *alpha*. I could spot an animal running through the forest on a new moon more than five hundred yards away and name the creature before I saw it. My senses were better than the best of my race. But I couldn't label something I'd never encountered before.

"Which is why I should be on it." Her stare was full of venom.

"You aren't human, though," I said, adding a low rumble into my voice, daring her to lie to me again. "What are you? You can tell me now or wait and tell me later. Either way, you'll tell me." I leaned a little closer, just in case she was too slow to realize the threat I posed.

She crossed her arms, being either obstinate or cold. Experience led me to believe it had nothing to do with the temperature.

She didn't stay silent long.

"Tell you what? You're the one who seems to have all the answers. If I'm not human, *you* tell me what I am." She shrugged, her nonchalance in strong contrast to the heat in her eyes and the anger seeping into her voice.

There were a million other things that needed to be done right now, and none of them included arguing with this odd female. I wanted to grab her by the shoulders and rattle her until she spilled all the answers. There was a strange strength about her that promised a longer fight, maybe to the death, if I wanted something she wasn't ready to give.

I grabbed her wrist, since her heartbeat was so soft that I could barely hear it with all the chaos and movement around us. She immediately pulled at my grasp, but I held her until I got what I wanted. Her pulse was racing, and so erratic it was hard to tell if it was adrenaline or if she had some kind of condition. I let her go. It didn't tell me anything that helped identify her, and there were a million other things to handle. Frankie's dilemma was becoming much clearer.

She wrapped her hand around where I'd grabbed her,

eyes narrowed and accusing, as if she couldn't fathom how I dared to touch her.

I softened my tone, trying a different angle. "Can you at least tell me how long you've been here? I'd like to let one of my doctors look you over. You don't look like you're in great shape."

Hope flared in her eyes and guilt swelled in my chest. If she wasn't going to be forthcoming, I'd have to get my information however I could.

She looked down at her feet. There was the subtlest shake of her head as she said, "I'm not sure." She spoke so softly that I wasn't sure if she meant to answer me. "What's today's date?" she asked, looking up at me, her voice slightly louder.

"October first," I answered, not allowing myself to pity this girl. It wasn't usually an issue, but it was already clear she'd been living in that hell for longer than my sanity would've lasted.

"Ten months," she said, staring at the ground again, as if she couldn't quite believe her answer. She jerked her gaze back to mine. "But I'm fine. I can go with the others. I don't need a doctor."

Ten fucking months and no puncture wounds on her neck? They weren't feeding off her, and they hadn't killed her. They'd kept her alive, barely. The vampires didn't keep anything that wasn't useful alive.

That answer told me more than she realized. If the vampires had kept her, she must have some sort of worth that wasn't obvious. She couldn't be released, not without answers.

Frankie had moved farther away, directing shifters, but Jobo was still nearby waiting.

The second I turned my back on River, she took the

opportunity to head toward the bus the humans were boarding.

I wrapped an arm around her waist, hauling her back. "Oh no, you're not going with them."

"You said I could leave." Her voice was breaking, as if I'd offered her the ticket to freedom after all this time, and then ripped it up before she could snatch it from my fingers.

I dropped her back at the same spot. "No, I didn't. And I won't until you tell me what you are."

I waited, expecting to see tears. All I got was anger so thick it nearly roiled off her.

"I'm human," she said, but her words lacked the same energy of before, as if she knew the farce had come to an end.

I signaled for Jobo to near. "She's not going with the rest of them. She's coming back with us for a while. Keep an eye on her until we leave."

Jobo was one of my tougher guys, someone who wouldn't typically be wasted on a baby-sitting detail, but he seemed to realize things weren't that clear-cut. He watched her with an intensity that was usually reserved for hundred-year-old vampires.

I put some distance between myself and River, something about her sticking in my craw more than it should.

Frankie finished with another shifter and then headed over to me. "Do you know what she is?"

"She's not a shifter, vampire, human, or anything I've ever encountered." There was no clear box to put her in, but I'd find one, even if I needed to build it myself.

"What do you want to do with her?"

What *was* I going to do with her? It would be so much easier to shove her on the bus, with the rest of the humans, but there were too many creatures in this world that had been rearing their ugly heads lately. She might not appear to be a threat—or an asset, for that matter—but some of the most vicious things I'd ever encountered were wrapped up in cute packaging. I didn't have the luxury of guessing wrong.

"For now, drive her back with you. Bring Jobo along, just in case."

"You think I'm going to need backup?" Frankie's eyes went wide as he looked past me to River, as if we'd discovered some rare creature capable of killing with a glance.

"I'm not sure, but until we get a better read on her, and what she is, we're going to use caution. She's your responsibility until I figure out what to do with her."

"Okay," he said, and started walking toward her as if he'd been told he was taking home a class pet or something.

"Frankie," I called.

He turned back to me. "Yeah?"

"Get her a blanket and some food. I don't want her dead before we figure it out."

And that *was* the only reason I cared. I couldn't have her die before I learned her riddle or unloaded her.

CHAPTER 3

R *iver*

The door to the bus full of humans closed, and my insides tightened as it pulled away. When these shifters raided the vampire lair, I'd thought I was going to die. Considering I'd been waiting for death in that cell for nearly a year, the amount of dread and fear that flooded me had taken me aback.

Then they'd let the humans out of the cells, telling them it would be okay and that they were free. I'd gone from the depths of despair to a high that you could only experience having lived through hell. They'd come to my cell, and just as they had with the humans, they'd told me I could leave. Finally free, after all this time, and it hadn't lasted more than a few seconds.

And now here was Frankie again, walking over with a blanket held out, as if he were still helping me.

I looked at his hand, ignoring his offering, preferring to freeze to death.

The bus's taillights were almost out of view as Frankie pointed in the direction of a camo-painted pickup.

"You're coming with us," he said, as if I were too dim to have figured that out on my own.

The bus was gone from sight. Other trucks were loading up and moving out, and yet my two escorts were standing there, waiting, afraid to touch me.

I turned, giving them the haughtiest stare I could muster, which was fairly impressive.

"Really? It takes two of you?" I raised a brow and then shook my head.

They both flushed. Jobo looked at Frankie, as if to silently ask, *Are we idiots?*

I didn't bother fighting. There was no point. I'd go with this group and find a way out later. I turned and headed toward the pickup, knowing they were following.

I sat in the middle of the seat as they plastered themselves to the doors on either side. They were putting in a lot of effort to keep from touching me.

"How long did the vampires have you?" Frankie asked a few minutes after he'd gotten the truck on the road.

"Too long," I answered, bitter that I'd fallen for that question before. Dante had been sneaky. I hadn't seen the trap coming, but damned if I'd answer another question without thinking on it long and hard. From here on out, anything else I gave these shifters was going to be hard won.

"Look, I know you might not want to come with us, but it won't be as bad as what you just went through. I promise," Frankie said.

"Sure." He spoke like a man who'd probably always been free. A cage was a cage. Would I be better fed in this new one? Maybe. Was it something to celebrate? I'd hold off on the party invites.

This was simply starting off as a politer version of what I'd already experienced. The vampires asked me what I was too, and I'd declined to answer them as well. Then they'd locked me away. The storyline was following a very familiar arc.

After the vampires' initial curiosity passed and their tests hadn't given them answers, they forgot about me. The days had rolled into weeks, into months. I'd lost nearly the entirety of my twenty-sixth year in that basement. Considering that my kind could live centuries, it burned slightly less, but not by much. We might have centuries, but very few made it that long. I wouldn't lose another year of my freedom.

"Seriously. Dante gave me responsibility for you. I'll make sure you're well treated," Frankie said, as if he were conferring some great privilege on me.

I shook my head and rolled my eyes, neither of which he probably noticed, as he was driving.

Jobo did and smirked, looking out the window as if he wanted to laugh. At least I wasn't the only one who realized Frankie sounded like an idiot.

"You don't talk a lot," Frankie said, trying one last time.

I let out a sigh, trying to keep it inaudible but not succeeding. The kid didn't seem that bad, and he *was* going to be my top jailor in charge. Making the tiniest effort wouldn't be the stupidest move on my part and might help grease the future cell door hinges a little.

"Nothing interesting to say." That was the most I could offer up at the moment, but at least I'd answered.

"Some reason, I doubt that," Jobo said.

Luckily, everyone stopped talking after that. The only

communication was when Jobo reached into the glove compartment and handed me a protein bar.

I declined, the bile in my throat too thick to swallow past. With them sitting on either side, I'd even lost my option for jumping out of the truck. It probably wouldn't have made a difference anyway. There were trucks in front of us and trucks behind. My abilities would've been stretched thin with so many people, and in this weakened state and this setup? I was utterly useless.

My situation was still looking up, though. The last ten months, it felt like my soul had been slowly ripped and shredded into pieces. It was only my sheer pride that had kept me from sobbing day in and day out. But even though I hadn't made it on that bus, I believed Frankie when he said things wouldn't be that bad for me. I'd bide my time and be free soon enough.

Many years ago I'd made a promise to never give up, never quit. There weren't many of my kind left. I didn't have the luxury of giving up—not that I ever would.

A few hours later, we pulled through iron gates into what looked like an old college campus. There'd been a well-known university in this area before the vampires and shifters took over. I'd never seen it, but this fit the description. Stately buildings were spread across the lawn, ivy growing up some of the larger buildings' stately facades.

Frankie pulled the truck in front of one of the largest structures and got out, motioning for me to follow. I took it all in, from the distance to the gates, to the shifters. There were quite a few walking about, as trucks had pulled in before and after us, unloading in various spots. I couldn't tell a shifter from a human, but I'd bet they were *all* shifters. If I was going to survive and escape, I needed to see as much as I could, gather as much intelligence as possible.

Jobo was asking Frankie if he should come as well as I stood silently, not making a fuss, but noting everything around me.

The entire campus was probably walled off with that same high brick wall. The buildings were all masonry construction. It was a well-thought-out pick for a stronghold.

"River, this way," Frankie called from the stairs of the building. He'd already lost his companion. This might end up being easier than I'd even imagined.

I turned toward a solitary Frankie, acting the obedient captive. No need to get his hackles up or give him a reason to watch me closer.

He held the front door open for me, as if I were a guest. "This building is used for all different purposes and gatherings, business meetings and such. Sometimes members from other packs will stay here when they're visiting for a while," he explained as we walked down the halls of the grand building. The signs had mostly been taken down, but there was a random name plaque on a door here and there with "dean" of this or that.

We took the stairs to the third floor and continued down a long hallway. There was a window that looked into another room.

"This was an old science lab," he said.

And my new cell. He'd been right about one thing: it wasn't nearly as bad as what I'd left, with a bed, a nightstand, and a desk on the other side. It also looked like there was a bathroom. But best of all? There was a window with drapes covering it.

He walked through the door, waving a hand around the room. "You can get settled here. Dante is going to want you to see the doc after he finishes up with the injured."

"I don't need a doctor. I'm fine." I followed him in, knowing there wasn't a choice.

"He'll probably want you to be checked to be on the safe side."

Sure he would. Doubt the doctor would figure out the mystery that was me, but each new contact upped the odds.

"I'll be back in a few with something to eat and a change of clothes."

I nodded, refusing to thank him. If he'd let me go, I'd be able to get my own things.

He walked out of the room, and I made my way over to the wall, my hand trembling, hesitating to pull back the curtains in case there was nothing but brick on the other side. I yanked the panel to the side, and then the other.

Even in the dark, I could see the trees, and the night sky was ablaze with stars.

I swiped an arm across my face, refusing to shed tears over a stupid window, but they wouldn't stop. For the first time in nearly a year, I was going to see the sun again.

There was a pile of clothes when I came out of the bathroom, the shower having been too much of a temptation to resist. I threw on an oversized sweatshirt and a pair of boy's pants with the excitement of a woman donning her wedding dress. If there were matches, the dingy t-shirt and jeans would've been torched. A good kick and toss into the trash can had to suffice.

I was grabbing another chicken wing from the heaps of food Frankie had left when there was a knock at the door.

"May I come in?" someone asked as they cracked it slightly.

"Sure," I answered, going along with the farce that I had a choice.

I glanced at the older gentleman, noticing certain tells about the shifters, like their gait. Even older, as this one appeared, his stride was lithe and more youthful than a human's would've been at a corresponding age.

"My name is Dr. Farrat. Dante asked me to check on you."

Again with the politeness. It was a hard act to pull off when you were applying it to a person who was locked in a room.

"Thank you for coming by, but I don't really need a doctor. I feel fine."

His smile faltered. Clearly he wasn't used to being put in situations such as this.

He had one hand on his bag as he glanced back to the door. He looked at me again, like he was in some sort of medical purgatory.

What were the odds he'd recognize my kind? As unlikely as the others, but with each new face, those odds narrowed a bit more, and my heart rate rose.

If my take on Dante had been correct, this examination was going to happen whether either of us wanted it to or not. Might as well not torture the old guy completely. I could stall and give him a few scraps of knowledge, plus, it might help me a bit as well. He just didn't know it yet.

"If it'll make you feel better to check me out..." I shrugged. "Should I sit or stand?"

"You can sit in that chair if you'd like." He nodded too enthusiastically, giving the sense he wasn't used to unwilling patients, or how to handle them.

I kept my posture and expression as calm as I could,

considering I wasn't sure how my vitals would compare to humans or shifters.

He felt for my pulse, and his brows got a hair closer.

"Little fast, but that's to be expected." He nodded, trying to reassure me all was okay.

He had no idea.

He moved on to my blood pressure, squinting a little. He hummed, pulled out his stethoscope, and listened to my heart.

"Do you have a..." He was looking upward, as if he couldn't figure out a condition that would make the rhythm of my heart acceptable.

"A what?" I asked, as if I couldn't fathom what he was talking about.

"Nothing. It's all good." He put his things back in his bag and took a needle out. "Would you mind if I took a blood sample?"

And this was where the ruse was going to come to a close.

"Yes. I would. I have a terrible fear of needles." I got up from the chair and put half a room of distance between us. "The last time I was poked at, very bad things happened." I let out a loud sigh and shivered.

"I can promise you I'm quite experienced. I'd never hurt you," he said.

His kind eyes made me believe he was speaking the truth, not that it mattered. No one would be getting a sample of my blood unless they were running me through the heart to get it.

"It's not you. It's what happened to the person who took it. It's just..." I shook my head again. "You seem like a very nice man, is all."

He put the needle back in his bag without a fight. "You know, you look dehydrated. It's probably for the best to wait on that anyway." He scooped up his things, heading to the door. "Let me know if you need anything else."

"I will, and I'm sure your kindness will be rewarded. Thank you."

The door closed on the nice doctor, another hurdle cleared. I went back to the inspection of my new, plusher cell, noticing Frankie had left a bag of books and magazines as well.

This stopover hadn't been in my plans, but it didn't seem like it would be hard time, as long as I got out of here before Dante got too nosy. That one was definitely going to be a problem.

CHAPTER 4

D*ante*

Frankie walked into the storage room where all the documents we'd found at the vampire haven were getting piled up. His hair was shooting up in every direction. He had a habit of repeatedly running his hands through his locks when things weren't going smoothly but hadn't achieved this level of disarray in ages. The crazier the hair, the rougher the seas.

I gave the other guys in the room a nod toward the door. A couple of them looked at Frankie's hair as they left and shook their heads on the way out.

"You get her settled?" I asked, betting this was going to be about River.

"Yeah, she's in. I just dropped off some clothes and food, too."

He walked farther into the room, tapping on almost every box as he did.

"When's Doc going to see her?" I asked, trying to ignore the level of fidgeting. "I don't want her keeling over dead before he gets there."

"He knows to report to you as soon as he's done." He circled the room again, looking very interested in the box lids.

"Is there a problem?" I asked.

He turned and blurted out, "How long do you think you're going to be keeping her here?"

"Depends on how long it takes her to talk and what her answers are."

"Then maybe you could let her go sometime soon?" He crossed his arms.

"I can't answer that question. I don't have enough information." It was becoming clear Frankie might not be the best man for this job, but who else did I trust as much to both take care of her and not cross the line? No one.

"But it's not out of the realm of possibility that she could be released in a day or so if things go well?" Frankie asked.

"I highly doubt it. Even if she spilled her guts tonight, I'd want to verify her story before I did anything."

I grabbed another box, stacking it with the rest that would have to be sorted. Frankie stood there, watching me.

"What's your concern, Frankie? We're not harming her, so what's the issue?"

He leaned against the wall, looking like we'd lost the battle tonight, instead of having no fatalities. "She looks like she's had a rough go of it, and I don't think she's a bad sort. I don't want to put her through any more than she's already been through."

This girl was going to be a problem. There was something about her that made you want to help her. I'd sensed it too, but she seemed to be taking Frankie down in one fell swoop. He was losing all objectivity, and she hadn't been here a day.

"You don't know what she's been through. We don't know why they had her. They weren't feeding off her, but they didn't let her go or kill her. She might be a monster for all we know, with a long list of atrocities." And unlike him, I didn't have the luxury of being soft. When I made mistakes, the pack paid for them.

"I'd hate to think we're piling on an innocent. She was so sad as she looked out the fucking window, like she hasn't seen the sky in a decade, and—"

I spun on him. "And you don't think that might've been for your benefit? She knew she was being watched?"

He straightened off the wall as the idea of being duped actually entered his mind for a second.

"Frankie, she's comfortable in a room and being given everything she needs. She's not being tortured. All she has to do is tell us what she is." Tomorrow I'd make a list of other possible candidates for the job of guardian. Hopefully she wouldn't be here long enough for me to need a replacement, but I'd learned long ago to always have a Plan B, C, and D ready.

For now, Frankie seemed like he was coming around to some common sense.

"You're right. It's a hell of a lot better than the place we broke her out of." His trademark grin was returning. "Oh, and you're not going to believe this. You know how I've been looking for a Fender Springhill guitar for my collection? After I got done getting River settled, I saw Logan on my way over here, and he'd found one in the stash we got from the vampire raid. He put it aside for me."

"See? If you were doing something so bad, would you be so lucky?" I asked, playing into his superstitious nature, even if I didn't buy any of that crap myself.

"Yeah, you're probably right." He left, looking more at ease, but I'd still be making that list of replacements.

* * *

I nodded to Marshall, who was posted outside of River's door, and headed over to Doc. He was watching River through the glass, stroking his jaw.

"Thanks for checking her out, Doc. What do you think?"

He let out a low whistle as he continued to watch her through the one-way mirror. "I'm not sure what to think. Her blood pressure is too high, but that could be explained because of the duress and strain she's been under. But..." He looked down and shook his head.

"Her scent?" I offered. After the day I'd had, waiting for him to spit it out was taking twice as long as I had the patience for.

"Oh, her scent is definitely *way* off. But no, not that."

"Then what?"

River was standing by the window, staring out at the moon, her hair falling in soft waves, varying streaks of light blond to warm honey brown.

She was prettier than I'd figured, and would probably be even more so after her cheeks weren't so hollowed out and the dark smudges under her eyes faded. They'd had her trapped in that musty basement without a shred of light for a year. It was shocking she wasn't a babbling idiot by this point. That kind of treatment would've broken some of my toughest men. I didn't have the luxury of feeling bad for her, but if I did...

Doc squinted as he too watched her. "It was her heart-beat. It wasn't the normal 'ba-boom, ba-boom' you normally hear." He patted his chest in time to the heartbeat he'd expected.

At least there was one. She was technically among the living. In this day and age, a heartbeat wasn't a given.

"What did it sound like?"

"It was scattered, all over the place and way quieter than normal, like a tiny rock band lives in her chest, but almost muted. I'm not sure I could replicate the sound, it was so—*odd*."

"Ever hear anything like it before?" I rested my shoulder on the frame of the window, watching her move about the room, looking so innocent and fragile.

"Nothing even close," he said, sounding mesmerized.

I refused to let myself get lured in by some siren's song, but there was something about her that drew the eye. It took me a few moments to jerk my attention away from her, to realize that Marshall had joined us, staring at her too.

I stepped away from the window, breaking off every-one's fixation on River.

"Doc, let me know what information you get from her blood," I said.

"Uh, I didn't take any," he replied like someone who knew they'd given the incorrect answer.

Marshall was suddenly only interested in getting back to his post outside the door.

"Why not?" I asked.

"She didn't seem inclined to give me a sample, and considering her health, I didn't see the harm in letting her have a few days to get back on her feet."

A different day, a different doctor, I might've told him to go back in and get a sample. That didn't mean he'd do it. One of the reasons I liked Doc so much was he stood by his principles and instincts. One of the biggest issues I had with him was his unwillingness to follow orders if they deviated from said principles and instincts.

"A couple of days," I said.

He nodded noncommittally and took off while the getting was good.

I glanced back at River, and she was looking at where I stood, as if there wasn't a mirror on her side. Physically, she'd been through hell, but that look in her eyes said she hadn't given up the fight. I'd seen that look in my toughest shifters.

Still, she needed to understand the way things would be working here. I opened the door and walked in her room. She immediately fixed her attention on me, watching every move as I entered her space, as if I'd lunge at her. I was a predator by nature, and anything smaller or weaker would be stupid not to recognize it, and yet it bothered me that she was looking at me that way.

"You can sit. I'm not going to touch you."

She stayed by the window, ignoring my words. It was a smart move. She didn't know me.

I grabbed the chair from the desk, swung it around, and took a seat, waiting for her to settle down, finding myself slightly swayed to Frankie's opinion and wanting to throw the door open, and tell her to leave. As the alpha, I didn't have the option of softness.

She watched me and then leaned against the wall, the lines of her form smoothing out a bit.

"You need to tell me what you are. If you don't tell me, I'll figure it out anyway, but it will take longer." I leaned my forearms on my legs and clasped my hands together, hoping she'd see the logic.

"I already told you what I am." The stubborn set of her chin said she wouldn't be cooperating anytime soon.

Those huge, beautiful eyes were glaring in my direction, but her scent drew me even more. With her skin freshly scrubbed, she was filling the room with this intoxicating aroma that was almost addictive.

"That you're human?" I did nothing to hide my derision, and hardened my voice to let her know I wasn't fucking around. "I will be getting that blood sample, and you will tell me what you are if you ever want to get out of this place."

She leaned back against the wall, continuing to try to roast me alive with her stare. It should've pissed me off, but it made me like the chit more. I'd seen where they'd kept her, and yet she stared at me like she could kill me if she chose. Full-grown shifters didn't provoke me the way she was now.

I got up, knowing I had to leave before I tried to nibble on her skin to see if she tasted as good as she smelled.

"Knock on the door when you're ready to talk. The guard will be waiting. And when the doctor comes back, you will give him a blood sample or I'll hold you down while he collects it."

She didn't speak, just continued to give me the evil eye. I walked out, wondering if whatever she was had some strange pull on werewolves or just me. Either way, I needed to get her out of here.

I called up a fellow alpha that I'd recently made an alliance with.

"Cole, I need a favor. I need you to come and take someone off my hands. It's a bit of an unusual situation."

CHAPTER 5

R *iver*

How to Live Your Best Life, Positive Thinking, How to Succeed and Thrive...

There had to be something better in this box of books than this crap. Did Frankie think this was some sort of self-improvement retreat? Did he notice he locked the door every time he left?

I dug a little deeper, past the next couple of layers of books in the box, skipping over anything that had an ocean or sky on the cover, and finally found some good stuff: *Dune* by Frank Herbert, a couple of oldies but goodies by Stephen King, and, last but not least, Anne Rice. This would definitely work. Another couple of layers down and there were some shirtless men. Now those looked like they might pass the time nicely.

There was a knock at the door, and the shirtless men got buried.

"Hello?" I called hesitantly when no one appeared.

A petite woman with a wiry build, gray curls, and strong features walked in. She could've been forty or eighty. The way werewolves aged, it was hard to know for sure.

"My name is Henrietta. Frankie said you were here. Figured I'd come by and bring you a few things to help you get more comfortable." She put a bag down by the nightstand. "I didn't know what size you were, so I brought an assortment."

"Thanks."

She glanced around, taking in the pile of clothes sitting on the desk. "Not many drawers and a bit barren, huh?" she asked.

"Seems the decorator was more into a utilitarian style." Did this woman realize I had bigger problems than décor?

"Dante says he's not letting you go until you tell him what you are." She scoffed and waved her hand. "I'm not going to lie and say you smell human, but you also don't have an evil feel about you."

I nodded. That she hadn't asked any questions yet hadn't gone unnoticed. They might still come, but the way she was surveying the room, it didn't seem a high priority at the moment.

She moved about the area, adjusting the lamp on the nightstand and then fixing the drapes into neat folds, before putting her hands on her hips. "I should've brought some flowers. There are some beautiful Montauk daisies in bloom right now. I'll bring them tomorrow," she continued, not really asking me at all.

She looked around again. "Maybe a nicer blanket and some more pillows as well." She pointed to the corner. "A big couch in that corner, too, right under the windows."

"That would be great. Thank you." I didn't need a bull's-eye floating over her head to see a possible ally when one smacked me in the face. But why? If she followed through on all she was saying, which I believed she would, I'd have other opportunities to ask.

She turned back to me. "You might as well be comfortable, not that you're going to be here that long. Dante's not a bad man. He'll come around and let you go soon enough."

She might know him better than me, but there was a veil of distortion that seemed to be happening with this woman and him. I'd seen the look in Dante's eyes. He wasn't letting me just walk out of here.

"Are you his mother?"

She smiled warmly. "His aunt. He's my sister's boy, but she's off in a different pack."

Aunt. That made sense.

"Can I ask you another question?"

"Ask whatever you want," she said, peeking into the bathroom, probably trying to inventory soap or something.

"Why is it that there's a group like this? In other places, the shifters all live spread out."

"Dante thinks it's safer if there's an attack. They can't pin anyone down alone and pick off our numbers."

They were the vampires, obviously. And maybe me.

"Yeah, well, Dante seems to fear I'm some evil mastermind about to take down his pack as well."

"He'll see some sense. It might take him a while, but he will. He's stubborn but not stupid." She walked over. I was about to jerk back, but she hugged me before I could. I'd been imprisoned for nearly a year, but I hadn't been hugged in way longer than that.

She let go. "Sorry, but you look like you needed that."

Don't cry. Don't. Cry. What the hell was wrong with me? Was I becoming the biggest ninny going?

"Thanks," I said, trying to keep it together.

"I'll be back soon. If you need anything, anything at all, you tell whoever's at the door to tell me."

I nodded, feeling like I might lose the battle against the tears at any moment.

Thankfully, she walked out. She might've been sent here as some sort of spy, a slow game to gain my trust, but that hug was too genuine.

If she was a spy, I'd already lost the war, because that woman was good.

CHAPTER 6

D*ante*

Henrietta walked into my house without knocking. Normally it didn't bother me. No one around here knocked. It was the *reason* she was here that had my hackles up. Word had already spread that she'd checked in on River. Just as Frankie had jumped to do her bidding, Henrietta had been giving orders about what needed to be brought and rearranged to make River more comfortable.

She had that stubborn look in her eyes as she walked over. I held the coffee pot up. She ignored my offer. I refilled my cup before settling at the table, prepared to hear the tirade that was coming.

"Why are you holding that little girl hostage, and for no good reason? It's been three days. That's not the kind of wolves we are." She was in full-blown mothering mode.

"Because I'm the leader of this pack, and it's my job to assess threats. That little girl, as you call her, looks at me like she wants to slit my throat. Don't underestimate her." I was aware it wouldn't make a lick of difference to Henrietta. Once she decided to champion someone, she wouldn't let it go, and because I was her nephew, I was going to sit there and listen to her harangue me until she tired.

"I've known you your entire life, so I know you're not stupid. That girl is not a threat." Hands on hips, she stared at me like I was ten.

"She isn't human, and she won't say anything else. The vampires were holding her but not feeding on her. Clearly there is more going on."

"Our kind was held at times too, or do you not remember?" she said, with the fierceness of a mama wolf protecting a cub.

Now we were getting to the heart of the problem. Way before I was born, my aunt had been one of the shifters held by humans. It hadn't been long, because our pack tracked her down and broke her out of the research facility they'd taken her to. They'd only had her for a month, but my mother said Henrietta was never the same after.

She never talked about that time. Whenever anyone asked, she simply said it had happened and it was done. She wouldn't relive it to appease anyone's curiosity, and it was her cross to bear. Her silence said more than any story of horrors could've.

I sipped my coffee, thinking how if I'd left here fifteen minutes earlier, this conversation might not be happening. "Of course I do, and I'm not going to keep her here forever."

"She might be beaten down, but that girl is no quitter. She's not going to tell you what you want unless you torture her, and that's not happening. What are you going to do then?"

There was no debating that she could be right. I'd seen

the strength Henrietta talked about. It was impossible not to see it.

"You're right, and it's not going to be an issue. I have someone coming to get her."

"Who? And taking her where?"

I threw the rest of my coffee in the sink. There was nothing I wanted as much as getting away from Henrietta right now.

"Cole's pack over on the East Coast. They've got better resources." And they should've been here by now. It wasn't *that* far away. What the hell was taking them so long?

"You can't just ship her off to get poked and prodded. You don't know what they'll do to her. I've heard stories about that place, weird chemistry that shouldn't be happening and strange doctors."

So had I. It was what made me think it was where River belonged—not that I'd share any of that with Henrietta.

"I know you mean well, but I *can't* just let her go because everyone feels bad for her." I walked out the front door, praying she wouldn't follow but hearing her steps behind me.

"*Why* can't you let her go? You're the alpha of this pack. You can do whatever you choose."

"And this is my choice. I'm not going to argue about the situation," I said, my voice growing rougher as I walked.

She didn't follow me this time, obviously hearing the edge in my tone. Instead of doing the million other things that needed to be handled, I found myself outside the East Building, where River was.

Marshall was at the door, guarding her room.

"She knock or ask for anyone?" I asked, knowing I would've been alerted immediately if she had.

He shook his head and then looked down, assuming the news would annoy me.

He was right.

"What about the doc? Did he come by again?" There was word Doc had stopped by several times, but instead of drawing blood, he was drawing cards. Apparently River shared his enthusiasm for gin rummy.

"Uhm, yeah, I did see him." Marshall cleared his throat and went back to his paper, as if he'd been dismissed.

"And? Did he get a sample?" I took a deep breath. It wasn't Marshall's fault that I couldn't get a handle on one stubborn female.

He looked up. "You know, I don't think so, but I might be wrong."

I was going to have to get a new doctor. This one had too many principles by far. Even if I held River down, he'd probably refuse to stick her with the needle if she didn't want it.

I looked through the one-way mirror. The place looked like a day spa, with plants in the corner and pictures on the wall.

River was reclining on the sofa underneath the window, flipping through a magazine and glancing up at the sky.

Why did she have to keep staring out that fucking window? If she wanted to go outside so badly, all she had to do was tell me what she was and I'd let her go. Or I most likely would, as long as whatever she was didn't pose a threat to my pack.

She suddenly closed the magazine and stared at me again, as if she could see me, and smiled. It wasn't a welcoming smile but one of those fuck-off smiles, when someone thinks they have you beat and are screwing with you.

Oh no, this was done. I swung the door open, startling her but not enough for her to get up.

"You ready to talk?"

She answered by turning away from me to look out the window.

"There is a limit to my patience. If you think you're going to sit here and not give me answers, things *will* get worse for you."

She didn't speak. Why would she? Who'd believe it when her accommodations kept getting better and better? This place looked better than my cabin.

"So that's where we're at? You think the silent treatment is the way to handle this?" I said, crossing the room.

She looked up smugly. "There's nothing I can say that's going to make you happy anyway." Then she rolled her eyes.

"Fine. We'll do this the difficult way."

I walked out, leaving the door open so she could hear me as I talked to Marshall. "I want this room cleared out of everything. Nothing is to remain. Not the bed, a blanket, nothing."

She didn't say a damned word or even glance in response. I shut the door.

"I have to take everything?" Marshall asked, looking at me like I'd told him to beat his new puppy.

"It'll be fine, Marshall. The quicker she talks, the better. This is going to speed things up."

That was another thing. I was sick of having to reassure my people that River would be just fine.

CHAPTER 7

R *iver*

The door opened and Henrietta looked around the barren room.

"He emptied this place out. That son of a bitch," she said.

"It's fine. Marshall sneaks a sleeping bag and pillows in every night. My books are in the bathroom. It's really not bad." I put my magazine down. "Want a cupcake?" I asked, and then finished up the last bite of the one I'd been eating.

She shook her head. After her reception of the cupcake, I didn't bother telling her about all the food Marshall and Frankie kept bringing me out of guilt. My cheeks were already filling out from the nonstop pastries, meats, stews, and various dishes I couldn't even name. Then there were the visits with Doc, who was always good for an hour or so of card playing. If she thought this was rough, she needed to see the basement I'd been in.

She stood next to me. "Get up. We're going for a walk."

"We are?" This was a new one. A walk would be nice. The view from the window was good, especially when they had that party on Saturday night and there was lots of people-watching to be had, but some fresh air? Wasn't turning that down.

"You're coming with me, and we're going for a walk today and every day after until we get you out of this fucking box."

Henrietta had never sworn before. She looked like the type to F-bomb the world, but when she opened her mouth, it was all homemade cookies and hot toddies.

"Can you do that? Are you going to get in trouble?" I was already on my feet. If she was game, I certainly was.

"I'm his aunt. What's he going to do?" She grabbed my arm, tugging me with her to the door.

Marshall jumped to his feet as he saw me walking out with Henrietta, stepping in front of us.

"What, uh..." He pointed at us. "What are you doing, exactly?"

"We're going for a walk. Move," Henrietta said, her short frame somehow towering over the foot-taller Marshall.

"I mean...okay. But if Dante hears, I'm telling him you swore to me he said it was okay."

And the plot thickens. That was a pretty far step, farther out on the limb than just busting someone out for a walk.

I held my breath, waiting for Henrietta's response.

"I can live with that," she said, and tugged me forward again.

No one stopped us on the stairs, even as we caught a couple of looks. No one blocked us as the exit came into view.

The moment we stepped outside, we caught the attention of everyone in the area, but Henrietta continued to walk, as if we were doing nothing wrong.

The air was warm for a fall day, and the sun felt strong. Maybe it was because it had been so long since it had touched my skin.

"Thanks, Henrietta. I really needed this."

"You don't have to thank me for giving you something you should already have." She pointed to the side. "That's the greenhouse. The next building down the way is where Doc is set up." She continued to name places and buildings like I was a guest visiting.

We'd made it to one of the parklike clearings, and a lull in the conversation, when I couldn't hold back anymore. This wasn't a planned conversation, but it had to be said. Whatever her intentions for being so nice to me, it had to be out on the table.

"I can't tell you what I am. I would if I could, but it's not something I can say without endangering others."

She stopped walking to look at me. "I'm not asking you to. I never would." She rested her hand on my arm. "Secrets should be shared willingly, not traded or forced."

"You're not mad at me?" I hated that I cared. It would've been easier if she was mean or manipulative. That was easy to shrug off. Niceness was my downfall, maybe because it had been so sparse in this past year.

"Of course I'm not mad. You can tell me as little or as much as you want, and it's your choice, always." She wrapped an arm in mine, tugging me along. "I'm going to share a secret with you, no strings attached. I don't like to talk about this much, but there was a short stint in my life when I was held somewhere against my will. It was a very bad time for me. If I can help you, I'm going to, and I don't care what anyone says about it, because I wish someone had helped me."

She didn't offer any more details, and I didn't press for any. Just as I didn't feel like talking about how many times I'd nearly lost my mind in that vampire basement, how I screamed in pain when they tried things to figure out what I was, she could keep her secrets as well.

We continued to walk, a camaraderie being forged with each step.

There was nothing like having a nice moment and then having it ruined. Dante was heading toward us.

"I'll handle this," she said, sounding more annoyed than fearful.

"What will he do?" I asked, hating that there would be a cost for her being kind to me.

"I'm his aunt. I changed that boy's diapers. He won't do anything but bluster."

We stopped walking as he approached. His eyes looked darker than ever as he stared in our direction.

"What are you doing?" he asked Henrietta, but looked at me.

"Getting her out of that barren room after you took all her things."

He broke his attention from me. "They're not her things, and if she wants out of that room, she knows what she has to do. Now take her back."

"When we're done with our walk," Henrietta said, sounding as fierce as Dante. You could see the family resemblance.

"Don't pick a fight you can't win." He stepped in between the two of us.

"We'll see about that," she said, and then walked away from both of us with an intent in her step that gave me the sense her destination was already determined.

He turned and stared. "Would you like to walk, or will you need to be carried?"

"I can't even imagine how you two are related," I said, and then gave him my back as I headed toward the building, ready to spit nails after the way he'd treated Henrietta. "You're a horrible person if you haven't figured that out yet."

"The worst," he said, like he'd heard it many times and cared about it less than the ant he crushed under his heel.

He followed me all the way up to my room, holding the door open.

I walked through it and then turned to him. "You're just pissed off you can't get me to do what you want," I said. "The big alpha laid low by little ole me."

He seemed like the type who always had control of his temper, but my shots were definitely hitting their mark if the bulging vein in his neck meant anything. Good. I was pissed off, so why shouldn't he be?

"Tomorrow the window gets boarded up and the lights get turned off," he said, his tone ice cold.

"Fuck. You." I walked into the room and settled on the floor by the window. "I'll be taking my nap now, so if you don't mind…?" I dismissed him with a flick of my fingers.

He shut the door, but before he did, I heard Marshall ask, "Am I really going to have to board up the window?"

The door shut.

I smirked in the direction of the mirror. Sometimes I'd turn that way and smirk just to screw with anyone who might be watching. Let them think I could see them.

It was hours later when I watched them below, gathering outside. They seemed to do this casual party of sorts one night a week. I always turned off the light so it wasn't as obvious that I was sitting there, staring at them.

They'd talk, eat, and mingle. Sometimes there would be someone, or a few people, playing instruments. Other times there would be speakers set up. At some point, at least a few people would dance. I couldn't seem to tear myself away from the window, having never been part of a community like this, not even before the takeover.

My race had been in hiding for decades as a matter of survival. You didn't have parties because that drew attention. You didn't go places with lots of people because, again, you couldn't draw attention to yourself. I'd never even been this close to a party in real life. They all looked so...*happy*.

Dante walked into the group a little later, and someone handed him a drink. One of the younger kids ran over and wrapped his arms around Dante's leg. Dante ruffled the kid's hair.

Was it his kid? For some reason I'd assumed he was single, but maybe not. A woman who looked in her thirties walked over. Was that his girlfriend or wife? She was curvier than I was, especially right now. She tugged the kid off his leg and seemed to be making small talk, friendly enough but not overly so. She waved and walked off, looking as if she were leaving the party.

He turned his profile to my window, not looking directly over here, but I could feel his attention. I backed away farther into the room. He remained still. Was he thinking about me? Why did I feel as if he didn't like this situation either? I had magic, but I wasn't psychic. Still, I couldn't shake the feeling he was watching me, wishing the situation were different.

CHAPTER 8

D*ante*

Frankie was leaving the East Building as I was approaching the next day.

"Anything?" It was the same question I asked every day, and I'd probably get the same answer as the last ten times.

"No, and I have to say, it's starting to really bother the guys. They feel like we're torturing her. Marshall told me you said something about boarding up the window. I'm not sure that's a good move. It's not going to go over well."

That much was obvious. *I* didn't like the idea, and it was mine. I'd misjudged River. There'd been fire in her eyes, but I thought dangling the carrot of freedom would make her cave. It was a rare situation that my gut instincts were at a loss. Now what? I had one option left, and that too seemed to be falling through.

"Cole's people should've been here by now. Hopefully

they'll show and we can hand her off," I said, losing hope by the day.

"Do you know when they'll get here?"

"I put in another call. I'm waiting to hear back." I walked past him, marching up to River's room, Frankie following me.

I looked through the window. She was lying on the tiled floor of the room, her head resting on her arms as she stared up through the window, looking content in spite of her sparse situation. I was running out of options. For some reason, I couldn't take her window, and I wouldn't withhold food, especially from someone who hadn't done anything against me.

It didn't matter. She wouldn't be my problem soon. I'd dump her on people with more resources in this department and move on.

My phone buzzed. "This is them," I said to Frankie. Were they close? This was it. She'd be leaving?

"Are you going to answer it?" Frankie said as I continued to stare at my phone.

I stalled another second, as if my finger didn't want to hit the accept button, but I forced it.

"Sassy, it's good to hear from you. I was expecting someone to be here by now. Cole said he was sending them."

Frankie's face lit up.

"That's because nobody's coming," she said. "I don't care what my mate said because he felt bad; you're not dumping your shit on us. I'm not handing some possible innocent over to be poked and prodded by these lunatics so you can forget about it."

I'd talked to her more than once, and she'd never had a lot of fluff. She didn't disappoint this time.

"But your doctor—"

"Oh no, that nutcase is not *my* doctor, and no one is becoming a pincushion under my watch."

We'd been in lockstep in every other area that had to do with the pact with the vampires—until now.

Sassy was some sort of shifter hybrid in a cute little package, but her teeth bit hard. Most people didn't like going head to head with her. That wasn't my problem. The chick behind the mirror was my concern, and I'd go against a haven of salivating vampires to unload her.

"She might not be an innocent. I can't let her go, and I don't have the same resources you do. We did agree to an alliance, correct?"

Frankie took a step back, running both hands through his hair as he picked up on enough of the conversation to lose his happy-go-lucky attitude.

"Oh yes, we agreed to an alliance, but nowhere in that deal is my doing your dirty work. Clean up your own mess. I've got enough crap of my own." There was a pause before she added in a softer tone, "Respectfully, of course." I could hear the laughter in her voice. In contrast, Cole laughing in the background was crystal clear. He was lucky he was states away or I might've punched him in the face.

"If you need anything else, feel free to ask. Have a nice evening," she said, sweet as pie, before disconnecting.

"They're not going to take her?" Frankie said, having heard enough.

I shook my head, pocketing my phone because there was no one else I trusted enough to take her. In the back of my mind, I'd always known Sassy would look out for River's best interests. Now I was utterly screwed.

Frankie immediately shifted his hands to his hair again, but then his face froze, distress morphing to dread as he looked over my shoulder, out the window.

"Oh fuck. The Hen Pack is coming. They've *organized*."

There was more dread in his voice than if Sally, some girl from a neighboring pack that stalked him, was on the lawn with her bags packed, ready to move in.

The Hen Pack was the name given to my aunt and some of the other matriarchal females that joined forces when they felt their interests—or the interests of a particular female pack member—were not being looked after. I didn't need to ask whose cause they were taking up this time, as I'd had a preview.

I made my way outside so I could avoid this confrontation in the building, where River might hear if things got heated. Plus watching her lying on the floor didn't help my argument. No matter how it might be spun, no bed, no blanket, not even a light? I looked like a monster. For all the death I'd doled out over the years, I was surprisingly not used to feeling like one.

The pack of females walked over and stopped in front of me. There were six in total, and none of them alone were much fun. Together? Vampires would've been easier.

Henrietta led the pack—hence the name—and stood in front.

"What can I do for you?" I asked, acting like this wasn't going to be a shakedown.

"We're here to talk about the girl you've locked up," Henrietta said. "We understood why you did it, so we gave you some leeway, but this isn't going to continue. We're getting on to two weeks now, and the conditions of her situation have been getting worse and worse. We've decided that there needs to be an intervention."

Lucy, always one to put her two cents in, stepped forward. "You know there's female alphas and pack leaders now, right? We aren't living in the dark ages. You can't lock a woman up and think that we'll stand by and do nothing. This shit isn't going to fly, not in this pack."

Giselle squeezed past Lucy. "We will not tolerate this."

I lifted my hands in a sign of surrender. "I've heard you. You might have a point. I'll have a solution for you tomorrow."

They had no idea that they'd just given me an escape clause from a situation I found nearly as repulsive as they did. I'd killed many, but I'd never caged anyone. No matter what people might think, something in me twisted every time I saw River in that room with nothing.

I'd give them exactly what they wanted. The pack would think I was taking in the majority's wishes, and I could let River out of that room without looking too weak. I wanted to hug and kiss each and every one of the Hens, but I kept my face straight, as if this wasn't a win-win for me.

"One more night. That's it or we're busting her out ourselves," Clancy said from the back.

"She will be resituated tomorrow. I give you my word," I said.

The Hen Pack stood their ground for a few more minutes, giving me their best collective glare. No one, most of all them, had expected such an easy win.

"You better," Lucy said. The other women were waving at her and nudging her in the arm.

"We'll return tomorrow," Henrietta said, before ushering off her group.

"For heaven's sake, Lucy, can you never win graciously?" Clancy said as they walked off.

Frankie, who'd been hanging back because the Hen Pack scared him more than a raid, finally found his balls and moved closer.

"Now what? Are you really planning on letting her out?"

There was a little too much hope in his tone. I was

afraid if I didn't let River out soon, my guys would protest next. She had to be let out or this situation was going to get uglier by the day. The girl wouldn't break, not unless I was willing to stoop to levels I couldn't stomach. It was time to switch gears and figure out another solution.

"They're right. I can't lock her in a room forever with no sunlight or fresh air, sleeping on the floor. We might not know who or what she is, but she's not going to give up her secrets that easily. I'm not sure I can do any worse to her. The stick isn't working. It's time to try the carrot, but to be honest, I don't have much faith in that either."

"What are we going to do with her, then? Can we let her go?" he asked.

"I might've underestimated how strong her will is, but my gut is screaming that we can't let her fall into enemy hands until we learn more."

The sense that her secrets were much larger than we knew had been growing since she got here. She wasn't holding out for something stupid, like she had one-eighth fairy blood, or some other trivial thing. No. There was something big here. I could feel it.

"Then what do we do with her?" Frankie asked.

"Find her a place to sleep where she won't be able to sneak out in the middle of the night but that appears free. Then find her a job with people who can keep an eye on her during the day—keep her close enough to watch, but enough leeway that she doesn't look like she's being jailed. That should make the Hen Pack let up before we get pecked to death, and maybe it'll inspire her to talk a bit. Even if it doesn't, it'll be more sustainable if she's here for a while."

CHAPTER 9

R *iver*

Frankie swung open the door to my room, or more accurately, my cell. It might have a window, but the door was still locked. It was leaps and bounds better than the basement I'd been living in for the past year but was going downhill fast, especially if they took my window away.

Frankie walked in and settled on the floor next to me. This was it. He was trying to figure out how he was going to break it to me that my window was getting boarded up. The anger was building so thick and fast that it was hard to swallow. If Dante took my window, it was going to be war. I might even do something stupid, and I no longer cared what the repercussions were. He wanted to play dirty? He had no idea the depths I'd go.

"Dante has decided while you're here, you should be contributing to the community."

I still had no words, but for a reason other than pure

rage. Contribute to the community? Had these people lost their minds? How the hell was I supposed to contribute while I was locked in a...

Wait a minute.

Was I going to get out of here? Have something to do all day? Maybe even go...outside?

Don't get excited. I'd probably be escorted to the bathrooms and back every day. These people weren't trying to help me. They were either so shorthanded, probably due to running around and getting into fights all the time, that they needed free labor. *Or* they were going to torture me with latrine duty.

"What did you have in mind?"

Anything that got me out of here, got me closer to freedom, would be a step up, even if it was scrubbing on my hands and knees.

For someone who'd come in here looking determined, he was slumped against the wall, deep lines forming on his forehead. Had Dante given him specific instructions? Had Frankie given this any thought before approaching me?

As the silence stretched out, I plucked some lint off my leg. "You know, I'm decent in the kitchen if something has to be arranged."

His eyes widened. "Really? Because the kitchen is one of the openings that really needs to be filled. That's what I was coming to tell you."

I shrugged. "I guess I don't have a choice, do I?"

Relief spread across his face. "No. I mean, Dante's orders need to be followed."

"What kitchen job specifically?" I asked.

"There are a lot of people here who prefer to grab a quick meal and don't have a lot of time to cook. Most of us don't trust local restaurants. There've been a couple attempted poisonings."

He was causal enough that the damage couldn't have been too bad. But still, his agreeing the kitchen was a good idea might not have been his brightest move. I'd be willing to take it as long as I could get it, which would probably only be until the first person thought they had the runs, but whatever.

"Would I be coming back here every night?" I asked, trying to flush out the rest of the details that he didn't seem to want to tell me, or maybe didn't know.

He rubbed his palm on the top of his legs. "You'll be moving out of here. This wasn't really meant to be a long-term setup."

I was getting out of this room for good? I was almost free, from the way this was sounding. Except why did he look like he was about to doom me to a worse hell?

"Where will I be going?" I asked when he didn't offer up any more details.

His hands shifted from his legs to his hair. "You know, if you'd talk to Dante, tell him what he wants, you could leave. He doesn't want to keep you."

If it were only that easy. My kind had been getting used by every other race in existence from before they'd started tracking time. It wasn't until we'd been so depleted that they thought we were extinct that we were left alone. I wasn't telling anyone anything. I wasn't going to be the one who let the world know that some of us were left.

"I'm not a threat. If he can't grasp that on his own then there is nothing I can do to help him."

"Well, either way, if you help out around here, maybe be seen more, you'll gain a little trust and he'll come around. It's better than being stuck in here," he said, as if I wasn't still waiting to find out where I was going to be living.

"Frankie, where am I moving to?"

He attempted to smile before giving up and blurting out, "Dante has an extra room in his house."

It felt like the floor had fallen out from underneath me.

* * *

Dante

Again, a mention of "the eight." No names, no locations, only that they must be protected at all costs. Every stash of confidential information I'd come across had some mention of the eight, but never any other details. But why? Who were the eight all these vampire documents alluded to? Were they the key to defeating the vampires?

I was opening the next file on the computer we'd taken from the last vampire raid when Frankie walked in.

I nodded to him as he stopped in front of the table in the storage building, where everything with potential intelligence was. The vampires were like an oversized, bloated government with their formalities and all the crap that they tracked. It was shocking that they had time for anything else.

"I gave River a job. I think it's going to go pretty well. She was slightly hesitant, but I think she'll see the benefit," Frankie said.

"Good. What do you have her doing?" The less I knew, the better. I'd decided that it was best I avoid her while she was here. She had a strange effect on people, and I needed to keep a clear head. But the Hen Pack would surely come calling for details.

"Helping in the kitchens," he said.

"Good choice. Natalie's been asking for more staff for months, but I didn't have any free hands." I glanced up at him before adding, "Make sure you tell them to keep an eye on her."

"Yep. Definitely," he said.

I went back to the files as he rocked back and forth on his heels, creaking the floor every time he moved.

The only thing that was worse than the monotony of this vampire writing was Frankie's stare. His hair wasn't standing on end, but that didn't mean things were going well.

"Was there something else?"

"Yes, actually, a minor detail. Nothing too important, but wanted you to be aware of it so you weren't surprised."

"Which is?" This wasn't going to be good. What had he done?

"Well, since you wanted her moved from the building, I went through all the options. There weren't many." He shrugged, as if already relieving himself of the blame.

"And?" I asked, wishing he'd spit it out already.

"Your extra room was the best candidate."

Why had I decided Frankie was the best man for this job?

"*My* house? You can't figure out anywhere else to put her?" I shut the laptop, standing as he took a step back.

He threw his hands up. "You said you wanted her somewhere we could keep an eye on her. You're the lightest sleeper in the entire pack. Nobody else would even know if she was gone. Plus your place is the most centrally located. It seemed the best option."

He moved a little closer to the door, looking for an opportunity to bolt.

"Best option? Having her underfoot every moment of my day? You're telling me there was nowhere else?" I said, and then blocked his exit so he couldn't run out the door the way he clearly wanted to.

"You don't understand. Most of the suitable places, the people who are in those places, who asked to not be named, were hesitant because they've heard some things and don't want to be in a position to piss her off." He crossed his arms and then waited.

"Why is that?" I shut the door, making it clear he wasn't getting out of this room until he explained the rest.

He ran both hands through his hair and groaned. "What I'm going to tell you sounds absurd, and I know it, but they think she's a witch or something."

"What?" This had to be a joke.

"You don't understand. When she was in the cell, things would—*happen*." He threw his hands up as if to say the universe worked in mysterious ways.

"Like what things?" I'd known River was going to be disruptive, but everyone was taking leave of their senses.

"Remember how I got the guitar after bringing her supplies? Well, every time I bring something for her, good things happen to me shortly after, and I'm not the only one. It happened with Marshall, Doc, everyone, and word sort of spread."

"She's *something*, but she's not a witch." They were all losing their minds, and now I was going to be stuck with her at my place, my two-bedroom cabin. The only space I could get away from everyone, and the main person I wanted to avoid would be there.

"It's not like they don't exist," Frankie said quietly, moving his knee back and forth.

"I know they exist, and I've met more than a few. She's. Not. A. Witch."

Unfortunately, it might not matter. Sometimes what people believed had more impact than the reality.

It was probably better anyway. I couldn't have her

staying with people that feared her. It screwed up my life, but how often was I even there?

I walked back to the table and took a seat again, and Frankie followed me.

"I didn't know what else to do with her. It seemed like the best option. She's already got the Hen Pack doing her bidding. I didn't want to put her closer to any of them or we could end up with an outright revolt."

I held up my hand. "Leave it. It'll be fine. It's the right call." Nothing about this was fine, but it would have to be. She'd be in and out of my house every single day. There was something about her that set my nerves on edge, and now I wouldn't be able to retreat.

"You mean that?"

"Do I say anything I don't mean?" I opened up a new file, needing a distraction.

Frankie was beating a quick retreat.

"Wait. When is she moving in?"

"I have her…uhm…" His hair was standing on end from the amount of ruffling it was getting now.

"*When?*"

"Tomorrow morning."

I took a quick breath, trying to hold back a temper I didn't used to have. I'd prided myself on self-control until recently.

"Fine."

He was gone before I'd finished saying the word.

CHAPTER 10

R *iver*

"Well, here's the place." Frankie stood beside me in front of Dante's home.

It was a small cabin. I'd been hoping for a bigger place, not because larger was better, but because there'd be more room to get away from him. That was not going to be a possibility here.

On the plus side, it was further toward the outskirts of the campus, though not incredibly so. The East Building had been smack in the heart of things. The cabin was also quite charming, with a Goldilocks type of appeal. If I didn't know who lived in the place, I might be excited to move in.

But it was *his* house—the man who was keeping me here against my will, had taken all my furniture and my vase of flowers from Henrietta, and threatened to board up my window.

I wasn't exactly sure how the situation here would play

out, but he better not think I was anything beyond a platonic roommate, one who had zero desire to speak to him and every inclination to kill him in his sleep. There better be a lock on that bedroom door that worked from the inside.

"I'll just leave your bag on the porch steps and get out of your hair," Frankie said. I hadn't realized he'd been standing by the stairs waiting for me to move.

"Thanks," I said.

He dropped my bag and left. I'd seen cheetahs running after prey that were slower.

Well, I couldn't stand here in Frankie's dust forever. I needed to go in.

The door was open, and I stood on the threshold, staring into the place that looked like a hunting lodge, minus the heads on the wall. Everywhere, it was wood, stone, or leather, as if Dante were allergic to anything not found in nature or that he hadn't personally killed.

I lifted my hand to knock on the frame, not looking to be his next meal if caught unaware.

"Come in," he said, stepping out of a hallway and into the main room.

I grabbed my borrowed bag, filled with secondhand clothes that were nicer than anything I'd ever owned, and crossed the threshold. I stopped short, as if I were a criminal waiting for a verdict—a very *angry* criminal that could go on a murdering spree given the slightest provocation.

We sized each other up like two boxers before the heavyweight championship.

His gaze said he had me dead to rights. Mine replied that he didn't know what he was up against. I might look weak, might even *be* weak at the moment, but I wouldn't go down without a fight. He'd better bring whatever he had, because I wouldn't be leaving anything off the table.

"You put on weight," he said, as if I didn't know he'd been watching me through the one-way mirror on more than a few occasions.

Anyone who'd seen me a couple of weeks ago would presume that was a compliment. Did that mean he wanted to start this situation off on a good foot? Wasn't possible, not when both of mine felt like they'd been encased in cement shoes, thanks to him. If he thought we were going to have some polite chitchat, he'd learn fast.

"Your jail serves better food," I replied. The most he deserved was to be tolerated.

"That's your room." Unaffected by my lack of reception toward his olive branch, he pointed to a door that opened off the small hallway.

I leaned forward, trying to get a better sense of where I'd be sleeping. Would this be an upgrade from the last room, or did this one have a bed of coals?

The corner of a plaid coverlet was visible, along with the footboard on an iron bed and a wood dresser. Looked livable enough.

"That can't be it. It's got furniture." It wasn't smart to pick a fight with a guy in a higher weight division, but I wasn't feeling particularly bright and shiny at the moment. Today I was grungy, tarnished, and looking for a fight, even if it was a losing one.

I took a few steps toward the door, pushing it open a bit more to get a better view. There was a vase of daisies on the dresser and throw pillows with hand-knit coverings. Henrietta had been here.

"It can be emptied out," he said, having snuck up behind me.

I turned and glared up at him, refusing to back away. He needed to know how much I hated him.

"Take whatever you want. It makes no difference to me."

Up close, his smell reminded me of a summer evening in the forest, woodsy and carnal, like a magical concoction of everything primal and male. As I knew what he looked like as a beast, his features were almost too perfect in human form. His deep-set eyes were unreadable as they scanned my face, which was equally blank. He wanted to test me? Act as if he were so cool? I'd be Antarctica. He'd never know how his nearness unsettled me.

"How long do you plan on continuing with these games of yours? Insisting that I'm some type of threat to you? Should I block out my calendar to, let's say, New Year's? Do you think you'll get some common sense before then? Or do you have so little entertainment in your life that you'll need to keep me around longer?" I crossed my arms, waiting to see if he'd take the bait, if he'd reveal anything about his plans.

The man obviously had a lot going on, considering he'd found me during a vampire raid. That didn't mean he was above some poking. Big men often had big egos that went *swoosh* when popped. Who knew what might come out?

He crossed his arms, leaning a shoulder on the door-jamb. "Any idea on when you're going to stop lying? Or is that the only thing you know how to do?"

Well, that hadn't worked. Talk about popping an ego. Mine was making a sad little whizzing noise as it took the hit. I'd been lying my entire life, but not because I wanted to. I'd hated it from before I knew exactly what I was doing. The only thing I hated more was being used, so that little pop was going to get a patch as I continued lying until I was out of here.

"Why do you feel that you're entitled to know everything about me? Is that part of this whole alpha act, or some inherently spoiled part within?" I pointed toward his chest, and whatever black and rotten thing that resided in it, stopping short of actually touching him.

"So you're admitting you aren't what you say? Could you finally be making some progress?" he asked with mock intrigue.

"You aren't entitled to know anything about me."

He straightened and leaned closer, planting a hand on the wall beside me. "And I say I am. Since you're here, and can't seem to leave, that would make me correct."

"So your philosophy in life is might makes right? How very"—I let my eyes make an obvious path up and down his form—"*predictable*."

"You forgot to add true." He smiled, showing no shame at all.

I smiled back. "You know who coined that phrase?"

"No. Why don't you enlighten me?"

"I can't. No one knows. It was such an idiotic thing to say that no author ever wanted to own it."

He didn't seem to notice the insult. His inflated ego seemed stubbornly hard to pop.

"Unfortunately for you, it's true. Why don't you make things easier for both of us? You don't want to be here, and I don't want you here. Tell me what you are and odds are it'll be as unimpressive as I'm assuming and you can leave."

He was staring at me like this bullying act, this looming behavior, would work. If it was only about me, I would've probably tried to strike a deal the night I'd arrived. Truth was, lying was exhausting. He had no idea how much that option called to me.

"Like I said, I'm human. If you can't figure that out then there's nothing I can do to help you." I turned, giving him my back.

His hand wrapped around my arm, pulling me back to him. His stare was more intent this time.

"I'm letting you out so you can contribute to the community. If you try to leave, I will catch you, and you'll be back to your cell in the building with no bed, no lights, and no window. Just know that the youngest of my pack could hunt you down and find you on their break from hopscotch."

"I know. You're all so very smart and talented. Oh, and so scary too." I gave a fake shiver.

He had no idea how I could lay this place to ruins if I was willing to pay the price, if it weren't against everything I was and raised to be. He'd never know, because that would be the deepest betrayal to my people, and I'd die before I did that.

"What exactly are you that you hold no fear of me? Is it stupidity that gives you such brazenness? Or do you over-estimate yourself that much?"

He was looking at me in a way that was more unsettling than his threats, as if I'd given him another little nugget in this last conversation somehow. How quickly I'd forgotten how adept he was at uncovering information. This conversation needed to be shifted, and fast, before I gave anything else away.

I looked down to where he was still holding me.

"I can tell you what I'm not, which is your maid or your prostitute, and I'd prefer as little contact as possible."

I yanked my arm out of his surprisingly light grasp, turning to get settled into my new room, but not before I caught the smile. He knew exactly what my game was. I was going to have to be extra careful around this one.

And now I lived with him.

I'd thought getting out of the room with the view was going to be better, but I wasn't so sure. This place exuded his energy, his smell, *him*. He'd put me on edge from the second I met him, and it wasn't getting any better.

I flopped onto the bed. No, it was better here. Even though he put me on edge, he wanted to avoid me as much as I did him. I'd adjust, get past the cooler months, replenish, and get out of here by spring.

CHAPTER 11

R *iver*

The kitchen was in full swing, with chopping, mixing, and all-around hustle and bustle. Two girls around my age were chatting over some carrots they were chopping. Another young guy was lugging a couple of bags of potatoes across the room. An older, stout woman with bright red hair in a messy bun, and not in some attempt to be fashionable, walked out of a pantry closet. She stopped short at seeing me standing in the door.

They all seemed to notice me at the same time, turning my way and staring.

I raised a hand in a weak wave. "I'm River. Frankie said you had a job for me."

The older woman nodded. "That's right. Frankie said you'd be coming." She motioned me forward. "I'm Natalie. I run the kitchens. That's Amber." The girl with big brown doe eyes and blond bologna curls waved and smiled. Natalie pointed at the raven-haired girl. "Carly."

She pointed at the smiling guy with rumpled brown hair lugging more potato sacks across the room. "That's Sanjay."

Natalie waved for me to follow her into a small office and did a quick sweep of my form before she grabbed some stuff from the open shelving. "Here's an apron. You need to do something with all that hair, too."

"Sure," I said, already beginning to braid it. You didn't need to be a genius to know that a grunt person in the kitchen was right around the bottom on the totem pole, but it got me out doing something other than twiddling my thumbs all day. I wasn't looking to get booted my first morning on the job.

Natalie was on the move again, and I kept pace. "You can start by helping Amber."

Amber had moved from chopping vegetables to cracking eggs into a large bowl, several dozen still waiting beside it.

"Once the crowds come, you'll be on the serving line," Natalie said.

She was short and to the point but didn't seem altogether horrible. She seemed like the type that left you alone as long as you did what you were supposed to.

After tying on the apron Natalie had given me, I started cracking eggs and dumping them into a larger bowl.

Amber leaned forward slightly, her nostrils flaring. "Wow. I'd heard you smelled different, but I hadn't believed it could be *that* different."

"I've been told I have a unique scent, but I don't notice it myself." I cracked a few more eggs, waiting to see where this went. It wouldn't be a horrible surprise if there were orders to watch me, maybe learn whatever they could. Although Amber didn't strike me as the brilliant spy type.

"It's not a *bad* smell," she said, shrugging as she cracked some more eggs. "It's actually a bit nice."

"Thanks." At least she was pleasant enough if I was going to be working here every day.

"Carly, come over here and smell River." There was something about the familiarity of the way my name flowed off her tongue that lent the impression she'd said it many times before.

Carly walked over with a neutral enough expression that alarm bells didn't go off.

"Don't be goofing off," Natalie called to us from across the room.

"I'm helping them crack eggs because the toast slices are done," Carly yelled back.

Natalie scowled but seemed to be willing to let it go as she walked in the office.

Carly stopped beside me. "My God, you do smell delicious, like dessert at a wedding feast."

"Thanks," I said, waiting for questions about what I was that didn't come.

Amber leaned in closer. "So what's the deal? We heard Dante was keeping you locked up, but then the Hen Pack had a fit and he let you out?"

So, that was why Dante had let me out. Henrietta had browbeaten him into it. The day she walked off, she'd stormed away like a woman with a mission. Apparently it had been accomplished.

I looked up from the eggs. "Hen Pack?" I asked, already knowing it was Henrietta but knowing the rest of the players in the gang would be nice.

"It's what everyone calls Henrietta and the pack of old

hags she runs with," Amber said, getting a giggle out of Carly.

Old hags? Was that how they viewed their elders? If they'd grown up without them, they might value their presence a little more. I'd been raised by someone barely older than myself, and I would've killed for someone with some wisdom and knowledge.

I wasn't going to be here that long. What they did, who they disrespected, shouldn't be my business. But Henrietta? She'd gone to bat for me.

Keep your mouth shut.

I wasn't in a position to make waves, nor did I need to. Henrietta could handle herself easily against these two idiots, even if I did want to lend a hand.

"So why'd he have you locked up? You don't look very dangerous to me." Amber said it the way you'd tell someone they *aren't all that.*

"Everyone is supposed to keep an eye on you, but to be honest, you don't strike me as an evil mastermind," Carly said, then the two of them erupted into laughs.

That's right. Treat me like a nobody and spread the word. Do my dirty work for me.

"I really don't know why he thinks I'm a problem. I mean, like you said, I smell different, but I'm painfully boring."

That got a couple more smiles as they glanced at each other knowingly.

"Where are you staying now? Are you still in the East Building?" Amber asked.

"No. Frankie moved me." This wasn't going to go well. Not with these two, not in any world would they want me near Dante.

"Where to?" Carly asked. "Is he putting you in one of the dorm buildings? We're in the little brick one at the edge of the property by the front gate. Maybe you can ask him to move you there? That's where a lot of the single girls are."

"Really?" They had me at "front gate," even as I kept my face blank and my voice bland.

"It's sort of like our little sorority house," Carly added. "We don't typically allow humans inside, but we might be able to get some of the other girls to go along with you staying there if we vouch for you."

Amber nodded. "You know, tell them you're willing to help out around the house, do little errands and such. It's just that, being a human, they'll expect you to help out to a certain degree."

Oh yes, everyone knew exactly how humans were treated these days. They wanted a live-in maid. As much as the idea of picking up after these two, and a houseful of their friends, made me want to vomit, they'd never notice me sneaking out in the middle of the night. Could I suck it up and clean up after them for a couple of weeks? That was the least of what I'd be willing to do.

"That would be amazing. I'd be so grateful if you would vouch for me, and I'd be more than happy to help out. It would be the least I could do in return for getting to be around all of you. I'll ask Frankie if he can move me."

Amber and Carly exchanged smiles.

"What building did you say you were in?" Amber asked.

"Where'd Frankie put you?" Carly asked.

Sanjay headed over like a shark that had smelled chum in the water. "Frankie's not moving her anywhere. She's in Dante's house." His brows were nearly to his hairline as he smirked in my direction, as if we shared a mutual secret.

"*Oh*. Is *that* how you got out?" Amber asked, her friendly stare turning ice cold.

"I'm not sure why I was put there. Trust me when I say

Dante doesn't want me there. He *hates* me." Where I really wanted to be was under a rock, and not because of what they were insinuating. That I was trying to placate these two was enough to make me want to scrub a few layers off my skin. But what was more important was getting out from under Dante's watchful eye. If these two useful idiots could help, I was all in. I'd go to bed with the devil to get out of his place, or in this case, the devil's dimwitted henchmen.

"No one ever rooms with Dante, but you just *ended* up there?" Carly dipped her chin, glaring.

As stupid as she might come off, it was a good enough question to make me wonder myself. How the hell *did* I end up there? It wasn't for the reasons they thought. He couldn't stand to be near me. But why put me there? Unless there was no other place he'd felt safe leaving me?

"I went where Frankie told me. I'll gladly move and help you out. I *want* to help you, I swear. I can wash, fold, iron, cook. I'm all-around great at domestic stuff." I added enough pleading to my tone to impart some sincerity. As to all the domestic stuff they wanted done, I'd be out of there before they knew how many of their shirts I'd burned or how that red rag had gotten in with all the whites.

As if we'd conjured him, or more likely because he'd been given instructions to check up on me, Frankie walked in. He headed over casually, as if this were a regular stop for him.

Amber didn't wait a second before she pounced on the opportunity to get a maid, turning to Frankie with a flirty smile.

"Frankie, speak of the devil. We have a question for you." She pointed to me. "River wants to know if she can move in with the girls. You know, slumber parties and all that good fun." She was smiling like he'd be invited to them.

Frankie didn't seem to be tripping over himself to get an invitation. He was a good-looking kid with a great build and an easy smile that outshone everything else. I didn't need to be the sharpest tool in the shed to know his date card was probably full.

He glanced my way. "If you want to make the move, I'll see what can be done."

This was too good to be true. I had to bite my cheek not to smile. "I think it might be easier for everyone, is all."

"Okay, give me a second to clear it, but I think it would work."

Frankie walked to the other side of the room, putting his phone to his ear.

I smiled at Amber and Carly, as if to say, *See? I'm just some schlub you can use.* I'd get moved in and use these two idiots right back, walking my way out of here.

Frankie turned back around, giving me the "sorry" smile. It needed no translation, understood in all languages. He followed it up with the sigh of regret and the *I'm helpless to do anything more* shrug. By the time he'd finished, he didn't need to speak at all.

"Yeah, the relocation isn't going to fly. Dante wants to leave you where you are," he said.

"Did he say why?" Was there any shot at all? A glimmer of hope? Something? If I was going to get out of here, I needed some distance from that man and not be in the middle of a kitchen, with coworkers.

"He didn't say. He just doesn't want you to move." He flipped his phone over in his fingers, waiting for some sort of acknowledgement that I was going to accept my lot in life and not blame him for it.

"Thanks for trying," I said, letting him off the hook, not

that I would've done anything anyway. Frankie might technically be the enemy, but I couldn't seem to neatly put him in that box, no matter how I tried.

"Okay, well, I'm off. Have other things to handle," he said, seeming happy to get away from me before my mind changed.

Amber and Carly's smiles dropped the second the door shut.

Sanjay, on the other hand, was laughing. "Told you so," he said.

"I guess it's too convenient for him to have a whore in house," Amber said.

"It's not like a shifter female would stoop so low as to be used like that," Carly added. "Well, she can't be very good at whatever she's doing if she's in the kitchen."

I didn't bother saying anything as they continued. In order to be willing to fight with someone, I had to care enough to bother. Those two were annoying the way fruit flies I couldn't swat away were. The only thing upsetting me was not managing to get out of Dante's house.

CHAPTER 12

D*ante*

River was standing behind the counter, handing out roast beef, carrots, and mashed potatoes during lunch service. I bypassed the food and dropped into the chair across the table from Frankie.

"How's she doing?" I asked.

"The younger women don't like her, but they don't seem to be doing a very good job of antagonizing her," Frankie said, laughing.

"Why don't they like her?" I asked. Everyone I'd seen around so far liked her *too* much.

"Because she's beautiful and staying in your house, and every young woman in this pack thinks that they are the alpha's true mate." He laughed again before he continued, "Between me and you? She's tougher than half the alphas I've met. I mean, I knew she was tough, but I swear this chick impresses me more and more."

"Really?" Nothing about that surprised me. I would've been more surprised if she *was* rattled.

"Yeah, Amber and Carly keep leaving their stations every time Natalie steps into the office, leaving River to man all the stations, but she doesn't get riled at all, just continues on. Sanjay brought over a tray of gravy, dripping it on her—intentionally, if you ask me. She ran a rag over it and continued as if she'd barely noticed. That or she really doesn't care. It's like she's got this air about her that none of them matter a whit."

"You didn't get involved, right?" The way he was watching the group of them, it was obvious he was having a hard time staying in his seat.

"Just as you ordered, don't do anything unless it escalates. Although I have to say, it's not that easy to watch their petty bullshit and not call them out on it."

"If it's not bothering her, why is it bothering you?" I scanned her clothes, finding the spots. I took a few deep breaths, so as not to go punch Sanjay in the face. It had nothing to do with her. Nothing at all. Only a weak man picked on someone weaker than himself. I would've wanted to punch anyone that had done that.

"You know I hate bullies," Frankie said, expressing all the disgust I kept buried.

"Leaving her in the room wasn't working, but I can't have her getting so comfortable that I never get an answer out of her." I forced my gaze from her and her coworkers, afraid I'd ruin all my good words by beating someone to a pulp soon.

"Yeah, I get it," Frankie said, and then sighed as if he didn't get it at all.

I wasn't sure this was going to work either. There was a limit to how much abuse I'd allow. Plus, there were other ways to get the information needed.

"Did Doc get a sample yet? He was supposed to stop by."

Frankie shrugged and then took the largest bite anyone had ever attempted to fit in their mouth. He'd rather choke than answer the question. Frankie had never been like this before River.

"Why is it that you can't seem to answer half the questions I ask about River?"

He scoped out the nearby tables, taking a head count of who might be within hearing distance before speaking. "Remember what I told you about what I thought River might be?" His voice was so soft that it was a strain to hear him even for me.

"How could I forget?" He was going back to the witch crap.

"You can think I'm nuts, but I'm not the only one who feels that way. Ask him yourself." He tilted his head slightly, almost as if to say that the Doc's believing it added credibility to his theory.

"I'll see you later." I walked out of the cafeteria, forcing myself not to look at River as I did.

Doc had a larger building toward the front of the campus, which served as his house, office, and surgery when needed. No matter how many other residences he'd been offered, he refused to sleep anywhere away from where he worked.

I caught him as one patient was leaving and another was waiting to go in.

"I'll just need a minute," I said to Angela. She was often seen on Doc's stoop. Werewolves weren't often ill, but Angela swore she had something every other week.

Doc waved me inside. "I don't see you here much. What's amiss?" he asked, fiddling with a pile of paperwork on his counter while avoiding my gaze.

I continued to stare at him and do little else. "I thought you were going to take a blood sample from River today? Is she refusing?"

"Um…" He turned, looking for something else to use as a distraction. "She's not exactly refusing, but she doesn't seem interested."

When he continued to fidget, I said, "Doc," in a strong enough tone to direct his attention fully to me. "For the pack's safety, we need a blood sample. We need to know what she is. If you need help, I'll hold her down myself, but this *has* to be done."

Doc shrugged. Before he spoke a word, it was clear this wouldn't go well.

"I can't do it." He was shaking his head in a dejected sort of way.

"You *can't?*"

"It's not that I don't *want* to." His voice dropped. "But I'm scared of her."

Another one? "More scared of her than disobeying orders?"

He went to the drawer and pulled out a needle. "I can talk you through it, but I can't do it. I understand if you want to get a new doctor, but I just can't do this."

I couldn't afford to have him leave. He was the best doctor I'd ever met. He was irreplaceable.

I grabbed the needle from him.

I'd never been told no so many times in my life, and because they were scared of *her?* I was the alpha of this pack. What was happening here?

"Do you need instructions?"

I didn't bother answering as I opened his door to leave.

"I'd go with you, but I don't want her to think I'm part of this," he yelled after me.

CHAPTER 13

R *iver*

No one walked me home from the kitchen, but that didn't mean I didn't have an escort. There were eyes on me as I made my way, even if I couldn't put a face or name to the watcher. This was to be expected, and so was them slacking off after they'd been doing it a while. The only person that might not slack was Dante.

I entered the cabin and stopped short when I spotted Dante sitting at the table, looking as if he'd been waiting.

He pointed to the chair opposite him.

I took a seat and then looked at the needle sitting on the table.

"I'm taking a blood sample. Tonight," he said.

I folded my hands on the table, glancing at the needle and then back to his cold stare.

"It's not going to tell you what you want," I said, buying

myself enough time to do a silent chant in my head. This wouldn't take too much to thwart.

"That you're not human?"

Point taken. My credibility might not be sterling and was definitely going to be in question after a sample.

"I won't let you take it," I said, hoping for my sake he heeded my warning.

"I'm not buying whatever tactics you're using on everyone else to scare them. The game ends tonight. You're giving me a blood sample if I have to hold you down to do it."

It was always going to come to this. I'd known that. Dante was much harder to coerce than the others.

"If that's the way you want to do things, but it's not going to work," I said.

He stood, and so did I.

"Running is useless," he said.

Hopefully I wouldn't be running too far. If things progressed the way they typically did, it wouldn't be necessary.

I dashed toward the door, my chair crashing to the floor. He lunged after me, taking me down with him. He flipped me, and I was trapped underneath him. His hips were flush with mine, our legs entangled.

"You had to make this difficult," he said, almost toying with me, gloating. He had no idea he'd already failed. I was having a hard time focusing on it as he lay on top of me.

"I guess I did," I said, trying to keep my focus.

There'd always been a strange tension when I was near him, but pressed against him, I was discovering a name for it, and it wasn't one I'd welcome.

"I'll be getting that sample now," he said, his voice growing rougher. Whatever I was feeling, it seemed to be mutual and growing.

"Do your worst." I looked to the needle in his hand, anything to break the strange connection that was building.

He followed my gaze to the needle and then looked closely at it. The tip was broken off.

"You knew I wouldn't be able to get a sample, didn't you?" he asked.

He wasn't smiling anymore, but I could hear it in his tone that he was slightly amused over being thwarted.

"It was a hunch." I hadn't been positive, but the odds had been on my side.

He didn't move, still hovering over me, his face inches from mine. Our breath mingled, and I licked my lips as his eyes shifted to them.

"You're not the witch they think you are, but you're definitely something." He smoothed his fingers over my cheek. "What *are* you?"

He was going to kiss me.

If he kept looking at me the way he was, as if I were someone amazing, I might not stop him either. My entire life, I'd been pitied, feared, threatened, but not once had anyone ever looked at me with the heat and want in his gaze right now, and it was undoing me.

He was a shifter, a barbarian by every other race's standards. And yet every part of my body felt like it was tingling with the feel of him. It took a conscious effort not to arch into him, to move against the erection that pressed into the junction of my thighs.

His head dipped, and I turned mine, denying him, even as my breathing stuttered.

His forehead leaned against my temple, his words feathering over my ear, making it that much harder to resist. "I know you want me. Why fight it?"

"Because you're you, and everything that entails." I took

a small breath before forcing the rest of the words out. "And I'm me."

He had no idea what that meant, but the gravity of it was enough for me to stop something that could only end badly.

"What does that have to do with this moment?"

His jaw rubbed against mine, the roughness sending a shiver through me.

I looked at him, wondering if he'd noticed my lack of fight, could sense my weakening, my utter wanting of him for no rational reason other than that something about our chemistry seemed to draw me to him. Was it an opposites-attract thing? Was his being so strong and fearless instinctively attractive to someone whose race had always been hunted? I didn't know, and it didn't matter. This couldn't happen.

"To you, I guess nothing. But to me it means everything." My kind didn't mate casually. There were no one-night stands and frivolous dalliances. When we mated, it was for life.

"Then tell me you don't want me," he said.

I hesitated, trying to force the words out. I couldn't, not when he kept staring at me like I was the most beautiful woman he'd ever seen.

My hesitance was all he needed to lean in again, and this time I didn't turn my head. I should've. But I couldn't seem to pull away. What was one little taste?

His lips grazed mine, and it felt like a blowtorch was taken to me with that small feathering. He slowly nibbled, brushing his lips over mine as he shifted against me, rubbing where my need was beginning to throb.

I opened my mouth wider, inviting him in even more. He sank his hands into my hair, tilting my head for better access, and everything else faded but him. The reasons I shouldn't be doing this were washed away by the taste of him. All the concrete obstacles, why this was a lethal decision, it all crumbled away with the feel of his weight.

All he was doing was kissing me, and it was enough to obliterate everything else from the world. I'd live a life worrying about shielding myself and all that mattered right now was him.

The door swung open.

"Hey, Dante, where are you? We got... *Ooh.*" Frankie's voice died on the vine as he belatedly noticed us on the floor.

I didn't know if Dante was glaring at him because I was too red-faced to look.

"I'm—"

"Get out," Dante said.

"Yep." Frankie had his back to us. "I didn't see anything, though, just so you know. I'll be out on the porch here, just taking in the night air and not paying attention to anything."

Dante got up and held out his hand to help me. I was already scrambling to the other side of the room. I would've run out the front door if Frankie wasn't there.

Something had happened with Dante that definitely shouldn't have, and it wasn't the kiss. Well, it *was* the kiss, but more. There was a strange connection, a weird pull, that shouldn't exist, definitely *not* with him.

"River," Dante said as I tried to escape to my room.

"Yes?" I asked, turning around as if nothing had happened, and I wasn't utterly unraveling over a single stupid kiss.

"You okay?"

Had he felt it too? Could a different race feel that? He looked off, and he surely had many more kisses in his life than I had.

I scrunched up my face, as if shocked by the question. "Yeah, of course. Why wouldn't I be? Because we kissed for two seconds and we shouldn't have and it'll never happen again because it's idiotic and we hate each other? I'm fine." I stopped talking. Fewer words might've been better. I should've stopped after "yeah."

I'd never prattled on like that in my life, and it was adding to the need to flee.

He nodded. "Agreed. It won't happen again."

I nodded and then ducked into my room, shutting the door. There was no discussion that would make this better. Only space and time had a shot. Well, on the plus side, at least I'd told him it wouldn't be happening again, and he clearly agreed. That was something.

Because it wouldn't. It couldn't. Too many more moments like that and I'd become unhinged, telling him anything he wanted to know. Whatever I'd felt passing between us, it had been nothing but feeling a connection with another warm body when I'd had so little interaction for so long.

CHAPTER 14

R *iver*

A week had passed, and we'd reached a sort of status quo. I'd hear Dante coming home in the wee hours of the night. By the time I woke in the morning, he was long gone.

I worked in silence, not speaking to the other kitchen staff other than Natalie, who was all business but seemed very happy with me.

When Dante walked in the house tonight, it was the first time I'd seen him since the kiss. He gave me a nod, his movements stiff, as if our interaction was like lugging around a two-ton boulder.

I tried to reciprocate the gesture but struggled to even hold his gaze for more than a second. My boulder was even heavier, and had tripled in weight since that night.

He walked past me, and the shower started a few minutes later. It was Saturday night, after all. Time to get cleaned up for "the gathering." I'd overheard them talking

91

about the festivities I used to watch from my cell. The middle grounds of the campus would have firepits lit up as they roasted meat and drank beer and wine.

The cabin here didn't have a view of where they would gather, but that was okay. Watching everyone else have fun wasn't as entertaining as it might sound.

I went back to sorting through the books that were shelved in the living room, deciding on which one I'd read tonight. There was a lack of romance selection, but I'd found some good fantasy novels. The layer of dust made me wonder if they'd come with the house.

Dante reappeared half an hour later as he walked past me again, but this time on his way out. He skipped the nod as I sipped my tea as if I hadn't seen him at all.

As much as I'd initially dreaded this living situation, the short time I'd spent here hadn't been altogether horrible. After our awkward moment, he'd barely been around. This was the most he'd been around in days. As long as I didn't look toward his bedroom, it was almost as if he didn't live here at all.

Henrietta walked into the house ten minutes later to find me sprawled out on the floor, surrounded by books in different stacks. There were the definite, maybe, and never-going-to-happen piles.

"What are you doing?" she asked.

"Deciding what I want to read. Would you like a cup of tea? I found a wonderful oolong in the cabinet, and I've got some brownies I made last night." There weren't quite as many brownies as there had been when I wrapped them. If I was going to pretend that I lived alone, I'd have to assume mice got to a few or it ruined the delusion.

"It's Saturday. Once the weather gets too cold, we won't be having the gatherings as often, and then you'll really be stuck inside. But while it's mild, you can't sit here and do this." She shook her head and waved at my piles. "You're young. You need to get out of here and be around people."

I pulled another book off the shelf. "It's not that I don't appreciate the offer, but I don't plan on being here that long, and, well, you get it, I'm sure."

From the scrunching of her face, it didn't look like she *got* anything.

"Get what?"

Yep, just as I feared. I was going to have to spell it out.

"I'm not a shifter. I'm sure most of the people there aren't going to appreciate me crashing their party." Nor did I have any strong desire to do any kind of crashing. Instead of a little crack in the windshield, my arrival might be more like a bulldozer through a greenhouse. She might think a night in reading sounded awful, but there was going to be a nice fire, some more tea, and at least one more brownie. It didn't get much better than that. A few months ago, this was all I could dream of.

"I don't care if you stay a few weeks. It's good for you to get out and meet people, get back in the swing of things a little."

"I don't know. There's no reason to make things awkward." Henrietta probably thought it was a fear of crowds after I'd been locked up for so long. She was partially right—I didn't really relish the idea of a crowd—but that wasn't the only issue. The more people I met, the more anxious I was that someone would figure something out.

She fisted her hands on her hips. I'd seen that expression. She'd taken on the alpha of this pack with a look like that. I didn't stand a chance. She'd be dragging me out of here by my hair if I didn't go willingly, or gathering the Hen Pack to come for me.

I got up, dusted my hands off on my jeans, and asked,

"Can I go like this?" If my jeans, sweater, and boots didn't cut it, it wasn't happening. This was as good as it got.

"You're perfect. Nobody dresses up for these things." She looped her arm through mine then dragged me along, assuring me on the walk over what a wonderful time I'd have.

The music was flowing and the firepits were lit. People were gathered around different fires, and the aroma of roasting meat filled the area.

I followed Henrietta, catching more than a few stares but a couple smiles. The farther into the gathering I got, the more stares, some of them feeling like bull's-eyes, seemed to line up on my head.

Henrietta, who'd gotten a few steps ahead of me, slowed her pace. "They're not used to strangers at the gathering. We're a standoffish race, but you'll never find someone more loyal than a shifter. They'll warm up and then they'll embrace you."

No, they wouldn't. She didn't know what some of them were thinking, or clearly *repeating* over in the group off to the side, where Amber and Carly were standing. Shifter hearing wasn't needed to see them giggling as they looked my way.

They could laugh all night. I was here for Henrietta and that was it. I'd have a drink or two and then sleep soundly. The one thing living in a dungeon for nearly a year had done was make me immune to petty things, such as giggles from jealous girls.

A woman around Henrietta's age made her way over, smiling at us both in greeting.

"I'm Clancy. Glad to see you out and about," she said.

"Thank you." I smiled, faking that I was happy to be here. This was probably one of the Hen Pack who'd help liberate me from the room, which I was happy to be out of.

"Hen, do you have a minute? I have to talk to you." Clancy was glancing at me and then back to Henrietta.

"I'm going to go grab a drink." I pointed over to where a keg of ale was on the side, giving Henrietta an easy out.

"Okay, I'll come find you in a bit," Henrietta said, acting like a mother who was dropping her kid off at school for the first time.

"I'll be fine," I said, faking another smile for her sake, already feeling my cheeks getting sore from smiling more than I had in a year.

I'd hang out for a few and then head back to Dante's. There was nothing more distasteful than forced small talk, but this outing might not be all bad. Maybe as they got used to seeing me around, they'd start to disregard me. There were people watching me constantly. Even if I couldn't see them, I could *feel* them. I left the kitchen, they were there. I walked to the gathering with Henrietta, they were there, and they needed to get bored of watching nothing. For now, I'd lie low and gather intelligence until I could make my exit.

In the scheme of things, riding it out here over the winter wouldn't be unbearable. I could formulate more of a plan in the meantime. If I left now, I wasn't sure where I'd go. The place I'd called home might not exist anymore, if I wanted to take a risk going back there.

I neared the keg and grabbed a glass off the table beside it. A couple cut me off before I got to the tap with a glare in my direction.

Message received. I was an outsider and last in line. Not a problem. They could think whatever they wanted as I bided my time.

I sat on a nearby bench, waiting for them to finish filling their glasses as a swarm of people approached, all needing to suddenly top off their drinks. If they thought waiting for a beer was bad, they should know what it was like to wait for a bug to get closer to your cell because no one had felt like bringing you food that day.

I let them play their petty games while I surveyed the area, cataloging every face, seeing which ones hung together. Frankie was on the far side of the clearing. Anyone he seemed close to might be higher on the totem pole and a person to watch out for. The way he was leaning toward his current companion and smiling made me think this woman was more important for tonight than anything else.

Some heads turned toward the other end of the perimeter, and I followed their gazes to see Dante entering the clearing.

Everyone in the pack gave him his due attention—anywhere from discreet interest, all the way to drooling infatuation. Amber and Carly, mouths hanging open like wrinkly-faced dogs, were going to need a towel soon.

Dante's gaze skimmed the crowd before landing on me. "Want a drink?"

My attention snapped to the older, gruff-looking man that had a mug outstretched to me.

"You better take it. I'm not going to get dirty looks for a drink you won't even accept," he said.

I laughed a little. "Thanks. Not trying to get anyone in trouble."

He smiled as he perched on the bench next to me. "Trouble? Nah. Not from these young kids. They're not worth the energy of getting my hackles up, but you seem to know that well enough."

I nodded, keeping my comments to myself. It was one thing for him to criticize his pack, but that was a possible trap I wouldn't be walking into.

He continued to size me up. "You are a wise one, huh?"

"Not wise enough," I said, thinking of all the missteps I'd made in the last year. Anyone who'd ended up in one jail only to get busted out and end up in another wasn't winning any awards for cleverness.

"I'm Gus." He had a beard that was half black, half gray, and eyes that looked like they'd seen more than their fair share of action and intrigue, and yet somehow still saw the good in all of it anyway.

"River."

"So I see you're hitting it off about as well as fireworks in a tin shed." He had an infectious chuckle.

"Yes, I seem to be quite popular, don't I?" I grinned at him.

"You know what the problem is, don't you?" he asked, scanning the crowd.

"That I'm not a shifter or that I'm a stranger?" I asked.

"They think you're fucking the man *they* want to fuck." He chuckled again, probably one of the few people here that would find that amusing. "It's hard to say where your sensibilities lie, but if you fuck him, it's no one's business anyway."

Did nobody here cohabitate and *not* sleep together? Was it that crazy an idea that I wasn't sleeping with Dante?

I tipped my head in Dante's direction. "Does it look like we're together?" I said, feeling some strange compulsion to add to this one-sided conversation about my fictitious love life.

Gus laughed again. "Depends on which one of you I look at. If I were to only look at you, I'd think maybe, maybe not. You look like someone trying to keep to your-self, like you've got a wall a few feet thick all around you. I look at him, on the other hand… I say if it hasn't happened yet, it will soon."

I followed his gaze back to Dante, who was staring intently in my direction.

"Trust me when I tell you he has no interest in me at all. That's dislike you're seeing there." If he'd seen the way Dante was avoiding his own house because he'd kissed me on a whim, Gus would rethink those words.

"You haven't been around men enough if you think *that's* not interest."

"If there's interest there, it's because he's wondering why I'm here."

Gus let out another guffaw. "Yeah, I've seen Dante irritated before. *That's* not the look."

Dante kept directing his attention my way. If he didn't cut it out, everyone might make the same assumption as Gus and the kitchen crew. The more he singled me out, the more interest I'd receive from everyone else, and nothing about that was good. The last thing I needed was an entire pack of shifters all curious about me, wondering things, poking around, trying to figure me out.

Watching me everywhere I went.

I needed to blend into the background. Let them all get a good look and decide there was nothing interesting here. And what was Dante doing with his staring? Shining a big ole spotlight on me.

I chugged half my glass, the urge to march over and strangle him growing stronger by the second.

"Considering you might be here a while, I could give you some advice about getting along," Gus said.

"I won't be here that long, but thanks anyway."

I wasn't looking in Dante's direction and I could still feel his eyes on me.

"He's looking for answers, and I'd guess you aren't one to bend, so I'm thinking you might be here a bit longer than you intend. Either way, I'm around if you decide you want that advice," Gus said. He tilted his head back slightly, sniffing. "You smell as good as apple pie right out of the oven. You're not a shifter, but you're not human, that's for damned sure."

I raised my brows and nodded as I stood. "Well, it was nice talking to you." I knew when it was time to finish a conversation.

CHAPTER 15

D*ante*

When I left my place, River had been settled beside a stack of books with a tea next to her. I'd successfully avoided her for days and now couldn't seem to stop watching her, the way she kept her chin up. Half the pack seemed fixated on her, and the other eyed her like she was a pariah, but it didn't seem to bother her.

She glanced in my direction, her eyes burning but her lips parted. She'd fled like the devil was chasing her after our kiss. Thankfully, one of us had some sense. It definitely hadn't been one of my brighter moves.

Nothing had been normal about that night. I was the opposite of clumsy, and I'd tripped over nothing. She'd done it somehow. I didn't even know what she was, but she'd done *something* to thwart me—and yet that wasn't what was preoccupying me.

She'd tasted as sweet as she smelled, her lips like

sucking on honey. Then there was the way she melted into me, forming her body to mine as if we fit perfectly.

No. I needed to stop thinking like that. It couldn't happen again. This wasn't the place for her. She shouldn't have come. As soon as she told the truth about what she was, she could leave. The sooner the better.

She shot another glare in my direction before walking out of the clearing. Good. Hopefully she wouldn't come to one of these again.

Frankie was about to head out after her, make sure she got where she was supposed to, but Charlie followed her first.

I intercepted Frankie and, with a nod, followed instead.

Charlie was one of my least favorite pack members and a perennial pain in the ass. Someone spilling gravy on her at work was one thing, but I wouldn't tolerate anything that happened alone, in the dark of night.

If this was a shifter female, a warning wouldn't be necessary. Charlie wouldn't get out of line with a pack member because he'd know there was a price to pay. A human? All bets were off.

Charlie caught sight of me right away, stopping and turning.

"Not for you." I shook my head.

"Fine." He shrugged.

"Make sure you spread the word to everyone, because if anyone attempts the same, there will be a problem."

He nodded and blew out a breath but headed back to the gathering.

Charlie might try again in the future, when no one was watching, but he'd give it at least a week or two. One day I'd catch him doing something bad enough to kick him from the pack, but it hadn't happened yet, and it wouldn't be happening tonight.

Up ahead, River was winding her way around the back of the buildings. She was going in the right direction, but her picking the outer path in the deepest shadows didn't altogether reassure me that she'd end up where she was supposed to go.

I continued to follow. Even out here, in the open air, her scent was intoxicating. It was bad enough I couldn't get away from it in the house, where it literally clung to every surface.

I was about to turn around and send another pack member to follow her when she stopped walking.

"Why are you trailing me?" she asked, hands on her hips, staring me down.

"Why are you lurking around in the shadows?" I asked, getting closer.

"I'm heading back to my cell."

"You're free to return to the other room if you like that one better." At least that would get her out of my hair. As it was, I didn't want to go home anymore because of her. I didn't trust myself after the other night.

Her eyes narrowed, as if that wasn't a choice at all.

"Why did you have to keep staring at me tonight?" she asked, switching gears but with the same amount of gasoline revving her engine.

"Do you have any idea who you're speaking to? I'm the alpha of this pack. I'll do what I please."

"I want to know why," she said even louder, as if she hadn't heard me.

"Because I don't trust you. You're hiding things and lying, and until you come clean, I'll be watching you, whether you approve of that or not." I wanted to grab her and shake her, or worse, kiss her again. Whatever she was, it called to me like a siren's song.

She turned and walked a few steps but then stopped

again, as if she couldn't contain herself. "You're giving people the wrong impression—unless you *want* them to think you're sleeping with me?"

"As if you care what they think." Nothing about her read like she'd noticed all the angry stares in her direction, even if I'd noted them. But not her. She acted as if they weren't even there, so what was the real problem?

"*You* should. As their alpha, I'd imagine sleeping with me would be a very bad idea for you."

She spoke as if she were giving me a warning. The girl had the nerve to threaten me with my own pack's opinion?

"If I wanted to fuck you, I'd fuck you. They don't dictate who I'm with. But don't worry. It's not going to happen. That kiss the other night meant nothing. You're not my type."

It was all true. I'd always thought I had a type, and that was dark-haired, dark-eyed, and voluptuous—yet River kept drawing my attention to the point where I didn't even look at anyone else. But damned if I'd touch her again.

"Good. Because I don't want you," she said. "It's bad enough I have to live with you."

"Get back to the house before I no longer give you that option," I said, hoping she'd heed my warning, because I wasn't sure what else I was going to do with her if she didn't. She was an unsolvable problem that seemed to plague my existence, and yet it felt like it was a chore to stay away from her.

She was walking again before my sanity finally settled back in. She didn't care what the pack thought. It was their *attention* she didn't want. I'd seen the way she'd trailed along after Henrietta as she entered the gathering, like a kid heading into detention. She'd gotten dragged here, and then too many eyes were on her. What secret was she hiding that was so bad she was constantly fearing discovery?

I walked back to the gathering, located Jobo, and nodded in the direction I'd just come. He'd have to watch her for tonight, because I needed the space. I grabbed a drink, planning on killing enough time that she'd be in bed when I got back.

Gus, the only one who didn't fear approaching me when I was in one of these moods, walked over.

"You've got a look that's scaring everyone off tonight," he said.

"Long week, is all." I sipped my drink. He was one of the oldest pack members and saw way more than most, but tonight was not the night for the poking he sometimes enjoyed.

"Anything to do with your new guest?" he asked, not taking the hint.

"Not at all," I said, giving him another hint he might decide not to pick up on either.

"I was chatting with her," Gus said.

"I noticed." I finished my ale, wishing shifters got drunk easier, especially if he insisted on discussing her.

"She doesn't look altogether threatening. When I heard you were keeping her, I was expecting something a little scarier. Unless there's a different reason you're keeping her. She might not be a shifter, but she's a fine-looking female."

"Goodnight, Gus." I grabbed a bottle of whiskey on my way out, heading to the storage building. I'd sleep there tonight, like I had last night.

CHAPTER 16

D*ante*

Frankie barged into the storage building, which was becoming the place I spent almost all my time lately, between going over records and not wanting to go home.

"We've got a vampire heading toward the gates," he said, sounding a little winded, like he'd sprinted over here. "He's walking out in the open, as if he's coming to discuss something."

Now I had a damned vampire approaching. Vampires didn't stroll up to this place and ask to have a chat, especially not here. We were known to be uncooperative with their kind.

"Just one?"

"Yes. One male, already confirmed by patrol in the forest."

I'd been waiting to see what would come after the last

hit but had imagined an attack, not a lone vampire on a diplomatic mission. What were the odds it had something to do with River? My gut instinct said they were uncomfortably narrow.

"Where is she?" I asked, not having to name River.

"In the kitchens."

I closed out of the files I'd been scanning, shut the computer, and headed down toward the gates, Frankie following. The vampire in question was standing there, waiting on the other side. Two of my shifters were on either side of him, and more stood inside the gates, daring him to make a wrong move.

The show of force was a bit of overkill, but at least in my pack, we had no delusions that we weren't at war with these vampires.

The innate stillness of the vampire guest hinted at an age older than the hills around this place. It was as if they forgot what being human was after a while, and no longer cared to pretend. Everything about their unnaturalness repulsed me.

"Open the gates," I said to Jobo, who was closest.

The vampire proceeded to walk in and slowly approach, stopping at a reasonable distance. He wasn't here for a fight. That much was clear.

"I'm assuming you came to talk?"

He nodded and then looked about the place. "It's about a delicate subject. I'd appreciate it if we could go somewhere with a little more privacy."

I nodded and walked into the small building just inside the gates. He could follow me or not. I didn't care, and I wasn't concerned about being with a vampire alone, not even one of his age and strength. I'd gone head to head with older and stronger. I was still here. They weren't.

He followed me in.

"It's soundproofed. No one will hear us in here," I said.

He stood still for a minute, as if judging the silence for himself.

"My name is Heiko. I'm not from around these parts, but I was visiting a coven in the area not long ago. I was in the process of negotiating with them to acquire something, but when I returned to complete my transaction, the coven seemed to have burned down. I happened to pick up on the scent of shifters and traced the trail back here, so this seemed the most logical place to inquire."

"Inquire into what?" I asked, waiting for the threat to come, knowing what he was looking for. Hoping I was wrong.

"Accidents happen all the time, and I'm very understanding of that. As long as I can conclude my transaction, I don't see this situation having anything to do with me."

"And you think there is a way I can help you finish this transaction?" I leaned on the only table in the small room, waiting for him to offer more details even though I already knew exactly where this was going.

"There was an unusual female staying with them that I was interested in." His jaw clicked to the side and back, one of the only movements he'd made since he walked into the room.

I wanted to ram my fist through the wall. She'd already been more aggravation than I'd guessed, and it seemed the price of keeping her, trying to find out her secrets, was about to get steeper.

"You'll have to give me a little more information. 'Unusual female' fits an awful lot of people." Not to mention, admitting to having her was akin to admitting we'd raided the vampire coven and then torched it. The conflict between the shifters and vampires was on the verge of becoming an open war, but I wasn't above buying a few more months, especially not when dealing with this enemy.

"It's a female with an unusual scent. I don't think I need to elaborate any further." He tilted his head to the side, but unnaturally slowly, as if a fragment of humanity might still be lingering inside of him but was distorted by too many years of being a monster.

He didn't need to say any more, and I wouldn't bother to continue playing dumb. It had never been my strong suit.

"If I knew the location of this unusual female, why would I hand her over?" My skin was tingling and itching all over as the urge to shift and tear this vampire's throat out threatened to overcome me—not that he'd know. I'd lived long enough to learn how to keep my appearance calm, even when a storm raged within.

"Because I would make it worthwhile to make a trade. The unfortunate incident that happened to that coven doesn't appear to be widely known. By the time someone does notice, any trace of anything unusual will probably be gone—unless there was someone to say otherwise."

He'd do my dirty work and cover up a crime committed against his people, on behalf of the pack, just to get River? What the hell *was* she?

"She's a little more valuable than that trade, don't you think?" I asked, smiling, as if I knew. Common sense dictated she had to be, or this vampire had a strange obsession for her.

Heiko didn't flinch, as if he'd expected to pay more. "Name your price."

What in the hell was River that this very old, very

powerful vampire asked me to "name my price"? What would happen if I *didn't* name my price? There would be a cost for that as well.

"I'll need a little time to think about it."

He moved so fast that he nearly disappeared, and then he was standing beside me, placing a card down on the table. "Don't take too long. I'm not the most patient type."

If he thought that little trick was going to work, he hadn't dealt with too many alphas. He could bluster all he wanted. I made decisions when I was ready.

"*Like I said*, I need some time. I'll let you know."

His face was unreadable as he turned and walked out of the building. He was a blur out of the gates.

I was still leaning on the table when Frankie walked in. "What was that about?"

I didn't move or answer for a few seconds, trying to calm the urge to shift.

"He came here looking to make a trade for River," I finally said. "He told me to name my price." I picked up the card he'd left on the table and shoved it in my back pocket.

"Did you name it?" Frankie asked, looking paler than normal.

"I'm thinking about it," I answered. It wasn't an offer I could turn down out of hand, not when, strategically, it might be the right move. Even if the idea did turn my stomach, it deserved thought. "Where is she now?"

"Prepping in the kitchen for dinner service."

I straightened. River and I were about to have a moment of truth.

"Dante, you won't really hand her over to him, will you?" Frankie asked before I made it to the door.

I froze, forced to voice the truth. "I'll do whatever is best for this pack."

It was what I had to do as alpha. I couldn't put an outsider before our survival, no matter how distasteful the negotiation might be. Hopefully River gave me a reason to keep her.

But if not...

CHAPTER 17

R *iver*

Carly walked over as I was finishing up the last chop on the onions—somehow I always got the onions. She dumped all her celery in front of me and then walked over to chat with Amber, smiling and giggling.

The two of them always looked for ways to do the least amount possible, but I'd rather have busywork than die of boredom. They were the laziest pair I'd ever met in my life. No wonder Natalie had been begging for help.

The door opened, and Amber and Carly's gazes snapped to the newcomer. I'd barely glanced up when Dante wrapped his arm around my midsection and carried me into the kitchen's office. He shut the door, put me down, and then planted a hand on the wall beside my head.

The last time we'd been this close, we hadn't been talking. I tried to shove the memory from my mind, even as my body seemed to remember all too well. I planted my spine against the door so it couldn't curve into him of its own volition.

"I had a very interesting visit this afternoon," he said, his voice lower than normal.

I sucked on my lower lip, and his eyes fixated there. He was talking, and all I could think about was how close he was, the feeling of his arm wrapped around me. His touch seemed to short-circuit my brain at the very worst times. It was probably because I'd been deprived of any touch for so long, or hadn't been around anyone even mildly attractive, let alone Dante, who oozed sex appeal. I'd better find someone else to fixate on soon, or things might get weird. Okay, *weirder*.

"Why do you do that? Grab me around the waist instead of asking me to come with you?" If he hadn't touched me, I wouldn't be feeling all weird.

He planted the other hand on the wall, boxing me in. "Because I don't trust you to do what I say, and for good reason."

The guy had a point. I wasn't fond of orders. I'd want to know why, and he'd never bother explaining, not when he could carry me into the other room without asking me.

"I had a vampire asking about you today," he said, his gaze as intense as it was steeped in accusation.

Suddenly the feeling of his touch took a back seat as the prospect of sitting in a basement for the rest of my life loomed large. I couldn't go back to them, any of them.

When I came here, I'd told myself it was another jail, but that was a joke. This place was worlds better than where I'd been. And if the vampires were seeking me out, it could only be for one reason, one vampire. There was one who came right before Dante's raid, and he'd known something, or at least sensed something more than the others.

My spine was still glued to the door, but now it was because I was afraid I'd fall to the ground without it.

Dante dipped his head lower. "You're turning white as a ghost. Why don't you tell me what's going on and stop playing stupid? Why do they want you bad enough that I can name my price?"

My mouth grew dry. "Is that what they said?"

"Yes. Said they'd bury all the evidence of the raid and anything else I might want. All I have to do is hand you over."

"What did you tell them?" My heart was beating so hard that I was afraid I'd pass out before he answered.

He wanted to get rid of me. I'd overheard a lot of things lately, like how someone had originally been coming from another pack to get me but decided not to. Well, here was his opportunity to unload me.

"It wasn't a *them* but a *him*. Does the name Heiko ring a bell for you? Or do you know nothing about that either?"

My lungs stopped functioning as everything short-circuited. It was as bad as I'd feared, and now he'd tracked me down.

Dante's eyes were intense as we stared at each other.

"So you do know the name," he said.

I couldn't talk. I could barely think past the panic.

"You have a choice," he said. "You tell me what's going on, why he wants you so badly, or I hand you over."

He was asking the impossible. I couldn't tell him, not without betraying my people, however many were left. As long as I could feel some of us still out there, they had a chance, even if I didn't. If the vampire suspected what I was, and I was turned over, everything might be lost anyway, but I wouldn't betray them willingly.

"You need to tell me what's going on. I need to know what you are. Time is up. You get until tomorrow night."

I still wasn't responding. I didn't know what to say.

"Do you hear me?"

I managed to nod. There was only one option left.

CHAPTER 18

R *iver*

There wasn't a creak in the house. He hadn't been here when I got back from the kitchen. His ego was so big that he probably figured I was so awed and scared of his threat that I wouldn't go anywhere. He'd left me here alone, practically asking me to escape.

There was only one option. I got out tonight or I was done. I wasn't going to tell him what I was so he'd hand me over. I'd rather die trying to get out than live through that again. It was better to get shot in my back running than bowing at the feet of my captor. It was time to seize the opportunity.

I wouldn't be so brazen as to walk out the front door of the cabin. It might not seem like someone was watching, but there were eyes on me constantly. I'd slip out the window in my room.

I layered on two sweaters and then rummaged through

the refrigerator, grabbing a block of cheese and the end of a roast, then wrapped them and threw them both in a bag.

I turned the lights out in the bedroom then watched, waiting to spot movement. There was no way I wasn't being watched by someone. Then I spotted him. Marshall was in the distance, the light of a cigar flaring as he killed some time.

Dammit. I'd have to do something to get out of here, but if I did too much, it would backfire. I didn't have magic that worked offensively, or I wouldn't have been stuck in a basement for a year. It was a delicate balance when using it for my own ends and not leaving myself vulnerable after the repercussions hit.

Still, there was no option. I centered myself, giving the slightest push in his direction, and then waited.

His cigar dropped. He was looking for it, and then a small flame started by his feet. While he was busy trying to stomp it out, I opened the window.

I was halfway out when an arm wrapped around my waist, hauled me back in, and tossed me on the bed in a heap.

"Where did you think you were going?" Dante asked as he shut the window and then turned to me.

I jumped to my feet, shooting toward the door, some intrinsic part of me rebelling over his claim on my sovereignty.

I'd barely made it into the living room before his arm wrapped around my waist again. He hoisted me off my feet and dropped me back onto the couch.

He braced a hand on the back of the couch as he leaned forward, forcing me farther back.

"Did you really think you were going to get away that easily?"

I turned my head, refusing to answer.

"For someone who doesn't want to end up with vampires, you think strolling out of here is the smartest move? You don't think Heiko has people watching this place, hoping for you to make it easy on him?"

Actually, I *hadn't* considered that in my tsunami of panic, but damned if I'd tell him that.

"No? You don't have any interest in answering that either?" he asked. He pulled the chair closer to the couch, sat in it, and stared at me. "So what are your plans? You'd rather keep your secrets and get handed over? If that's the case, I'll call Heiko now. I might as well get something from the deal."

I glared in his direction but kept my silence.

"I'll take it from your expression that you do understand."

"I don't have a choice," I said, and then looked away again, trying to hold it together.

"You always have a choice. That's a cop-out."

"If you're telling me I either tell you everything or end up being traded to the vampires, I *don't* have a choice."

He kept staring at me, expecting more than I could give.

"Look, you're right, I'm not human—we both know that. And if I could tell you what I was, if there was an easy out, I would take it, but it's not *my choice*. So if you're going to hand me over, then just do it."

I stood, done with his games.

"Sit. I'm not done yet."

I sat again, knowing how easily he could force me to. And there was still a chance I could get out of this predicament. I'd cooperate if it would buy me some time.

"I'm going to ask you questions, and you're going to answer as honestly as you can. If you don't, I'll hang you out to dry and let him take you. Do you understand?"

"Yes."

"Do you know why the vampires want you?"

"I suspect, but I don't know for sure."

"Is it the same reason the others had you in the basement?"

"No. The others kept me for the same reason you are. They knew I was different, but that was all."

"Why does he want you?"

"Because of what I am."

"Which is?"

"I can't tell you."

I leaned forward, planting my forehead in my hands. He was going to hand me over. Why wouldn't he? I couldn't go back to that. I'd rather be dead. I'd have to die, because if Heiko got his hands on me and confirmed what I was, if other people found out…

"Please. Look, I'll do whatever you want, and I'll even be nice about it, but I can't tell you what you want."

"For fuck's sake, River, do you understand the position you're putting me in? If it comes down to you or my pack, my pack is going to win every time, and you aren't giving me anything."

"You should've just let me go when you found me. Stuck me on that bus with the others."

"Maybe I should've, but it's too late now," he said, sliding down in his chair and, for once, looking almost as miserable as I was.

"If you decide to hand me over, will you at least give me a little warning so I can prepare myself?" I wouldn't be used by Heiko. I'd grown up on stories of what happened to my kind. Death was preferable.

"Prepare how?" Dante asked, as if he could sense the depths of my desperation.

Maybe he could. Shifters had a sense of smell that

couldn't be rivaled, and surely dread had some hallmark scent.

"I think I deserve to know, is all," I lied.

He was in his chair and then he was there, putting his hands on my shoulders. "River, if you want to survive this, you have to give me *something*."

"All I can say is that if they're your enemy, you don't *want* them to have me."

He scoffed. "That's it? That's all you've got? I'm supposed to choose to keep you, possibly put my pack in a worse position, because you think it's better?"

I nodded, knowing how inadequate it was.

He shook his head, and I could see my fate neatly written in his expression.

CHAPTER 19

D*ante*

River wasn't going to tell me anything. I'd spent the entire day hoping she'd send me word that she'd changed her mind. She hadn't. She'd die first. As much as I respected that she'd protect her secrets, I needed to do what was right for my pack.

I'd been working a long time on piecing together the true hierarchy of the vampire establishment but only had hints of the true power behind the curtains. The older and stronger they were, the more sway and control they had. If I wanted to really hurt them, I had to go for the top. As of yet, I hadn't been able to figure out who the top eight that got mentioned sporadically were.

I dialed Heiko. "You want the girl, I want to know the locations and names of the top eight vampires. Not the ones who pretend to be in charge but the ones who really are. You hand that information over…"

My chest tightened. I knew full well what I was about to do, what I had to do for my pack.

"Yes?" Heiko asked.

It didn't matter if she was an innocent in this war, which wasn't even confirmed. My pack came first or I didn't deserve to be alpha.

"Give me that information and you can have her."

There was a pause, and just as I thought he'd say no, he said, "I agree. I can be there tonight to complete the deal."

Tonight. I'd have to hand her over to him tonight. Did it matter? Tomorrow wouldn't be easier, and this was the right thing to do, for me and every other shifter in existence. I'd given her an out, an opportunity to come clean. She hadn't taken it. She wouldn't betray her people. Well, neither could I. This wasn't on me.

It was midnight when I walked into her room, my chest tight and my skin tingling. The urge to shift had been strong ever since my talk with Heiko, but that wasn't unusual. It would be stranger if I *hadn't* had the urge.

River jerked her head in my direction as soon as the door opened. No sane person in her situation would've been sleeping. She sat up and stared at me like I was an executioner come to cut off her head.

"Get dressed. We have to meet someone."

"Where?" She sat there for a few seconds, frozen, as if stunned it had come to this.

"You know." She'd been warned. What had she thought would happen?

"You're handing me over?" Her voice was trembling. In all the time she'd been here, it'd never done that. My flesh itched and tingled with an intensity that was hard to ignore.

"Yes," I said, waiting to see if she would say anything.

She turned, dropping her gaze to the floor.

If she wouldn't help herself, what did she expect me to do? Put her before my pack when she wouldn't cooperate? No. This was her choice.

I shut the door, giving her a minute to change and get herself together.

She walked into the living room a few minutes later, dressed in jeans, boots, and her heaviest jacket. She moved past me toward the door, not glancing my way.

I followed her out, letting her lead the way, as she seemed to know to head toward the front gate.

I'd expected her to beg, plead, say *something*, but she was utterly silent as we headed out.

The only thing I saw was pure rage and venom in her eyes when she looked at me, and the grip around my chest grew tighter, the desire to shift even stronger.

Had she thought I'd pick her over my pack when she wouldn't even try to work with me? I was at war. Sometimes innocents got hurt. And who knew if she was an innocent? I knew nothing about her, and she refused to speak. Honest people didn't have anything to hide.

Frankie was heading toward us not far from the cabin. He kept staring at her, as if her inability to look at him was shredding him inside.

"Is he there?" I asked, forcing Frankie's attention back to me.

"Waiting in the gatehouse," Frankie said, as if we were about to meet the Grim Reaper. "He didn't come alone this time. There's another ten with him, waiting outside the gates. We've got more than twice that watching them."

"Good."

Silence fell, and I was the first to start walking again, not looking at River.

She'd follow. She had too much pride to make a futile attempt of running, and she was too smart to bother exerting herself.

We walked for another minute before Frankie made a suspicious sniffing sound. My second-in-command, my right-hand man, was fucking crying. This had to be a joke.

Frankie sniffed again. "It's cold out here tonight," he said.

I was silent. If I said anything, it wouldn't be good, and tonight was already ugly.

"I don't blame you," River said softly to Frankie. "I know it's not your decision."

He nodded, probably because he would've started bawling if he replied. It was good she was leaving, given what she was already doing to my men.

The light from the gatehouse was visible. This needed to be done. She was just another headache, and I had a war to wage. Handing her over was the smartest move. If Heiko was true to his word, he was going to give me information I might never be able to get, names and locations that were invaluable to our side.

Heiko moved to the window, watching our approach.

River's heart, usually too soft to hear, was beating like a drum, her breathing stuttering and stopping as she neared the building. She didn't look at me but continued toward it anyway.

I walked in first. Heiko wouldn't be touching her until the information was handed over. His eyes lit up as he watched her following behind me. Her chin was up and she met his gaze like a fucking warrior. Frankie, on the other hand, walked in behind her looking like he was about to be sick.

Heiko dragged his gaze from River to me, holding out a

folder. "This is the information you requested. Now for her."

River wobbled slightly as he reached out.

I stepped in front of her, having no idea why the fuck I did.

"I'll need to look these over first," I said.

Heiko dropped his hand. "Fine."

I flipped open the folder, skimming it and finding eight names and locations, having a hard time focusing at all with the clamoring her heart was making behind me. It wasn't like he was going to kill her, or even feed off her, or he wouldn't have paid so dearly. He'd keep her alive. After the war was over, I'd see if I could do something for her.

I pushed away the image of what she'd looked like when we found her. There was no going back. I'd looked at the names and gotten payment, a kind that couldn't be refunded. The deal was done.

"Are you satisfied?" Heiko asked in a tone that said I better be.

I shut the folder and took a step out from in between Heiko and River, barely able to withstand the urge to shift at this point. I hadn't had such a difficult time controlling my wolf since I was an adolescent. I literally wanted to tear off my own skin.

Heiko wrapped his hand around River's wrist in a hold so tight she flinched.

"I'm so happy to see you again," he said.

She'd kept up a tough exterior so well that when she finally cracked, trying to pull away from him, it rocked me.

He dragged her out the door as I watched.

The tingling in my skin grew, the urge to shift becoming so strong that there was no stopping it. For the first time since I was a kid, I had no control over what my body was doing. I shifted so fast that my clothing shot off me in shreds. I leapt out the door and in between them, knocking Heiko's grasp off her. River looked stunned, but Frankie leapt into action, grabbing her and tugging her out of the way.

Heiko bared his fangs as we squared off, toe to toe. The growls of my people sounded all around me as they shifted as well, staging their own stare-off with the vampires waiting at the gates.

"You'll regret this," Heiko hissed. "You broke our deal."

I answered with a growl that might've woken the entire pack, not budging from my spot in between him and River.

He looked beyond me, toward her, and I lunged, nearly catching his flesh but stopping just shy. This was the first time in my life I'd ever gone against my word. The least I could do was not kill him.

Heiko was hissing, but he slowly began to back up to his own kind, knowing he was outnumbered, knowing the bloodbath that would ensue.

"This will not be the end," he said.

He backed slowly toward the gates, and then he and his people were gone.

I turned and jerked my head toward Frankie. He immediately urged River farther away from the gates, in the direction of my cabin.

I headed after the vampires, the rest of the pack following, and made sure they cleared our territory, not sure when I'd be calm enough to shift back.

CHAPTER 20

R *iver*

Frankie shrugged out of his jacket and laid it on my shoulders as we walked back to the cabin. It wasn't going to help the shivering that was more from shock than cold. Was it done? Was I truly safe, or would Dante change his mind again? It had looked pretty bad, and the way Heiko acted... But what did I know of these things?

I stepped onto the porch of the cabin and crossed my arms, replaying everything that had happened only minutes ago in my numbed mind. I'd almost been handed over to Heiko, then in seconds Dante pulled a one-eighty, about to kill the vampire he'd made a deal with.

Frankie was standing beside me silently, as if he were trying to sort the situation out as well.

"Do you know what happened back there?" I asked.

He didn't look like he had any answers, but he must have more than I did.

His hands on his hips, he shook his head. "I have no idea what that was about, or why he changed his mind. The one thing I can say: that deal looks like it's *done*."

"Are you sure? Maybe Heiko will come back around and try to renegotiate?"

Frankie's brows nearly touched together. "Negotiations between vampires and werewolves don't happen often, and there's a certain etiquette you need to follow when dealing with them. After what happened out there, I don't know how there'll be any follow-up negotiations. Talk? No. Bloodshed? Possibly."

A well of nausea gripped my stomach. "Bloodshed? I don't want anyone to fight. I just want to be left alone."

He smiled slightly. "I wouldn't take too much of the blame if it happens. We were fighting long before you showed up, and we'll be fighting after you leave. This is bigger than you." He took a deep, calming breath as he looked out into the night. "I'm glad this blew up. I didn't like anything about it, not from the second I got a whiff of it. No one should end up with that abomination."

"Thanks. So am I." I shrugged off his jacket and passed it back to him.

He climbed down the porch steps and stopped at the bottom. "I'm going to head back and make sure they don't need me. You going to be okay?"

"I'll be fine."

"Do me a favor—don't try to disappear tonight, okay? The timing could be *very* bad with a forest full of vampires."

I laughed, sounding a little hysterical. "I won't."

Frankie disappeared toward the front.

I settled into one of the rockers on the porch, waiting... For what? Dante's return? Some explanation that would pop into my head? I didn't know, but sleep wouldn't be coming anytime soon, and as it turned out, neither would Dante.

* * *

I was chopping carrots in a sleepy daze, still running over last night's events in my brain. One second I was about to be handed over, and the next Dante shifted, looking as if he were about to eviscerate Heiko, who hadn't done anything to provoke it. There had barely been any talking between the two. Had there been some sort of nonverbal slight I wasn't aware of? What had I missed that made Dante change his mind so suddenly and ferociously?

Dante hadn't returned last night, which was probably a good thing. He'd been gone this morning as well. I was beginning to wonder when he'd come back.

What did I even say after what happened? From the looks of it, the negotiations were done with Heiko, but what happened if there was another taker? Would I be bartered again? Did I thank the man who'd stolen me from my last kidnapper for not handing me over to someone worse? Ask him if he was going to keep me around for a while?

Henrietta walked into the kitchen and smiled in my direction before heading over to Natalie. "Natalie, do you have that powdered sugar?"

"Sure do. Waiting on the counter for you over there. Had the girls measure it out this morning."

"Thanks!" Henrietta grabbed the bag and headed back to me. "Natalie, I'm stealing your girl for a few minutes," she yelled across the room, locking her arm with mine.

"She's not our girl. *Please*, steal her," Carly said under her breath. Amber giggled as if Carly had said something clever.

"You two, mind your Ps and Qs," Henrietta said as she tugged me past them. Not bothering to keep her voice down, she added, "Those two have always been bad apples, even when they were tots. You could see the rot right out of the basket."

I lifted my face to the sun, having never relished it as much as I did after being deprived of it so long and having a close call with a return to hell. The day was mild for late fall, the sun warm on my skin. The reminder of how I might've lost this freedom last night made it feel even better.

She waited until we were out of the kitchen before she said, "Those two better not be giving you a hard time. Because if they are, I'll have a talk with them."

"I believe they *think* they are, but it's hard to keep track of their silliness."

A couple of snide comments and pointed looks weren't shaking my foundation. You had to put more effort in if you wanted to get a wave out of this ocean.

We both laughed. "That always seems to be the way," Henrietta said. "The strong so often question their capabilities, while the weak imagine they can tackle the world. But I didn't come to talk about those two ninnies. Word's spreading fast about the visitor and what happened last night. I heard you were there and that Dante wasn't in a good way. I tried questioning him about it, but he wouldn't discuss anything."

"I was there, and Dante definitely was not in a good way." Given the deafening sound of Dante's growl last night, it would be surprising if anyone didn't know something had happened last night.

"I don't like the sounds of what almost went down." Henrietta, normally so composed, shook her head as she crossed her arms.

"I'm not sure exactly what happened, and I was there. He was about to hand me over, and then he shifted and lunged at Heiko, the vampire he'd made a deal with." I couldn't even look in the direction of the front gate without getting a chill over how close I'd come to being a real prisoner again.

"I can't believe he almost did that." She tilted her head, looking off in the distance. "But he's never been one to hold people against their will, either. I swear I don't know what's gotten into him lately."

"He's never kept anyone here before?" I'd assumed this was old hat for him.

"He's never kept an innocent, someone he had no beef with before. He's being beyond stubborn lately."

"He's nervous that I might be able to aid his enemies," I said. He had no idea how right he was.

Wait a minute. Had I just defended Dante? If I had, it was only because I might've made the same trade if it protected my kind.

"I mean, it's logical."

Henrietta hummed. "Surprised you see it that way. Well, I didn't come here to listen to you defend my nephew. I need to ask you a question."

"Of course," I said, not caring what she asked if it changed the subject. My heart rate had gone from its normal putzing around to a quarter horse in the race of its life.

Her eyes were darting around the place. "Do you want to be here? Because if you want to leave, I'll get you out."

My mouth dropped open as I processed what it sounded like she'd said. She'd help me escape? "You'd go against Dante? For me? You barely know me."

"I know what I have to do to live with myself." She

shrugged, as if this were the right thing to do, so there was no other choice.

I threw my arms around her, probably choking her with how tight my hold was. She patted my back patiently as she waited for me to pull myself together.

When that didn't happen right away, she said, "River, it's not that I don't appreciate the hug, but I'd rather not be so obvious about your gratitude if I need to get you out of here."

I backed up, noting how we'd already caught a couple of weird stares.

"Sorry. It's just..." My eyes were burning with the amount of gratitude I was attempting to hold back. Even if she weren't capable of doing what she offered, she'd *try*. It was more than anyone had done for me in a long time.

"You just need to tell me when you want to leave. I'll need time to figure things out, but I'll make it happen."

Having someone that would help me get out? Between the two of us, it could happen. All I needed was a little help and I'd be beyond these walls.

Beyond the walls that were probably serving a dual purpose right now. Heiko wouldn't give up easily. If he'd tracked me here, offered Dante whatever he wanted, he knew what I was, what I could do, and what I was worth. He'd be lying in wait, watching, hoping I'd make a move that stupid, where he could easily pick me off.

I walked a couple of feet to a bench on the side of the walk, not believing what I had to say. There was no other option, though.

"Actually, I think it might be best if I stay for a while, at least if Dante's not going to hand me over."

"Really?" Henrietta asked, sitting down next to me.

"Just until after winter passes and I can come up with a better plan, as long as another deal isn't made." If Dante did find another taker, or work things out with Heiko, I'd have to take my chances.

"If you're sure."

I nodded, not sure at all.

If she'd met Heiko, knew why he wanted me, she wouldn't be so surprised. When I'd thought I was being handed over to him, all I wanted to do was run. Now that Dante had decided to not turn me over, this might be the safest place there was, as long as he held strong.

"I'm not sure there is a better place right now, not for me," I said, feeling like I owed her some honesty after all she tried to do for me.

Dante had many faults, but right now, he was the one thing keeping me out of Heiko's hands, because not even a coven of vampires would be willing to walk into this place. Or at least I hoped so.

"I should probably be getting back," I said.

Henrietta nodded. "Oh, before I forget, it's Gus' birthday on Tuesday. I know you aren't in the best place, but he's really taken a liking to you, and he'd love to see you there."

When the person who was willing to break me out of her own pack invited me to a birthday party, I showed. She could've asked me to walk on hot coals and I would've done it.

"I'll be there."

CHAPTER 21

D*ante*

Last night's meeting had turned into a disaster and definitely not the right move for the pack. I didn't know if Heiko's names and locations would pan out, but if they did, and he'd held up his end of the bargain, I'd screwed him. He wouldn't be going away easily. There would be a price to pay.

Unfortunately, there was no way I could let River go, not even now, knowing it was a mistake. When I saw her skin go white as a ghost as she struggled to get away from him, when I remembered how she'd looked when we first found her...

But losing control the way I had? What the hell happened? It made no sense, not even to me. Even now I could feel the itch to shift. I wouldn't be handing her over. Right or wrong, it didn't seem to matter.

Whatever she was, Heiko wanted her, and badly. Even if

I had been willing to hand her over, it might have turned out to be a disaster. There was only one way to handle this. I needed to find out what she was, one way or another, and I was running out of ideas.

The halls of the library were empty. Where was that damned kid when I needed him?

I finally found him at the end of the aisle, on the floor with three books laid open. His red hair was sticking up in every direction, like his brain was on the verge of exploding. The kid was a human reference machine.

I stood in front of Macky for a full minute before he noticed me.

He dropped his book in his scramble to get to his feet. "Oh, Dante. Sorry! I didn't see you."

"I have an important job for you."

"You do?" His eyes lit up. As one of the weaker shifters in the pack, I didn't call on him for the tough assignments, or not physically tough. This was going to be a rough one.

"I need you to find a race that would fit this description." I handed him a piece of paper, detailing all the irregularities that River possessed, which weren't a lot to go on.

He skimmed the short list and then glanced up, clearly afraid to ask me the obvious question.

"Whatever your suspicions, I need you to keep them to yourself," I added. The kid liked to read more than interact with people, so that shouldn't be tough.

"I give you my word as a shifter that I won't say a word to anyone." He slapped a hand over his heart, as if he'd been asked to go on a suicide mission.

"Yeah, just work on it."

I left the library, passing the compound's mechanic shop. It used to be a science lab until we blew out a few windows and put in garage doors instead. With what was coming, we'd have to be as self-sufficient as possible.

Taking your car to an outside mechanic when you were in a war was a recipe for disaster.

Gus was under a lift, talking to one of the younger pack members, when he turned, sensing me. Even though he was older, his senses were on par with my own, which wasn't surprising, since he'd been the alpha of his own pack before he decided to retire.

He walked out, falling into step beside me. "There's some rumblings about what happened last night," he said. "Heard the growling myself but didn't feel like getting out of bed." He yawned, as if I'd screwed up his sleep.

"Little bump in the plan, but nothing disastrous." Not yet, anyway. We'd see what next week brought.

"Can't say I'm upset about that. I know in war sometimes innocents get hurt, but that one wasn't sitting well with me."

"Apparently it didn't with me either," I said, preferring not to have this conversation at all.

Gus looked at me for a few seconds and then let out a soft laugh. "You didn't mean to shift, did you?"

"No. I didn't," I said, owning up to more than I'd planned on.

"Well, this is very interesting, although I already suspected as much." He laughed a little more. Gus was lucky I liked him.

"I'm glad you're entertained, but if you're going to insist on talking about this, do you know of other instances where something like that happened? I can't afford slips like that, and I'd like to know what triggered it."

"It never happened to me, but I've heard of it more than a few times. Not altogether uncommon under the right circumstances," he said, laughter still thick in his voice.

"Which are?" If there was an explanation, it almost

made his amusement more bearable. I'd find out what the issue was and never let it happen again.

He waited as a few people passed us before he continued. "You sure you want to know? You're not going to like the answer, not being the way you are."

"Which is what?" I asked.

"You know, a little cold, closed off. Not one to show your feelings."

"I'm the alpha of this pack, about to head into war. How do you suggest I act?" Sometimes discussions with Gus were more aggravating than fruitful. Alphas who retired often went to different packs to make the transition easier. His decision to retire to my pack was a gift I was still trying to figure out. I was certain someone was having a good laugh about it.

"I'm not faulting you. I'm just saying you're not going to like the answer." He was smiling even wider.

"Gus, spit it out already." I'd never had time for cat-and-mouse games, not even for people I liked.

He crossed his arms. "The only time I've heard of an alpha losing control is when he feels that his mate is being threatened and his protective nature comes out."

I turned my head, giving him a look that made my opinion of his joke clear. His afternoon of amusement at my cost was over. "That's obviously not the case, so in what other circumstances does it happen?"

He shoved his hands in his pockets as he acted like he had to think long and hard about it. "Protective nature toward offspring, which *clearly* isn't the case here." He smiled, as if he couldn't be more amused.

"*Or...*"

"That's it. Those are the only two scenarios I know of."

"You're insane." I walked away from him, and he followed.

"I don't know why you're so opposed. I've seen the way you look at her, and I think the girl would make a great mate. She's a tough cookie." He was dogging my steps like an old matchmaker.

"She's not for me, and she's not my mate," I said, not caring who heard.

"You can say that, but I see the way you look at her. You want her, and you cared enough last night to shift," he said.

"There's a war coming. I don't have time for this." I picked up my pace, trying to lose the old man before I punched him instead.

"Then avoid her as much as you can, because all these feelings you get when you're around her aren't going away. The shifter in you has chosen his mate. It's over and done."

"I have to get back to work. Thanks for the talk," I said, even though it had been utterly useless. Gus was occasionally a good source of information, or he had been. It was obvious that he wasn't anymore. The old man was starting to go batty, and the Hen Pack was getting to him.

I was walking into the storage building when Frankie caught up to me.

"I couldn't find you last night. Everything okay?" he asked.

Not another one. I'd had Henrietta this morning, Marshall acting weird after her, then Gus, and now Frankie? I was done discussing last night.

"Everything's fine." Or it would be, because last night would never happen again.

I opened up one of the computers, trying to get to work.

"I'm still trying to understand what happened. Did I miss something?" Frankie asked. "I didn't see Heiko do anything, but there had to be something I missed." He dropped onto the chair in front of me.

What *had* happened? It wasn't the crap Gus was trying to sell me.

I leaned back. There was only one logical reason that made sense. My gut had told me something was off with that transaction, and my shifter side reacted. I'd been trying to get rid of her, so my judgment got clouded.

"Heiko wanted her too much. We were on the losing end of that bargain."

That. Was. It. That was why my inner beast had reared its head and wouldn't settle down. Finally something that made sense. Nothing as crazy as protecting my mate.

Frankie nodded. "When he offered to name his price, that was suspicious."

"Very."

"I should probably let some of the guys know, so they understand what went down. More than a few of them were confused. We were all wondering what we didn't see."

I nodded, not caring what he told them, but at least the problem was solved. He headed toward the door, seeming eager to spread the news that I hadn't gone crazy.

"Before you go, do we have any bungalows opening up in Henrietta's cluster?"

Gus was insane, but having River out of my cabin might not be the worst idea. How much trouble could she get into over there? She'd have her own space but be surrounded by the Hen Pack.

"There's one opening up. Claudia says she wants to move in with her sister."

"When is she moving?"

"Some of the younger pack are helping her box things up now. Figure she'll be done in a week. Why? Someone coming? Want me to hold it open?"

I'd get my house back. River wouldn't be there in the morning or at night.

But could I really trust Henrietta not to help her leave? She was soft on River. Even if I did let River leave at some point, and of course I would, it couldn't be chaotic and in the middle of the night. Heiko would have spies everywhere now. He'd be waiting for her to try to slip out on her own. And if someone was going to have her, damned if it wouldn't be me. She was mine.

My *asset*, that was. Not mine. An asset for the pack.

"No. Only curious. I saw some activity over there. Carry on."

CHAPTER 22

R *iver*

I'd felt eyes on me on my way to the kitchen this morning, and again every time I left the building for even the most trivial reasons, like taking out the trash. The only time I hadn't been watched was when Henrietta stopped by. Clearly they had no idea what she'd come to talk to me about or they would've watched us even more.

The smell of burning hit the air, and I ran over to the oven. Third batch of bread, all nice and toasty charred.

Amber and Carly laughed where they stood on the other side of the room, probably having caught the scent of burning bread way before me but not bothering to mention it.

Natalie walked into the kitchen and headed to the newest batch.

"I'm sorry, Natalie. I should've been paying more attention. I can't believe I ruined another one."

"It's all right. I know you had a rough night," she said, confirming that there wasn't a single person in the pack that hadn't heard what went down.

"I'll make another batch," I said, tossing the burned loaves in the garbage.

"No, no need to do that," she said, a little too quickly. "Wait here a second." She disappeared into the back for a few minutes, coming back with a bag. "Here, take this and take the rest of the day off."

"She screws up and she gets to go home early?" Amber said, walking over.

"She could come in once a week and get more done than you," Natalie said in her all-business tone.

Amber huffed but went back to her prep table, where Carly and Sanjay were all too ready to commiserate with her.

"Are you sure?" I asked Natalie.

"I've had to get by with them for years. I'll make it another day," she said with an eye roll in their direction. She shoved the bag in my hands and pushed me toward the door.

"Thanks."

I went back to the cabin, and while unpacking her supplies, I discovered a letter, which contained a recipe and a short note.

This is Dante's favorite. It can't hurt, right?

A couple of hours later, I was basting the roast again, careful not to ruin this meal. Not one part of me was delusional about how pathetic this was. It would be convenient to blame Natalie for how idiotic I felt, but I was the one who'd cooked the thing.

She was right. If there was any way to soften him up, it had to be explored. He might not make it home until after midnight, but I'd wait, because I needed to know where I stood. Every opportunity I had to sway him to my side had to be taken, because I couldn't even think about how close disaster had come last night.

The roast warming, I lay on the couch, waiting, wondering if he'd come home tonight. Normally I would've been tucked away in my room by now.

I caught sight of him approaching, and a knot formed in my chest. This was probably for nothing. He barely tolerated me. But I had to take a shot, and the next one, and every opportunity after...

He walked in and turned his head toward the kitchen, smelling the roast, before turning to look at me on the couch.

"Were you waiting for me?" he asked.

I shrugged, trying to figure out the best approach for groveling. I'd never done it before and was unaware of the etiquette involved, if there was anything beyond looking desperate. I wouldn't sell out my people, so it was groveling or...

Yeah, didn't seem like there were any other options. Groveling it was.

"I made dinner." I headed toward the kitchen, pushing past the heaviness of shame. I needed to embrace this pathetic, loathsome feeling that was growing in me, all while trying to not look in his direction and see his gloating.

It was hard not to notice him stiffen out of the corner of my eye. This wasn't going to go well. I should've asked for some pointers before attempting this.

"You don't need to make me dinner," he said, his voice harsher than one would expect after an offering of food that was supposedly his favorite.

Instead of taking the roast out of the oven, I braced my hands on the counter, keeping my back to him. Was it done? Was I done? Had Frankie been wrong? Was I still going to be handed over?

I forced the hurricane brewing inside me to not explode outward. Betraying any emotion at this point wouldn't help. The only option was playing it cool and regrouping. I'd have to take Henrietta up on her offer and hope Heiko didn't find me.

"Will Heiko be coming back for me?" How much time did I have? Were they already making plans? What if he was on his way back right now?

I'd been raised on the stories of how my kind had been kept alive to do the bidding of some king or queen. That wouldn't be my end. I wouldn't do it. I'd get out of this while I still could, one way or another, before that wasn't an option.

"He won't be returning." His voice was grave, as if he already regretted his choice.

I whipped around, not believing him, not when he didn't make any sense. There was no reason to keep me. Handing me over, at least with what he knew, was the best move. Why wouldn't he? It was the best thing for his pack. Was this a lie to keep me in line until Heiko showed up again? It was the only logical explanation.

"You really aren't handing me over to him?"

"No," he said, his voice clipped, as if he were angry at me for asking him.

Anger didn't deter me. I'd lived through worse than a bad temper.

"Whatever the situation, please don't lie to me. I can

handle the truth." Well, the groveling hadn't lasted long. It was idiotic to think it would work. If my skills had been lacking after being locked in a basement for nearly a year, why would they suddenly improve?

"I'm not in the habit of lying. I give you my oath as alpha of this pack: I'm not handing you over." He walked to the refrigerator and grabbed a drink, as if the matter were done.

He was telling the truth. Everything I'd heard of alphas was that they lived and died according to their word. I couldn't decide whether I wanted to collapse in relief or jump around the room.

I settled on offering him some dinner again, because hugging him was off the table, no matter how relieved I was. "Are you hungry at all? I made a roast."

He looked toward the oven and then me, his eyes not quite chilly but distant. "I'm fine," he said.

He didn't sound fine. He sounded annoyed.

"It's not poisoned, if that's what you're thinking." The guy wasn't throwing me to the vampires, and yet I couldn't be content. Why did I care if he wouldn't eat my food? The only reason I'd made it was Natalie.

He was looking toward the oven like there *was* poison brewing inside of it. "I know why you made it. I don't want something that was cooked because you thought you had to."

"Are you angry? I was trying to…"

Trying to be nice? Not exactly. I was doing what he'd said. Using it to try to show him in any possible way how it might be better to have me around. To try and wriggle myself into his favor.

In truth, I didn't want to eat the thing either. It was like tainted meat, spoiled by sad and depressing motives. It would probably taste like depression and sadness.

"You know, I'm not in the mood for it either. Do you think Frankie might want it?"

"I'll let him know it's here," he said, and took a step toward his bedroom.

"I might make myself a grilled cheese sandwich. Do you want one of those, for no other reason than I'm already going to be making myself one?" I asked, holding out an olive branch when I should've let him retreat. We weren't friends. I didn't know why he'd changed his mind and kept me. He probably had his reasons that had nothing to do with my welfare.

He turned back to me, and I knew from his expression that he wasn't grabbing hold of the extended branch.

"I need to make something clear: you don't owe me anything. I didn't turn him down to be kind. I'm not handing you over because I believe that whatever you are, it might benefit them to have control of you. So you don't need to make me roasts, dinners, grilled cheeses, or anything else. I'd actually prefer if you didn't."

He was watching me, his eyes cold and unmoving, probably waiting for me to tell him to go to hell.

It wasn't going to happen. It could be my relief that I was safe here for the moment, or that hearing the truth never bothered me. We weren't friends, and would never be, but at this moment, I didn't completely hate him, either.

"Will you tell me if something changes?"

He opened his mouth as if he were going to say something but then stared at me for another few seconds. "Yes."

"Like I said, I'm going to make a grilled cheese for myself. If it'll appease your conscience for saving me for the wrong reasons, I can burn yours a little, get it kind of crusty and black at the corners. I've been perfecting my technique at burning things all day."

He smiled, even though he was clearly trying to fight the urge. "Thanks for the offer, but like I said, I'm going to pass."

He retreated to his room, from me, and I didn't blame him. He was keeping his distance, the way I'd been doing, and needed to continue to do. Because if he ever found out what I was, things would probably change a whole lot, and not in a good way, but that was tomorrow's headache. Tonight was a good night.

Fifteen minutes later, Frankie showed up with a smile to collect the desperation roast.

CHAPTER 23

D^{ante}

Another gathering, this time a birthday, and another night of Henrietta dragging River along. River didn't look any happier about being here than she had last time. Actually, she looked about as miserable as I was that she was here.

Henrietta looked my way, and I tilted my head. She shook hers, but then walked toward me a few seconds later anyway, knowing there would be no avoiding me. Or she knew what I was after and wanted to voice her annoyance, which was more likely.

"Why did you bring her here again? And don't tell me it was her idea. She looks like a cat getting dragged into a bath. Can you never leave well enough alone?" I spoke as softly as I could, but in a group of shifters, keeping anything you said secret without a large buffer was tough.

"She works and then sits in the house all by herself. You think that's *healthy*?"

"It's not like she's here on vacation," I countered. I should've tried to look as if we were having a pleasant conversation, considering the attention we were beginning to garner. At the moment, I didn't care.

"Oh, we all know that," she said in her finest huffy voice, the one she used on me when I was a boy who'd gotten back late after running wild in the forest. "The least we can do is try to give her the nicest experience we can while you figure out what you're doing. How long are you going to force her to stay here? Or do you have plans to sell her off again?"

"I'm fully aware of what I'm doing, and I don't need to run it past you," I said, sounding nothing like the ruffian she'd helped raise and every bit the alpha—not that it would make a damned bit of difference with this woman.

"You're telling me that girl is a threat? That you really think she's going to turn around and kill us?" Her hands were on her hips. If my pissed-off expression didn't scream there was a problem, her stance was broadcasting it to the entire party.

"She's hiding things, and until she comes clean, she's not going anywhere." Let the whole pack know. Not that I cared. *I* wasn't hiding anything.

"And what does she owe you, exactly? Her life story because you plucked her out of one jail and dropped her in another?" Her mouth was in a flat line as she waited for an answer.

Even if I'd tried to disguise that we were having a disagreement, it wouldn't have made a damn bit of difference with all the huffing and puffing Henrietta was doing.

"You might have a bad history, but that doesn't change my obligations. I have to do what's right for this pack."

"This has nothing to do *with the pack*. I don't think you're keeping her because you're worried about what kind of threat she is. I heard about the deal with Heiko. If you were thinking about the pack, you would've handed her over—not that I agree with that, so don't even go there. But don't act like you're protecting anyone's interests but your own. You want her. That's why you won't let her leave."

So Gus had gotten in the ear of the Hen Pack, or at least its leader. "Do you know how insane that is? I want nothing to do with the woman. In fact, I want you to send her back to the cabin. She doesn't belong at these gatherings. They're for the *pack*, and no matter how much you want to include her, she doesn't belong." The last thing I needed was for River to start getting cozy with anyone else. Since we'd been arguing, I'd seen both Marshall and Jobo heading over to talk to her. She already had Frankie practically eating out of her palm.

Henrietta gasped, as if what I'd said was beyond appalling. "It's Gus' birthday. He wants her here."

"She's not part of the pack. We don't know what the hell she is, and you think she should be invited to birthday parties?"

Henrietta's face flushed as she rubbed her arm. My aunt didn't like to shift much, but it looked like she was having trouble holding back.

"*Gus* likes her, and it's *his* birthday. You look at her like she's a pariah, but you won't let her leave. You say she's not part of the pack, but she has no chance to be a part of us because of the way you act, the way you tell everyone to keep an eye on her. Are you trying to keep tabs on her or make it so *you'll* have a reminder that she's not supposed to be here?" She was rubbing both arms as she pointed to where another of River's past guards were nearing her. "I think she's fitting in with some of the pack a little too well for your tastes.

"Get rid of her," I said, not caring if Henrietta shifted or not.

She took a few seconds to visibly compose herself before she said, "I have a cake to go handle. If you don't like having her here, you tell her to leave. I won't."

She walked off.

I turned my attention back to River, who was refusing to look my way. She was sitting on a bench, Doc having joined her entourage.

The cake was coming out soon. I'd let her sing "Happy Birthday," but then the party was over.

CHAPTER 24

R*iver*

"Happy birthday to you, happy birthday to you, happy birthday dear Gus, happy birthday to you!" the crowd sang.

I stood somewhere near the back of the boisterous group, present but knowing my place. There was no delusion that I was part of this pack, or ever would be. I'd seen the fight Dante and Henrietta had a little while earlier, and from the way they'd kept looking at me, along with everyone else, I hadn't needed shifter hearing to guess what it was about. In some people's opinion, I was a barely tolerated guest. That was fine. I didn't have any long-term aspirations of fitting in.

"Blow out your candles, you old bastard, before your damned cake burns the whole place down," Clancy yelled.

Gus laughed, but it took him three tries to get all those candles out. How long did these shifters live? It was reportedly longer than humans, but there were a lot of candles on that cake. Clearly Henrietta believed in accuracy.

She was at the helm, handing out slices a minute later as Amber and Carly were giggling off on the side. They'd probably just found out someone's dog had died or heard Dante disparaging me. Either would do the trick.

Pushing them from my mind, I took a piece of cake from Henrietta.

"Thank you," I said, having had her cakes and cupcakes before, when the guys would smuggle them into my room in the East Building. I hadn't known then that she was the mysterious baker.

Her cakes were normally light, fluffy, with just the right amount of sweetness. I took a bite, and there was a saltiness to the icing that was completely different. I glanced around. No one was saying anything, but people were putting their forks down on their plates, slices barely touched.

Henrietta was talking with one of her friends, staring down at her slice. She toyed at it with her fork, shaking her head, a frown on her face. Her friend Lucy was shaking her head and patting her arm. Another of her friends walked over, making a show of eating a large piece.

It was something with the icing. Henrietta had picked up sugar at the kitchen, probably for this cake. My gaze shot to Amber and Carly, who were still giggling away on the other side.

Those little assholes.

I meandered over to the keg, which was close to where they stood.

"That old bag is always dragging that dumb chick everywhere. She deserves to get laughed at. She's a fool," Amber said, knowing I could hear her. It was one thing for them to mess with me, but they weren't messing with Henrietta, not while I was still breathing.

I filled my glass and then took the last couple steps and closed the gap. They glared at my approach.

"Having an entertaining evening?" I asked, not caring if they could shift and rip me apart in seconds.

"What do you want, freak? What? You upset your mommy isn't having a good time?" Amber sneered. I remembered thinking she was a cute girl when I first saw her. I hadn't known her yet.

"You're right. I am a freak, but I won't be running and crying anywhere." I smiled. "*You* might be by the end of tonight."

"Really? You're going to do something to me?" Amber said, looking as if I couldn't possibly hurt her.

"Yes, that is exactly what I'm saying." I smiled and stepped closer. "I know what you two did."

"We didn't do anything," Carly said.

"Sure. And neither will I," I said.

"Shoo, freak. We're done talking to you," Carly said, motioning with her hand.

"Don't say you weren't warned." I walked away from them, but not before seeing the rattled looks in their eyes.

I shouldn't do it. I knew that. Both of them at once? It would cost me. But something had to be done. Even if the crime was never known by the victim, there had to be payment. If it were anyone but Henrietta, I might've been able to leave it alone. But not the one person who'd shown me so much kindness. No. This was being handled, and now. Seeing their smug faces as they ruined Henrietta's hard work, I refused to let them go unscathed.

I'd also pay for what I was going to do, and that was all right. I'd gladly pony up.

I found a nice bench to settle myself on with my glass

of ale and prepared. There would be no control over exactly what happened, or how good or bad it would be. The goal wasn't to do any lasting harm, only enough to teach them a lesson. In this world, you reaped what you sowed, as I would after I finished.

I built up the chant in my head, the one that had been passed down through my family line. Every lineage had their own words, and they were sacred. They helped focus the magic that buzzed inside of me in the direction needed. The longer the chant, the stronger the magic, and the worse, or better, the results.

As the force built a little within me, a few of the more sensitive people in the pack looked around, as if they felt a tingle of something odd in the air. Most had never been around one of my kind and couldn't quite put their finger on what it was they were feeling. They looked around, saw nothing out of order, and went back to their evening.

When the right amount of force built, I directed it at my targets.

Amber and Carly walked across the clearing, heading in Frankie's direction. They talked about him often, both crushing on him hard, not that they'd say it. Not only would they pay a price, it looked like it would be right in front of Frankie.

Amber had stopped in front of Frankie when a loud fart hit the air. Carly stared at her friend's horrified face, but that quickly morphed into one of disgust, and then gagging.

The gagging seemed a bit much until I noticed Amber's white pants were now stained brown in the back. The spot was growing, traveling downward, and everyone near her took a step back, as it seemed to be leaking out of her pants and onto the ground where she stood. Amber broke into tears before running from the crowd, the entire pack seeing she'd shit herself. Carly was about to follow, to console her friend, but stopped short, leaning over and vomiting, splattering several people's shoes and pants in the process, including Frankie's. Sounds of disgust spread through the group as Carly took off next.

Jobo, with a friendly smile and warm eyes, came and took a seat next to me. "That was a bit of a mess, huh?" he asked. "Wonder what those two got into."

"Yeah, I wonder what happened," I said, then sipped my ale.

Dante walked over to us. "Jobo, I need a word with River," he said, his tone colder than normal.

I froze, my heart going from the beat of a waltz to heavy metal. Did he know something? Had I given myself away? Had he sensed the magic in the air?

"Yeah, sure." Jobo got up and gave me a last smile as he walked away, as if to say good luck.

I got to my feet, trying to prepare for whatever was to come.

"I think it's time for you to leave for the night."

He knew what I'd done. I should've stayed sitting because my knees felt like they were going to buckle. Now what? How'd he link that to me? What could I say? They were his pack members. Of course he was furious. How did he know, though? Could I deny it?

"Yeah, okay. I didn't mean to…" To what? Hurt them? Of course I had. Now I was going to lie on top of everything else? They deserved it.

There was a flicker of regret in his eyes before he continued. "I know Henrietta invited you, but these gatherings are for pack members."

Wait. What? My guilty conscience had kept me from holding his gaze, but now I couldn't do anything but stare. He had no idea that I'd caused that spectacle. He wasn't here because of *them*. He wasn't kicking me out because he knew I'd done them harm. He just didn't want me here.

Somehow it felt even worse than being found out. I continued to stand there, unwanted, feeling like the lowest slug. I straightened my spine in spite of it, refusing to let him see how deeply his actions cut me.

"Yeah, that's fine by me. I don't particularly want to be here anyway, not if you're going to be here."

I walked away with my head high, as if I were leaving by choice, even as it felt like I was slinking away. I made it all the way to the cabin, into my room, before I cried, because damned if I'd let him hear that he'd broken me.

CHAPTER 25

D*ante*

It was ten after seven. River's shift at the kitchen started at seven thirty. Did she think she could blow off her work assignments because Henrietta brought her to a party?

The door to her room opened, and then the one to the bathroom. I finished my coffee and headed out, knowing she was up.

I called Frankie on my way over to the back wall, where we were going through different options to safeguard this place better.

"Yeah?" Frankie sounded like he hadn't made it out of bed yet.

"I want you at the kitchen, and let me know if River reports to work on time." If she wanted to stay out on a Tuesday night, she better get her ass to work.

"Got it," he said, the bed creaking in the background and a woman's voice calling to him.

I was the first one at the back wall when Birger, my head engineer, showed up.

"What do you think we can do to increase the security?" I asked.

He walked closer to the brick wall that was already a good ten feet high. "From vampires?"

"It's going to be tough, but anything that might slow them down if there's an attack," I said. "They're good climbers, but they can't fly. There's got to be something else to hinder them."

"There's some rumors going around. Are we expecting an attack soon?" Birger asked.

"At this point in the game, you never know when it's going to come."

It was midday and Frankie hadn't called me, which meant River had probably reported to work on time. No matter what Henrietta might think about things, this had nothing to do with reminding myself that River didn't fit in. There were plenty of daily reminders as I continually tried to avoid her. I used to be able to grab lunch at the kitchen but hadn't done that in weeks because she'd be there. I didn't go home until late most nights, if at all, because of her.

So when I passed the kitchen that afternoon, after having left Birger and the others, I went in. I was hungry. This was my pack, my campus, and I was done rearranging my life for her.

River was standing at the buffet line, scooping out beef stew, eyes glazed and watery. I made my way closer, expecting her to look at me, the way she tended to when I walked in a room.

She didn't.

Her shoulders were sloped forward and her figure

strained. I weaved through the crowd and cut the line, stopping in front of her. Everyone swerved around me, taking the hint that the stew station was closed for the moment.

"What's wrong with you?" I asked.

She finally looked up at me, and as weak as she looked, she could still glare like no one I'd ever met. Or maybe no one had had the balls to look at me that way before.

"I have no idea what you're talking about. I'm working."

It wasn't a surprising reaction considering last night's events, which were justified whether she realized it or not. She could be as angry as she chose. Didn't matter to me.

I leaned closer. "How much did you drink last night?" She hadn't seemed drunk, but something was wrong.

I saw her chest rise and fall on a long sigh.

"Do you want some stew? If not, please keep it moving. You're holding up the line." She pointed to the people flowing around me with empty dishes, as if she were employee of the year.

I moved, but only to walk around to the other side of the counter. As much as I wanted to blame alcohol, she hadn't seemed drunk last night, and she didn't have a residual smell of it today. I went to lay a hand on her head. She jerked away, but I was faster. I planted a hand on her forehead while holding her still with my other hand.

She looked feverish but she felt like an ice cube. "You're freezing."

"I'm fine. This is how I normally am," she said, pulling out of my grasp and turning back to the line.

It didn't matter, as she had no one to serve. They all were speeding past her, and me. If they even thought about getting stew, I stared at them until they forgot and kept on going.

She was the only one who wouldn't take the hint,

standing there with her spoon and no customers. I grabbed it out of her hand and put it in the bowl. "Stop working and go home. Now."

She turned, and as cold as she felt, her eyes were burning.

"I can't go home, remember? I have to stay *here*, with *you*," she said, speaking to me like I was too thick to understand the conflict of my orders.

I leaned closer. "You know exactly what I mean. Now go."

"You said I had to do a job. I'm doing it. Now stop making a scene."

I leaned a hand on the counter beside her. "You want to see a scene? Try to scoop out one more serving."

She turned back toward me, eyes glassy and skin flushed. "Why are you doing this? You wanted me to work, I'm working. Now you don't want me to work?"

Even her scent was off. Weaker, diminished. She might be stubborn enough to stand here and make herself worse, but damned if I'd let her.

"If you don't walk out of here in the next five minutes, I'm going to carry you out, kicking and screaming if needed."

There was no doubt that we had every set of eyes in the place trained on us. If she wanted to avoid a scene, she should've left when I first told her to, but that wasn't who she was. It was as if after being tortured in that basement for so long, she was allergic to any kind of order, even if it was for her own good. She'd probably stand here until she dropped dead to prove she could.

As much as that sentiment touched on something familiar within me, I wasn't going to let her kill herself.

We stood, staring at each other for all of a second before she wobbled on her feet. She grabbed the counter, trying to cover up the slip, but there was no concealing it.

I raised my eyebrows and took the final step toward her.

"I'm going," she said, leaning away from me. She took off her apron and dropped it in the basket as she stormed out.

I looked to the back of the kitchen. Natalie wasn't there to handle things, so I signaled to Amber. "Take over her spot."

The girl had the nerve to huff as she made her way over.

"She drinks too much at a party she's not even wanted at because she's not pack and now I have to do her job," she grumbled.

Amber had been eavesdropping on my conversations last night, and of course was more than willing to share what she'd overheard. Probably had been repeating it all morning.

I waited for her to get close and then leaned in, as if to tell her a secret. Her eyes lit with excitement.

"You ever repeat one of my private conversations again, you'll be scrubbing toilets for a month," I said softly.

Her face blanched. She looked at me, as if hoping I was kidding. When she saw I wasn't, she turned, head down, picking up the ladle without another word.

I left the cafeteria, catching up to River, who couldn't be trusted to make it back to the cabin on her own.

"What? Are you going to tuck me in, too?" she asked, glaring over her shoulder. "Or am I not allowed to walk on the paths either? Should I stick to the muddy areas?" She actually moved off the walk and into the grass.

I watched her closely. She might still be fighting, but that didn't mean anything. She'd probably fight right up until she was in the grave. She wavered a little as she moved but righted herself before I had to grab her. She climbed the cabin steps a little slower than normal and walked straight into her room, trying to shut the door on me and failing.

She kicked off her shoes and dropped onto the bed in spite of me being there. If she hadn't already looked sick, that would've tipped me off.

"You don't have to tell me what you are, but I need to know if this is normal."

"I'm fine. I didn't sleep well. That's it."

I'd been told "I'm fine" by too many women in my life to not know that it meant the opposite.

She stopped talking. It was as if all the adrenaline she'd used to keep herself going was finally depleted, like a car running out of gas and stalling on the side of the road. She was sleeping like the dead a minute later.

I walked over, laying a hand on her head again, feeling the clamminess of her flesh. My skin itched as a burning rage built inside of me for no rational reason. She was an asset that I might lose, that was it.

"River? You need to wake up and tell me what's going on."

She didn't budge. Her eyes didn't flicker.

"River," I said, shaking her a little.

Nothing. Her chest was moving, but so slightly it was disconcerting.

"River," I said, giving her a firmer shake. She didn't even blink.

I grabbed my phone and called Doc. "You need to come with your bag up to my cabin, now."

"Everything okay?"

"I have no idea. That's why you need to get here."

I was watching her through the bedroom door when Doc walked in a few minutes later.

"What's wrong?" Doc asked, taking a few deep breaths while he rested his hand on the back of the couch.

"I need you to check River. I think something's wrong with her. She's sleeping like she's near death." I grabbed his bag and waved him in.

He walked, but not quickly. Doc needed to get out of that office and go for a run a little more often. It took an agonizingly long time for him to make it to her room.

He sat on the edge of her bed. "River?" Doc said softly.

She didn't budge.

"She won't wake up," I said.

He dug around in his bag and pulled out a stethoscope. "Let me check her vitals before we get too concerned."

"I'm not concerned."

He glanced at me, raised his brows, and nodded. "You sure?"

"She's an asset, is all," I said, looming over the bed.

"I thought she was a potential threat?" Doc asked, looking genuinely confused.

"Can you worry about that later and fix her first?" I pointed at River's limp form.

He listened to her heart, her pulse, took her blood pressure, even opened her eyes, flashing a light at her pupils.

Then he dropped his stuff back in his bag, standing as if he were done. "Her heart is doing the same crazy beat as it was before. Her vitals are all the same. Not knowing her race, I can only make a guess, but it might be some sort of healing sleep. I would leave her alone for now. If she doesn't come around by tomorrow morning, let me know. We'll try something else." He walked to the door.

"Leave her like that?" I said, pointing at her.

"I would. She might be fighting off a flu-type thing her

kind get. Nothing seems that off to me. To be totally frank, if it did, I'm not sure what I could do anyway. Something that might help us might kill her." He held up his hand, as if sensing I wanted to kill him. "But my instincts tell me she'll be okay, and I've been doing this for a long time now."

"That's it?" I said. "Just leave her?"

"I'll check back in tomorrow if she doesn't come around. I wouldn't risk doing anything else at the moment that could cause more harm."

He stood there, bag in hand, having never been so useless to me.

"Thanks for coming," I said, preferring him leave at this point.

I walked back to the bed, picking up her hand and feeling its chill while my phone buzzed in my pocket.

"Dante, where are you?" Birger asked. "I thought you were going to come back and look at some of the ideas I'd drawn up?"

"I'll be there in a..." I walked out of the room but stopped, looking back at River's unmoving form. "Something came up. Pick the best option and start planning without me."

"You're sure?"

I hadn't given a free hand in the planning of anything on this campus.

"I am." I tossed my phone on the dresser. I was getting her warm if it killed me.

I got the fireplace raging in the living room then grabbed the blanket and rolled River in it like a burrito. I carried her wrapped form and settled her on my lap in front of the fire, hating the way nothing stirred her.

She was still icy cold fifteen minutes later.

Fuck this wait-and-see shit. It was time for more drastic measures.

I carried her into the bathroom, laid her out on the blanket, and stripped off everything but her underwear, and then mine.

"You might think dying is the way to thwart me, but it's not happening. You hear me?" I said before carrying her into the shower with me.

CHAPTER 26

R *iver*

I woke, no longer feeling like an ice cube that would never thaw. I'd known I was going to pay for what I directed at Amber and Carly, but if I'd been able to make it through lunch, if Dante had left me alone, no one would've known something was off. I would've struggled, like an inferno that was running on the remnants of ashes, but toughed it out. But I felt a hell of a lot better having slept it off.

There was a creak from the chair across the room, and Dante's spicy scent was in the air. Why was he sitting in my room? I didn't want to open my eyes and find out.

And *why* did I feel like I was wrapped up like a burrito? I could barely move with how tight this blanket clung to me.

"I know you're awake," he said.

Of course he did.

I opened my eyes to see him reclined in the chair, right

where I'd expected him to be. His legs were stretched out in front of him and his arms were folded behind his head.

"How'd you know?" I asked, trying to get my arms free of the blanket from hell.

"Your heart has a strange, soft beat, but it picked up enough steam to let me know you were awake, and probably aware of me in your room."

It took me a few more seconds to get the blanket loose enough to get my arms free. That was when it became apparent that I had no clothes on.

"What... How..." I looked at him. "What happened to my clothes? I was fully dressed when I fell asleep." I gripped the blanket to me tighter than it had been wrapped.

"You mean when you passed out like you were dying? I put you in a hot shower," he said unapologetically.

"Why?" Was he a lunatic?

"Like I mentioned, you looked like you were dying," he said, and then took a sip from the coffee sitting on the table next to him. Along with his phone and a stack of paperwork and a computer by his feet. Had he been in here all night?

"I wasn't dying. All you had to do was let me sleep," I said.

No one had ever done anything like that. I couldn't remember my mother even doing that for me when I was little.

"I'm going to go take a shower," I said, needing to get out of that room and in a space to myself.

I hobbled into the bathroom, blanket still wrapped around me, trying to get my wits back. I turned on the shower, got in, and then rested my head against the wall, feeling more like banging it. The man was beyond infuriating. He'd kicked me out of a party, acting like I was the dregs of society, to then sit up all night watching after me? I wasn't even going to think about the shower.

He was up to something with all this. Some kind of mental warfare to break me. Nothing made sense anymore, but whatever his game, he wasn't going to win.

I walked into the living area half an hour later and there was a grilled cheese sitting on the table, with a cup of tea beside it. Dante was leaning against the counter.

"Is that for me?"

He looked toward the table and nodded. "Yeah. I thought you liked grilled cheeses."

I bit my lower lip, staring at the sandwich. He'd almost burned the edges a little, as if he'd remembered me saying something about liking it that way.

"What's wrong with your eyes?" he asked, watching as I didn't move.

"They're irritated. I got soap in them."

He didn't look like he believed me. *I* didn't believe me. That game he was playing, he might not win, but that grilled cheese was nearly undoing me.

The man had kicked me out of a birthday party. Was I really going to go soft over a couple slices of melted cheese? No. Absolutely not.

He was looking as relaxed as ever when he asked, "Do you plan on telling me what happened to you?"

Yep, the game was definitely still on. That's all this was.

"I didn't sleep well. Like you said, I drank too much."

His nostrils flared. "You smell different when you lie."

"I think your sniffer is off." My heart thudded in my chest, and I wondered if he could hear it.

"It gets even worse when you're nervous, like now," he said, watching me intently.

I walked over to the cabinets opposite him, doing my best to ignore him and his grilled cheese. I reached for a glass to get some water, not the tea that was there to lure me into his trap.

He followed. When I turned, he moved closer, putting a hand on either side of the counter, trapping me there with him.

"I want to know what happened last night. And don't tell me you were tired or drank too much. You have to give me something."

I knew I was going to have to give him something, but what? "What if I'm not human? What does it matter? I don't mean you or your people any harm. I only want to be left alone."

"You were lying there, looking half dead, and I had no idea how to help you. If something went wrong last night, or goes wrong in the future, I wouldn't have the first clue what to do."

His eyes were almost soft, as if he genuinely cared. This was the man who'd thrown me out of a party only a night ago. He was faking concern and I was feeling bad?

My God, he was good at this game. He'd almost had me. Had I spent a year in a vampire dungeon and learned nothing? You didn't trust anyone, especially people who were keeping you against your will.

"If I drop dead, it's not your problem. I'm not part of your pack. You'll be off the hook. Problem solved. Think of it like a gift," I said, steeling myself against his soft looks and trickery.

He even had the gall to look away for a second, as if he felt guilty.

"What am I supposed to do, apologize for speaking the truth? You aren't part of my pack. It's better if everyone knows where they stand."

At least that got him to move as he backed away from me, leaning against the other counter again.

"Which I guess excludes me from being invited to birthday parties, and that's fine. I prefer not to be anywhere you go." I walked back toward my room, ignoring the food and drink, done with his games.

"Riv, you need—"

I spun. "Don't call me that. My friends call me that, and I don't want the lines getting blurred about what we are. As you've already demonstrated, that's not what you want either." I shut the door and then leaned on it, trying to gather myself, feeling like it was all too much to stand at the moment. I'd been swallowing back my feelings for so long that I was beginning to wonder if I had them anymore, and then a grilled cheese nearly undid me. And then him calling me Riv. No one had shortened my name like that since I was a kid, because I hadn't had family in that long.

The door to the house slammed, and I still didn't move. I could do this. I could keep going. Just keep it together a little longer.

I got dressed for work and headed out, walking past the now-cold grilled cheese.

* * *

Natalie was walking out of the kitchen door as I approached.

"What are you doing here?" she asked, stopping short.

"What do you mean? I work here."

"Not today. You're supposed to take the day off, per Dante." She darted back in front of the door.

"There's no reason. I feel fine." There wasn't a thing wrong with me, not a sore muscle or a drop of fatigue. Why wouldn't I go to work? It was nice to have somewhere to go every day, in spite of Carly and Amber being here as well.

I tried to reach around her to the knob, and she shifted. "Dante said you were off today and that if you showed up, I wasn't allowed to let you work."

"Natalie, look at me." I stepped back, putting my arms out. "I'm fine. You can see I'm fine. I'll even do jumping jacks if you want."

"You could do a marathon. It wouldn't matter. The alpha tells me you aren't supposed to work, I can't let you work."

She stared at me, seeing that I was healthy, and still wasn't going to let me work?

"Okay. I'm not going to get you in trouble, but you do see how ridiculous this is, right?"

She gave me a half-smile and a shrug, refusing to actually say it in words.

We stood there for a few minutes, me because I didn't know what to do and her because she was afraid to leave the door unguarded.

I shoved my hands in my pockets, looking around and trying to figure out what I'd do with myself now. "Am I allowed to work tomorrow?" I asked.

"Probably? Haven't heard differently yet."

"Okay. I guess I'll see you tomorrow," I said, walking off, knowing she wouldn't move from the door until I was a good bit away.

I was meandering along the pathways when I spotted Henrietta heading toward me.

"How are you feeling? I heard you weren't doing so well last night," she said.

"I'm fine. I was just a little tired, is all. How did you know?"

"Dante asked me to come and check on you at the

cabin. When I didn't find you there, I figured you'd be at the kitchen."

"Yeah, well, I'm fine. He doesn't need to worry." I had to give it to him—he was really putting his all into this act.

"I understand why you're upset. Asking you to leave Gus' birthday party was uncalled for. He's acting quite unusual with you. He's typically indifferent to most people. Don't get me wrong—he'd die for his pack, but he doesn't get involved." She shook her head and sighed. "I've never seen him care who was at a gathering, let alone ask someone to leave. You get under his skin like no one I've ever seen before. I didn't think anyone was capable of jarring him the way you seem to."

"I guess it's only fair, because he's driving me quite insane as well."

"He is?" she asked, a little too quick and eager to hear that.

"Are you happy he's driving me crazy?" I asked.

"I'm sorry. Of course I'm not happy about how Dante is acting. Why would I be? It's horrible," she said, but with none of the normal fire she typically had when she was upset with him or thought he was in the wrong.

It was her nephew, though. She probably thought his pretending to care if I died relieved him of all guilt. She was buying into his bullshit.

CHAPTER 27

R *iver*

Amber and Carly glared at me from across the kitchen for the fiftieth time that day, before Amber broke off chopping carrots and walked over. I'd been waiting for one of them to finally break their silence.

"You spiked my ale the other night, didn't you?" Amber said.

Carly, who had been right behind her said, "Mine too."

"Don't you think you would've noticed me doing that?" I stopped chopping romaine so I could stare at the two geniuses. "You were both holding your drinks the whole time. Unless you're saying I've gone from near incompetent, as you've often said, to magician-like abilities, how would that be possible?"

The two of them looked at each other, trying to figure out what to accuse me of now. We all knew I'd done *something* to them. I'd warned them I was going to that night. It made me want to laugh, but it was almost cruel to mess with them any further. As it was, there had been a few people giggling during breakfast calling them the Stinky Twins and Poop and the Gang. Amber was obviously Poop, leaving Carly to be the Gang? A gang was typically more than one, but it was funny enough to overlook the error.

"You spiked the keg, then," Carly said, proving once again she was the dullest bulb in the room.

"If I'd spiked the keg, why didn't everyone get sick?" I asked, waiting to see what they'd come up with next.

Natalie walked out of the pantry while they were still attempting to come up with a new theory. She stopped short, looking at our group with suspicion.

"Why aren't you all working?" she asked Carly and Amber, even though I was barely working myself.

"We were checking on River, since she was so ill the other day," Amber answered in a sickly-sweet voice.

"Sure you were," Natalie said. "We need more mushrooms. Sanjay was supposed to go, but he's sick, *again*. I need one of you to go scouting, and I want those vegetables ready by the time I get back." Natalie pointed to Amber and Carly's workstations.

"You got it," Carly said, looking like a shark smiling, curling back to her station.

I had gone back to chopping when the feeling of my people hit me. I'd felt glimmers of them in the past, distant reverberations of their magic, but this was more intense, as if they were nearer. How close were they? Was this one person, or was it several in the same location? Was that why it felt stronger? There wasn't anything I could do about it right now, but it was a comfort knowing they were out there somewhere.

Natalie stopped in front of my table, raising a brow. I'd

proven to her that I was a hard worker, so her expression was more *what's wrong* rather than *what's it now?*

"Sorry. Got a spasm or something. Already going away." I waved my hand for a second before beginning to chop again.

Natalie gave a little nod. "I want those mushrooms picked before I get back," she said to Amber and Carly as she headed out.

As soon as the door shut behind Natalie, Amber turned to me. "We know you screwed with us somehow, so it's only fair you go get the mushrooms."

That was the retaliation? I'd have to go forage for mushrooms, away from them?

"They tend to grow the best on shit," Carly added, grinning.

Okay, *slightly* more believable.

I shrugged. "I'm not allowed off the campus."

"I'll draw you a map and walk you out the back way," Amber said. "Even if they do see you, they'll let you go if I say it's okay."

There was a back way out of here? One where I didn't have to rely on Henrietta or anyone else to escape? Even if I wasn't ready to leave yet, I was going to go eventually.

I grabbed my jacket, knowing there'd be some sort of payment for the knowledge I was going to gain and not caring.

Carly was loading a basket up with muffins. She shoved the basket to Amber. "Give these to the guards. If it's Henry and Macintosh, they'll be so busy stuffing their faces, they won't even notice anyone leaving."

"I thought they'd do whatever you said?" I asked.

Amber looked at me with pure disgust. "Just shut up and come on." She walked out the door.

She had no idea how much I wanted to do this. I would've begged her to go pick mushrooms.

I followed her through the campus, winding our way toward the back, Amber swinging her basket of muffins with a smile on her face. And for whatever reason, no one paid us any mind. The usual eyes on me seemed to be gone. Did they assume Amber would never help me? It wasn't a secret that she hated me. Was I going to be able to stroll out of here with her help?

She turned and motioned for me to stop at one of the buildings and then pointed around the corner. There was an iron doorway in the stone wall that surrounded this place.

"Take this. I put Xs where the mushrooms grow." Amber shoved a hand-drawn map at me. "Go around the building over there, where they can't see you. While I'm giving them the muffins, you slip out. Obviously they'll let you back in when you return, so that's not a problem."

She tugged down her shirt, which had already been displaying ample cleavage, but was now barely covering her nipples, and sashayed over. Any memory of her pooping her pants the other night was clearly washed away from the guys' minds with the invitation she was putting out now.

She strategically moved so that their stares followed her breasts and food, and they turned their backs to the gate. With their attention on her, I slipped out of the well-oiled gate with more ease than I'd imagined possible.

I couldn't believe it. I was outside of the campus, my heart thudding and a smile on my face. I was free, completely and utterly free for the first time in close to a year.

I leaned against the wall, scouring the forest. The reason I'd turned down Henrietta's offer to escape could still be hanging around. Heiko knew I was here. He'd certainly be watching this place. There was a good possibility a slew of vampires were waiting for me. Dante was no slacker either. It was well known he had a patrol in this forest.

Dante would know every single creature in his territory, so they wouldn't be that close by, would they? No, or Natalie would never have Amber or Carly coming out here for mushrooms. This area was safe, at least close to the wall.

Amber and Carly had probably led me out here hoping I'd run, then get trapped, thrown in a basement somewhere, never to be seen again. Run was exactly what I wanted to do, but I'd do it on my terms, prepared and ready, not like this.

Didn't mean I had to rush back. I could enjoy a few minutes of freedom, right? It had been so long since I'd walked outside without being watched, was able to breathe in the smell of the autumn leaves without an audience wondering what kind of voodoo I might be committing. I'd take a few moments for myself and collect some mushrooms.

Best part of all would be when the guards saw me walking back voluntarily, they might think I was allowed to leave. Might trust me to come back when I walked out for good.

I pulled the bag out and strolled around, looking for mushrooms. I was so enamored of the trees, the scents, the stolen freedom, that I didn't notice a problem until it was too late.

* * *

Dante

. . .

It was six o'clock and she still wasn't home. Correction: she wasn't *here*. As she'd said, this wasn't her home.

I called Natalie. "Is River still there?"

"No. She left."

I went and stood on the porch, figuring she'd be appearing any second. "How long ago?"

She hummed, the sound strumming my nerves like an out-of-tune guitar. "I'm not sure. I had to go run some errands, and the girls were handling things. By the time I returned, she was gone. They said she wasn't feeling well."

She'd been fine this morning and yesterday. "And what time was that?"

"About four. Is everything okay?" she asked.

"Fine. Thanks," I said, cutting any further conversation short.

I called Frankie. "Who's on River today?"

There was a pause that went on way too long, nearly as irritating as Natalie's humming.

"Uh, I don't remember. I gotta check the schedule," he said, with a wavering tone that gave me no confidence in his finding a name.

"Find out and call them. I want to know who had eyes on her last and get back to me." I'd seen Marshall, Logan, and the other guys that filled in throughout the day. So who had been watching her?

No one. I couldn't even yell at Frankie. I'd been pushing off the responsibility, not wanting to deal with it. I walked back inside, letting the screen door slam behind me.

If she had left, it would be better. It was her choice. Let her go, and screw whatever happened.

She'd left. I didn't know how she'd gotten out, and fuck

it, I didn't need to. She knew Heiko was out there and preferred that risk to staying here.

Did she, though? Or had she thought she could slip past them? Several of my men had caught the scent of vampires around the perimeter, about ten miles out. Did she think they wouldn't be waiting for her?

Quarter after six.

My phone buzzed, Frankie's name flashing on the screen.

"Yeah?"

"I think there was a slip-up," he said.

I took a deep breath, having expected this, but that didn't seem to make it better.

"Have you seen her?" he asked, sounding desperate.

"It's fine."

She was gone. Did Heiko already have her? Why did I feel like I was about to come out of my skin? She'd left. She'd chosen to put herself in that position.

"So she's there? I feel so much better. I'm really sorry about dropping the ball. I don't know how it happened, but—"

"I'm in the middle of something. I'll talk to you later." I hung up on him and flung my phone across the room.

I should go to bed and say screw it. Let her leave.

I walked into her room instead of heading toward the couch and the stack of documents I wanted to go through. The hiking boots that Henrietta had given her were still there, and her heavier jacket too. Today was mild, but if she'd planned to leave, wouldn't she have taken her better items? If she thought it would throw me off the scent, maybe not.

Screw it. Let her go. Life would be easier without her.

If I could only get the image of her standing outside, looking half-starved and barefoot out of my head...

I shifted before I got out the door. I didn't have Carly or Amber's numbers, not that those two dipshits would give me any reliable information anyway.

No one stopped me as I made my way to the kitchen. I picked up her scent immediately and started tracking it. I'd once told her that the youngest of us could track her with ease. That wasn't completely true, but I could with little trouble. With her scent so fresh, with no rain or snow to muddy it, I'd probably be able to find her in under an hour.

If no one had gotten to her first…

The trail led to the back gate, and I leapt over it, continuing to follow her trail and ignoring my people standing there.

CHAPTER 28

R *iver*

If I'd known I was going to get stuck in a hole, I would've worn my heavier jacket, but hindsight was twenty-twenty. No one ever *thinks* they're going to fall into a hole. It was one of those things that just happens.

I'd had quite a few hours to decide whether they'd planned for me to end up here or get taken by vampires. It was still too murky to decide.

I dug a little more, trying to create notches where I could put my feet, but it was getting hard to see what I was doing now that the sun had set. Not to mention I'd lost feeling in my fingers and my ankle was killing me. I huddled down for another break, curled in a ball, knees to my chest. It was going to be a cold night.

I'd never imagined I'd be in a place where Dante finding me was a good thing. Because if he didn't find me, someone worse might before I managed to climb my way out.

One thing was for sure: sleeping here was going to suck, especially with all these spikes sticking up out of the ground. I was lucky I hadn't impaled myself with the fall, or maybe that had been the master plan? There wasn't more than a foot and a half in between some of them. Clearly it was a vampire trap of some sort. Had it actually ever worked?

"What the hell are you doing down there?"

Dante was standing at the top of the pit, staring down at me, silhouetted by the moon. I never thought I'd be relieved to see him, but sleeping in this hole hadn't been an inviting thought.

"What do you think? I fell."

"Why were you off campus?" he asked with enough of an edge in his voice that I wasn't certain he wouldn't leave me here.

"I was collecting mushrooms, as I'd been asked to do," I said. With the moon behind him, it was impossible to make out his features. His tone held enough of an edge that it wasn't needed.

"On whose order? Natalie wouldn't have sent you off property."

Nothing about the accusation I heard in his voice made this better. Now I was a liar?

"I was asked to do it, and I did it. Are we seriously going to have this discussion while I'm sitting in a hole, or are you going to help me out?" I shouted.

"I *should* leave you down there."

Asshole. Did he think I'd beg? I'd spent nearly a year in the vampire dungeon. If he thought a night out here was going to break me, he was delusional. Maybe Heiko *would've* been better.

"Then leave me," I said, my stubborn streak biting me in the ass even as my teeth chattered. Right now, the way he was carrying on, I'd rather lose a few toes.

He stepped away from the edge, and I listened for his steps. Was he leaving me? I wouldn't call him back, no matter what. I'd figure out a way to climb out of this thing tomorrow, even if it killed me. I'd slept in worse conditions, been hungrier and thirstier. I'd survive. I always survived, and I didn't need any beast man to be nice to me. He could go run off. I didn't need anyone.

A sound at the edge of the pit had me looking up. There he was, lying on the ground, reaching down. "Get up and give me your hand."

If his tone was a touch nicer, I would've done it. But he was still speaking to me like *I* was the asshole in this situation, and it had the unfortunate ability of bringing out my inner five-year-old.

"No."

His breathing was audible. "Get. Up."

My chattering teeth warred with my bruised ego. If his tone had softened even a little, I would've bent. But it hadn't, and so I didn't.

"I'll get myself out." I stopped looking up at him and planted my chin on my knees.

"If you could have, you already would've," he said. "So you'd rather sit down in that pit all night?"

Never knew what a sarcastic ass he was until now. "Yes. I prefer it over my current accommodations and company."

"Well, that's not an option. I'm not leaving you here, so either get up or I'll be coming down and getting you," he said.

The words might sound tough, but he wouldn't leave me, even as I was telling him to. Every time I wanted to write him off as the worst person I'd ever met, he did something to prove me wrong. This nice side of him was just enough for me to swallow my pride and get the hell out of this hole.

"Fine." I leaned a hand against the dirt wall, realizing my ankle had gotten worse since I'd been sitting. I reached toward him, but I was about a foot shy of his grasp, even as he stretched down as far as he could.

"What's wrong with your leg?"

The edge in his voice was back. Now I couldn't get hurt accidentally without pissing him off?

"I fell. What do you think?"

He was breathing loudly again, as if it were some calming mechanism. In all my life, I'd never seemed to irritate anyone as much as I did him just by being alive.

"Can you jump?" he asked.

I tried to get some height, but I only gained a few inches with one functioning leg. I tried again, putting some weight on the bad ankle, but it didn't make much difference. I ended up banging against the wall of the pit. "I don't think so."

"Flatten yourself to the side. I'm coming down, and there's not a lot of room."

"What are you talking about? Don't come down. How does that help?" There was the sound of shuffling above, but he wasn't replying. "Dante, just go get a rope." Still no answer. "Dante?"

With a thump, he dropped into the hole, lithely missing the stakes. He was no longer in his human form. I didn't scream, but that didn't mean there wasn't one lodged in my throat, ready to be set free at a moment's notice. This was still Dante. He was there in the eyes of this beast, if nowhere else. I'd seen him in this form before, and he wasn't like some shifters who lost control. Even now, the man was still there.

His snout flared as he dipped his head, sniffing me. I froze, Dante or not. His beast form slowly breathed in my scent, and there was no way he didn't smell the fear.

He paused near my leg, the one that had taken the worst of the fall. One of the stakes had skimmed my leg, tearing my pants and leaving a nasty scrape that was now a dirty scab. His mouth opened, and I pressed against the dirt wall, closing my eyes, my heart stuttering as I waited for his blood thirst to kick in and giant canines to sink into my flesh. There was nothing I'd be able to do to get out of this situation. It was useless to even attempt to fight.

His tongue shot out and licked the wound. Was he —*tasting* me? Was this to check out my injury or to see if I'd make a good meal?

I didn't think of it long before I had other issues. He wrapped his large claws around my arm, pulling me toward him and then over his shoulder. A second later he leapt straight up like it was nothing. He dropped me to the ground, lacking human finesse in this form.

I grabbed a tree nearby to keep upright as he shifted back into human form, every part of him on display. He grabbed his clothes that had been discarded and then glanced at me. I turned away, my face getting warm in spite of the chill. It wasn't my fault. I'd been locked in a cellar for a year with starved humans. How could I not look? Didn't mean anything. It was only fair. He'd seen most of what I had to offer when he took my unconscious body into a shower.

By the time I looked in his direction again, he was walking back toward me with a determined stride.

"I can walk on my own," I said, hopping back.

"That's great, but I don't feel like spending all night

watching you hobble so you can prove you're strong enough to do it."

I limped backward and fell on my ass for the effort.

He knelt beside me. "You're hurt and cold. Let's call a truce for tonight so we can get back sometime before the sun rises?"

I was also thirsty, not that I'd mention it. My ankle was throbbing, but there wouldn't be talk of that either.

Dante ran his gaze over me, like he was actually concerned. Plus it was hard to forget about the grilled cheese the other day, even if I hadn't eaten it.

I shivered, and he reached behind him, grasping the back of his sweater. He pulled it off then slung it over my head and jerked it down before it was clear what he was doing. The man was starting to give me emotional whiplash.

"Okay," I said, agreeing to his offer of a truce, afraid I was softening when I should be hardening.

He scooped me up in his arms.

"Are you going to be able to carry me the whole way?" I asked.

"I'll be fine," he said, laughing a little.

"For your information, I've put on some weight these last few weeks," I said, feeling scrawny all of a sudden.

"I noticed. It looks good on you."

What? Why was the man who'd demanded I be thrown out of a birthday party being so civil all of a sudden? I stopped talking. It was easier and much safer.

He seemed to like the silence as well, or at least didn't mind it.

Neither of us spoke again until the back gate came into view.

"By the way, care to explain why your blood is blue and sparkly?" he asked, looking at me.

My breathing halted and then restarted with a deep breath. Between falling in a hole, his licking me, and the entire nightmarish day, I'd forgotten that I had a scab on my leg that blew my human subterfuge into a thousand pieces.

"I thought we were calling a truce for tonight?" I asked, failing to come up with anything else. After you'd claimed to be human for weeks, blue, sparkly blood wasn't a good look.

"I wasn't picking a fight. I'm remarking on something everyone is about to notice unless you do something."

Who was this man? What was he after now? There was a trick here somewhere, but my fatigued brain wasn't firing well enough to figure it out. I shifted, crossing my legs so that my injury was hidden.

"Why do you care if they know? These are your people," I said.

"I have no problem with you glittering when you bleed. But I'm assuming you don't want to share that, or you would've told everyone what you are already." He spoke calmly, as if he didn't care either way. So he was really just giving me a heads-up?

The guys at the gate opened the door as we approached, their expressions flat as we passed. When I glanced back, there were a couple of raised brows as they made faces to each other, clearly wondering what was up. I'd like to know too.

Most people were inside by the time we walked through the campus, but enough were awake to take notice of the scene we presented. There I was, cradled in Dante's arms, in his sweater, as he was shirtless. There'd surely be a whole new round of stories in the morning.

He walked into the cabin, heading toward the couch.

"Don't put me—"

He dropped me onto the couch, in spite of the dirt all over me.

"I'm a mess."

He grabbed the throw blanket from the side and placed it beside me, and then lifted and redeposited me on it.

"Better?" he asked, as if it were my couch getting dirty.

"Thanks, but I think I'm going to take a shower."

"After you eat," he said, moving into the kitchen.

If he made me another grilled cheese, I wasn't sure what I'd do. I was really hungry, even if it was from him.

Oh no. He pulled out cheese. The butter was next. Oh shit. He was slicing bread.

Ten minutes later, there was a grilled cheese sitting in front of me with toasty edges.

I took a bite and then sniffled.

"Why do you look like you're going to cry every time you look at a grilled cheese?" he said.

"I'm fine. I don't want to talk about it." I dragged an arm over my face.

"Okay." He backed away. "Do you want tea?"

"No!"

"Got it. No tea." He put his hands up.

I'd finally figured out how to get him to leave me alone: look like I was on the brink of tears. Wasn't the most dignified method, but it seemed to work like nothing else had.

CHAPTER 29

D*ante*

Macky was at the table in the corner the next morning, five different books spread out.

"Any leads?" I asked.

He nearly jumped out of his chair, just noticing me.

"No, but I haven't quit. You gave me a job, and I won't fail you. I will read until my eyes can't open anymore." He was standing, his hand on his chest again, the way he'd been doing the other day.

"That's great." I waved my hand toward the chair, preferring he sit and try to act somewhat normal. "I have something else to add to the list."

He was waiting for me to speak as I fell silent. Why did I feel like I was betraying River by sharing this? She wasn't part of my pack. I owed her no loyalty. This was getting ridiculous. I had a vampire that was monitoring my pack's day-to-day movements. I'd increased the risk to everyone here, and she wasn't willing to give me answers. There was no choice, and yet I couldn't stop myself from adding, "Don't forget, this doesn't get discussed with anyone else."

"I would never betray a confidence between us, ever." His voice was deep and grave, as if he'd chug poison first.

This kid actually might. As much as the loyalty was appreciated, he always made things feel a little weird.

"Add blue blood to the list of what you're looking for."

"You mean she's an aristocrat?" he asked, then started chewing on his nail.

"No. I mean in the literal sense—her blood is blue when it hits the air, not red." The way the kid was tilting his head already, I didn't want to add in the next detail. "It's also…" I was not calling it sparkly again. Even if that's what it was, it felt like I was an eleven-year-old girl talking about nail polish. "It's iridescent."

He was staring at me as if I wasn't speaking English. "What?"

"You know, shimmery, with hints of other colors," I said.

His mouth gaped open for a few seconds before he said, "You mean like…sparkly?"

Dammit. "Yes. It's sparkly."

This situation was getting too odd to talk about. Now the kid was staring at me like I'd lost my marbles and was making this shit up.

My phone buzzed as Macky continued to stare.

I stepped away to answer.

"Dante, can you swing by the kitchen?" Frankie asked.

I'd told him I wanted people stopping by the kitchen. I didn't care what excuses they made up. After yesterday, I wanted to know what was going on in that place.

"What's the issue?"

"Not an emergency, but I might need your assistance."

"I'm coming." I'd swear I hadn't had a peaceful day since River had arrived.

*　*　*

Frankie was standing outside the kitchen, looking in the window and then scanning the area for my approach. The second he spotted me, he headed toward me. Whatever the problem, it couldn't be too bad if he was out here.

"What's wrong?"

He looked back at the kitchen again before shaking his head. "I was doing what you said, checking in on her but trying to stay out of the way. It's not going well."

Did it ever with River?

"What's the issue now?"

"She's standing at the table, and she won't sit because all the chairs are *suspiciously* broken. I know you don't want me to intervene, but she can barely stand, and she's not very good at listening to reason. So I insisted she either had to sit or go home, because she doesn't look good. Of course she ignored me." He threw his hands up. "That's when I called you, because I have no idea what to do at this point. I didn't want to carry her out without asking you."

"You can go. I'll handle it." I moved past him, having heard enough.

Frankie didn't linger, taking his out while he had it.

River was limping across the kitchen, barely able to walk, lugging a bag of potatoes along with her. The sight was enough to make my skin tingle and itch, but that was becoming old hat.

"Where are you working?" I asked, looking around the kitchen for a chair in front of one of the stations. There wasn't a single one to be found in the room.

Amber and Carly were keeping their heads down,

chopping carrots and stirring something on the range.

"Why? I'm fine," River said, leaning all her weight on her good leg, her face set stubbornly.

"Because I don't see a stool or a chair." I grabbed the sack from her and dropped it onto a nearby table.

"There aren't any available, and that's okay." She spoke loudly, looking across the kitchen as she added, "*I don't need one.*" Clearly she didn't understand shifter hearing. She'd been so loud that Frankie probably heard her from halfway across the campus.

Amber and Carly were continuing on as if they hadn't heard anything, but a grin broke out on one down-turned face. The itch to shift increased.

In that second, there was a very clear choice. I needed to either remove River from this kitchen or I was going to rip those two women apart. I chose the saner option.

I walked over and scooped River up as she squirmed.

"What are you doing?" she asked, trying to shift in my arms so she could keep her eyes on the kitchen.

"I'm taking you home to sit on the couch."

"Natalie needs my help. I can't leave. I have a job." She was grabbing at my shoulders like she could climb over me and get back to work.

"She was fine before you came, and she'll be fine now." And if I didn't get River out of here, Natalie wasn't going to have a staff left to do anything.

"You can't carry me through the campus again. People are watching. This is starting to look ridiculous."

"I don't care."

She huffed loudly, making sure I heard her displeasure. She crossed her arms in front of her chest, refusing to put one around my shoulders.

"Why didn't you just turn?" she asked, her voice shooting higher, and she started squirming around again.

"What are you doing? Why are you walking us through the center of the campus? Are you trying to make this as embarrassing as possible? Do you want every person here to see this?"

Something like that—not that I'd tell her.

"You still didn't tell me how you ended up being the one who was collecting mushrooms," I said, even though I'd pieced enough of it together on my own. I had a hunch but had been willing to extend the benefit of the doubt until this afternoon. Clearly I needed to send a message.

"I offered," she said, becoming more and more distracted by all the eyes on us. As we walked through the campus, every single person took note. By the time we got back to the cabin, the message was clear: River was officially under my protection. The only person left who didn't know it was her.

I laid her on the couch, and she sucked in a breath as soon as her leg touched the cushion. The pain was worse than it had been last night.

"Were you planning on standing on it all day until you couldn't stand at all?" I walked over to the refrigerator, pulled out the ice bucket, and dropped it a little harder than necessary on the counter. Grabbing the dishtowel, I made an ice pack.

"I had stuff to do. I *still* have stuff to do," she said.

"Someone else will be doing it." I grabbed her calf, swung her sideways on the couch, and laid the ice on top of it.

"Why? Are you firing me? I like working." She was trying to prop herself up, as if she thought she was going to get up and go back.

I grabbed her good leg, tugging her forward so she fell back into a lying position again.

Now what? If I let her go back to that kitchen, and they

did one more thing, it wouldn't end well. For all I'd told Frankie and everyone else to stand down, it seemed impossible to follow my own directives.

I caught sight of the stack of books on the end table.

"I was planning on telling you tonight that I'm moving you. You're needed more in the library. We're understaffed there as well."

"The library?" Her eyes lit like she was a kid offered a job at a candy factory.

It gave me the craziest urge to kiss her, but everything seemed to do that, including carrying her here.

She dropped her head back, groaning. "Natalie really needs help, though..."

"I'll get Natalie someone else." I grabbed the throw blanket and tossed it over her, as if the weight of the material would keep her on the couch. She could barely stand, but I didn't put it past her to crawl out of the house just to prove she could. "I need to go handle some things. Stay here."

"When do I get to start at the library?" she asked, her eyes big and nearly glowing with enthusiasm.

"As soon as you can stand," I said. "If your ankle gets worse, you'll have to wait."

She mouthed the word *shit*, as if it killed her to make that agreement. "Fine. I won't move."

I moved her stack of books to the nearby table, shifting her attention, and then got out of there before she forgot that reading might be a good way to pass the afternoon.

I barged into the kitchen five minutes later, stalking over to Amber and Carly.

Amber dropped her knife, and it clanged on the table as both their faces turned white.

"Listen to me closely, because I'm only going to say this once. Your scents were all over what happened to River last night. Now today, her ankle looks worse and there are no chairs. Fuck with her again and I *will* throw you out of this pack." I'd turned a blind eye for too long to the mischief some of the lower pack members were creating, but it was stopping now.

"For her?" Amber whined, her eyes watering.

"But she's not part of this pack." Carly crossed her arms. "We're just trying to help you see how weak she is. How she doesn't belong here. You need to get rid of her, for her own good. We're just doing this for her. We heard that you didn't mind if she had a hard time."

I wanted to curse and scream, but mostly at myself. What they said was true. I'd wanted River to experience hardship so she'd want to leave bad enough to finally tell me what she was. This was partially my fault, and there was no getting around it. The rage that had built since I'd seen River, the fury that I'd been trying to control, was now pointed inward. But it was over now, and I'd make that very clear to all.

"One more incident and you're both out of this pack. Do you understand?" I added an extra layer of ice to my voice and stared at them, waiting for an acknowledgment.

"Okay," Carly said.

"Yes," Amber agreed, dropping her head.

Natalie walked in right as I was finishing. "Oh no, what did they do now?" she said, looking over my shoulder to the two guilty faces.

"Nothing, but River won't be coming back."

"Oh shit," Natalie said, looking legitimately upset.

"I'll get you someone else."

I walked out as Natalie turned to them and said, "Great. I had one person around here that was actually a good worker, and you two had to ruin it. I hope you realize you didn't do yourselves any favors."

CHAPTER 30

R*iver*

It was Saturday night, and instead of walking past me, Dante stopped in the living room. "Are you coming to the gathering tonight?"

He couldn't leave well enough alone? Obviously I was sitting here, a book in my lap and a cup of tea beside me. Nothing about my current appearance would lead him to believe there were plans to go anywhere, but he had to have it confirmed. He couldn't leave the peaceful situation we'd had for the last couple of days alone. Even though I hadn't seen him much, I hadn't hated him either. When I had seen him, he'd been almost--pleasant? And I'd been somewhat cordial in response.

"No. You'll be happy to hear that I won't be forcing myself on your pack."

He walked closer and stopped in front of me.

"I'm saying you should come if you want."

My attention was jerked from the book I was using as a pretense to ignore him. "You are?"

"Yes." He shrugged, looking more handsome than should be allowed in his sweater and jeans. Plus, he was doing that *pleasant* thing again. He was actually pretty good at it when he wasn't being a total dick.

"You didn't want me at Gus' party not even a week ago. But it's okay now? Is it birthdays you want me to avoid? I just want to know what the rules are," I said, raising a brow.

"I shouldn't have forced you to leave. I'm sorry."

I nearly choked on the tea I'd just taken a sip of. Had he just apologized? It sounded like that. He was really upping his *pleasant* game tonight, that was for sure.

"It's the last gathering of the season," he said. "Henrietta makes a big deal out of it. I know she'd want you there, but it's up to you."

"Yeah, I mean, you know, maybe." I sounded like a stuttering fool, but it was hard to react any other way when shock was stealing all your brain cells.

He was watching me, as if he was disappointed that I was noncommittal.

I went back to attempting to read, looking to break the awkward moment. He walked out a few minutes later.

The best plan of action was staying here, reading, and leaving well enough alone. But he had to go and bring Henrietta into it. If she had been looking for me to come, had put him up to asking me, how did I not go?

I tried to read a few more pages, and then reread them. Then I sat there and drank my tea for a little while, but it tasted like guilt. *Had* Henrietta said something to him? Had she made him apologize and invite me? No one but her could've pulled that off.

I tossed my book onto the couch. It was time to find my best jeans and sweater.

I made my way down to where the gathering was, limping only a tiny bit at this point.

"You came!" Henrietta burst into a huge smile and then hugged me. It wasn't clear why she liked me so much, but the feeling was mutual.

"Had to. Heard this was a big shindig of yours." I gave her a big smile and squeezed her back.

Gus swung by and handed me a drink, and then Frankie and Marshall, Doc and Jobo, plus a few others I'd gotten a bit friendlier with showed up. Friendlier, almost as if I had *friends* here. I guessed I sort of did at this point.

But there was something odd about the mood of the whole place. Was everyone already drunk? I scanned the crowd; no one was glaring at me. Carly and Amber seemed afraid to even look in my direction.

"Henrietta, I need to talk to you for a second," I said, tugging her away from our little group when she came close enough.

"What's wrong?" she asked, her brows immediately dropping, as if she were going to have to kill someone.

"This is going to sound odd, but is something going on? People seem a little happier."

"Oh," she said, giggling. "You mean they're being nicer to you? Well, when the alpha makes a showing like he did the other day, they know they'd better not step out of line."

"Showing? What are you talking about? What showing?"

Her face scrunched up like she was confused, and then it was like seeing a light bulb go off. "You know, I keep thinking you know our ways, but you have no idea, do you?"

"None."

She took a deep breath, as if gathering steam for a doozy of an explanation. "You know how he carried you all throughout the campus the other day?"

"Yeah…" It was hard to forget. It felt like every single person had seen us.

"That was his way of saying you weren't to be messed with. That you were under his protection." Henrietta actually glowed, as if what she had said was a good thing.

I wanted to fall off the bench I was sitting on. As it was, I put my hand flat on the table. In my entire life, no one had ever stepped up for me in that way. And now, of all people, Dante was?

He was standing across the way, and our eyes met. He raised his drink to me, as if to say he was happy I'd come. I barely nodded, trying to digest what was going on.

"Why would he do that?" I whispered.

"Because he cares about you," Henrietta said, smiling as if that made any kind of sense.

I hadn't even meant to ask the question to her, let alone get an answer, and definitely not *that* answer.

I took another sip of my ale, and Dante's gaze met mine again. This time, neither of us looked away.

There was an attraction that was undeniable. When we kissed, it had nearly overwhelmed me, but it wasn't a real one. I hadn't seen a good-looking man for too long, or at least one with a heartbeat. So yeah, maybe my hormones got a little out of whack when we touched. That didn't mean it was anything other than superficial want.

I was probably a novelty to him. He was the alpha of this pack, and the women all fawned over him. Maybe he liked a challenge, and I had presented him one? Again, nothing that meant a thing.

If this actually progressed, it wouldn't lead anywhere good. Not to mention the other complications that came from being what I was. I walked away from the clearing, needing space to think and distance from him, space from whatever was going on between us.

I wasn't back for more than ten minutes when he walked into the cabin. I tried not to look at him when he walked in, tried to focus on my steeping tea. Despite my efforts, he still snuck into the corner of my eye. It seemed the only way I'd avoid noticing him was if I ripped my eyeballs out of my head, and even then they'd probably roll in his direction. If he'd walked in five minutes later, I would've been tucked into my bedroom, but I'd lingered in the main part of the cabin, almost as if I hoped he'd follow me.

He walked over to me, leaning so near that he was impossible to ignore.

"I know you *want* to hate me." His tone was almost playful.

There was the *I'm the alpha and this is how things are going to be* Dante, and then there was *this* Dante. The latter was way harder to ignore than the former, and much scarier to my psyche. With Alpha Dante, it was easy to give him *break your teeth on me* hard. This Dante made me feel gooey, like I was just taken out of the oven.

"You're wrong. I *do* hate you." I tried to make my tone hard but failed pathetically. I was afraid some of my gooey-ness slipped into my tone. "Or at least dislike you," I added, trying to salvage my hard-ass demeanor.

"Maybe you do, but you also want me."

Oh yes, he'd picked up on the scent of the melting chocolate and warm dough.

I spun, refrigerator at my back. I would really have to figure out my retreats ahead of time, or where to have my standoffs. The kitchen had too many obstacles.

"You're absolutely—"

"Don't forget, I can smell a lie on you." He leaned his forearm on the wall near my head.

"—drunk," I said. Still a lie, but a less embarrassing one to get caught with.

He smiled as if he knew my game. I hated when he smiled. It added charm to an already heartbreaking face. It was a combination that was hard to deny, especially after what I'd learned today. That he'd sent a message to his pack, his people, not to bother me.

I needed to hang on to saner thoughts. Didn't matter what he'd done. It would be crazy to get mixed up with him, and yet I couldn't stop my spine from bending toward him. Or maybe I just wanted a warm body. I'd been so lonely for what seemed like an eternity that the thought of him touching me made me ache, rational or not.

"If you can find some pleasure in this world, you should take it. You never know what tomorrow will bring." He reached out, pushing my hair away from my face, looking at my eyes, and then his gaze drifted to my lips. "I've never wanted anyone the way I want you. Ever since we kissed, I can't think of anything else."

Those lines should be repeated over and over, to generations of women, so that they were armed for when it might be used against them. That way maybe they could come up with counterarguments that worked while they still had a functioning brain.

Me? I was done for.

Since I knew he'd felt it too, that thing between us undid me. When we kissed, the longing had gone from a want, to a need, to a must-have in seconds, where the world and our differences ceased to exist. I hadn't cared who he was, and he'd nearly devoured me as well.

In the end, though, it wasn't what he said. It was how he was looking at me as he said it, as if he were mesmerized.

The way he touched me, as if I were something priceless and he was filled with amazement.

And he didn't even know what I was. He just wanted *me*.

He tilted my head back, brushing his thumb over my lower lip as I parted my mouth, inviting him in. He leaned close, his breath mingling with mine, as if savoring the nearness before he consummated the kiss.

The tension continued to build until I was the one who finally bridged the distance, needing to prove what I'd felt before wasn't true. How could it be? This wasn't the one I should be with. What sick trick of fate would put me with a shifter—an alpha, no less?

I licked my lips and then grazed his, the feeling of rightness, of longing, swelling up so hard and fast that I pulled his head toward mine.

Not that I had to encourage him much.

He took my invitation like he'd been waiting for a decade. Like a man who'd been starved for years and was handed a meal. His lips feasted on mine, and no matter what he gave, I wanted more. He slanted his head and then grabbed my hair, tilting mine when I didn't do it fast enough.

He lifted me and spun us until I was sitting on the counter. He spread my legs and stepped between them, pulling me close. He wrapped his other arm around my hips, and the yearning was so strong that it still didn't feel like enough. Like it could never be enough.

My shirt was tugged off, and then he unbuttoned my jeans and tugged them off my hips. He backed up, stripping off his shirt and then unzipping his pants. His massive erection sprang free.

I jerked out of my daze of wanting as pure fear replaced it. We couldn't. If we did, he might find out. Then what?

My heart seized.

"Wait, no. I can't do this. I don't..." I put up a hand as I jumped off the counter.

"You don't what?" He froze for a second before he asked, "Are you a virgin?"

He looked almost as jolted as I was, as if coming out of the same trance and realizing what had almost happened.

"I'm... It's just that it's... I can't." What else could I say? *The second you have sex with me, if you give a shit at all, things might get a little strange?* How did you have a conversation like that after telling someone you were human for weeks?

He stood there, looking as if I'd told him I was the Loch Ness monster.

I pulled up my pants and grabbed my sweater, holding it to my chest.

"I'm going to..." I tilted my head and took a step toward my room.

"Yeah, okay."

I retreated to my room, like I should've done as soon as I got back here.

CHAPTER 31

D^{ante}

River was a virgin. I didn't need the head trip that came with being a woman's first, and definitely not *her* first. It wasn't like this relationship would ever amount to anything. Whatever she might turn out to be, a casual fuck was not it, and I didn't need to be labeled the jerk who fucked her and left her.

I still didn't know what had come over me. She said I was drunk last night, but that hadn't been true. It was very hard for shifters to get drunk the way she was envisioning, but I *had* had more than usual, all in an effort to forget about her for a night. Then what did I do? I followed her back here and kissed her.

It had made it ten times worse. All I could think about was touching her, feeling her body moving against mine. Something happened when we came together, which didn't feel normal but did feel righter than anything else in my life.

Unfortunately, that didn't change anything. I was still the alpha of a pack that was about to be at war. She was—unknown at best. This wasn't a relationship anyone could afford, not her and definitely not me.

She walked out of the bedroom and slowed for a second at seeing me still there before continuing. She took a mug from the cabinet and poured herself a cup of coffee, acting as if nothing was different.

Maybe I should do the same.

She took a couple of sips and then turned, glancing at me, and I knew something would be said.

"Last night—I don't think that should happen again, okay?" she said, staring up at me.

So much for ignoring the elephant in the room.

"I didn't know you were... I wouldn't have started anything if I'd realized." Or at least I *hoped* that was true. With her, all bets were off.

She bit her lower lip, looking torn. And in spite of what I'd said, all I wanted to do was kiss her again.

"Our situation is complicated enough," she said, as if I needed to be sold on the idea.

"Agreed." Even if I wanted to rip her clothes off right now, I wouldn't. But the urge was stronger than anything I'd ever felt.

Was this some sort of trick she did? She could make things happen. Was she driving this attraction somehow? Toying with me to distract me? Was I being manipulated? Yes, she was pretty, but I'd had prettier. I'd had more outgoing, funnier, more of everything, and yet I couldn't seem to shake this want for her in particular.

"Are you doing some..." Had I lost my mind? I couldn't ask her that on a half-assed guess.

"What?" She turned, looking too intent.

"Nothing." If this wasn't something she *was* doing, that might be the worst possible question to ever be asked.

Her eyes narrowed. "No. It wasn't nothing. You think I'm doing something?" She put her mug down, as if she wanted her hands free to beat me with.

"Like I said, it was nothing." I made my way out of the kitchen, knowing when a battle was lost.

She was following, not looking like someone who was guilty, which made it all the worse.

"Why? Because you *want* me? You think you wouldn't unless I'm doing some kind of voodoo? And that even if I *could*, I would? You know how I told you last night couldn't happen again? Don't worry about that, because I'll make sure it doesn't. If you touch me again, I'll chop your hands off."

She strode away from me and into the bedroom, slamming the door.

I took a step toward the door, knowing the right thing to do was apologize. Then I turned and walked out anyway. It was better this way.

* * *

River

No one noticed as I walked into the building. The place was empty except for a young guy reading books at a table.

"Macky?"

He glanced up, taking a deep breath. "You must be River. I run this... Well, not really run, but I try to keep things in order. I've organized every book on these shelves." He stood up, knocking over books in the process.

"Oh shit, I'm sorry," he said, as if he'd done something to me.

"You're fine." I knelt down, helping him gather them up.

Macky smiled, his cheeks flushed as he piled them back up.

"Dante said you needed help here?" There wasn't another soul in the place. It was so quiet that you could hear the clock ticking on the wall.

"Oh, yes, a lot," he replied, his eyes widening.

"Well, I'm very happy to help. What can I do?"

He swallowed, staring at the ground for a second. His head popped back up, and he seemed to come back to life. "We're very disorganized. Whoever sorted them before did a horrible job."

He walked, and I followed.

"See these books?" He waved his arms wide. "They have shifters, vampires, all sorts of races listed in fantasy, which clearly is not the case, as we can all agree on now. This is quite a mess, wouldn't you say?"

He was so eager for approval that I didn't even look before I nodded. "I completely agree with you."

He let out a breath. "So you see the problem, then? They all need to be re-sorted, which is going to lead to all sorts of filing issues afterward." He made a few exaggerated sighs.

Clearly Dante wanted me out of the kitchen enough to create a job from nothing. Only moments ago, Macky told me he'd organized every book on these shelves. I had a choice to make: continue to dole out food, buffered by two women who hated me, or play with books all day. The twinge of guilt for Natalie was the only issue, but it wasn't like Dante would roll over. If he wanted me out of the kitchen, he'd get me out of the kitchen, and I didn't like the place enough to go to war over it.

"Absolute disaster to be sure," I said. Between the cathedral ceilings and the smell of books that was better than any perfume ever made, I probably would've agreed with anything he said.

"I think we're going to get along really well," Macky said, a gleam in his eye.

"I do too."

The breeze was blowing, fresh air filling my lungs as I sat on the lawn. According to Macky, lunch break was two hours long, not that I planned on taking that. This library job was the biggest scam going. It was like being a union rep with a no-work job. The work I did was too pleasant to be an effort, and when I left the library, no one seemed to be watching. I could probably leave right now if I wanted.

That was exactly what I should want after the other night, and then this morning. How could Dante kiss me like that and then think I'd made him do it? I couldn't decide whether to be flattered that he had so little self-control around me that he didn't think he was responsible for his actions, or insulted that he didn't think he would've acted like that without some sort of voodoo.

Didn't matter anyway. I couldn't leave yet. I didn't have any good options at the moment. My family was dead. The rest of my race, the ones who were left, I didn't know and might not like. Getting to them wouldn't be easy either, not with Heiko lurking beyond these walls. Even if I surmounted those obstacles, and I could find some of my people, my kind weren't like werewolf packs. We didn't necessarily all want to be together. It drew too much notice, and our talents didn't lean toward self-defense. Staying until the spring might not be the worst idea, as long as I could keep my distance from Dante.

When I did eventually leave, I would miss this place a little. The lawn was sprawling, and I could see the kids playing down at the bottom of the hill, where a gymnasium had been set up. People were out, catching the last of the nice autumn afternoons. Yeah, there was something comforting, almost happy about this place.

But it wasn't meant for me.

CHAPTER 32

D*ante*

The day was stunning as a lot of my pack ate their lunch outside, taking advantage of one of the last mild, sunny days left in the year.

There wasn't much time before my next meeting, but the perfect weather's call was too much to resist as I stood on the porch of the East Building.

Musical laughter carried across the lawn. River was sitting there with her lunch, smiling up at Henrietta, who'd stopped to say hello.

I'd barely seen her smile before, let alone laugh. Her eyes lit in the daylight like gems. Her hair nearly sparkled. There was something mesmerizing, almost ethereal, about her. Even if I hadn't known she wasn't human before, I'd know now with a single glance.

Henrietta moved on, and I met Charlie's gaze as he

walked in River's direction. He kept walking, as if sitting beside her hadn't been his intent.

Frankie walked over a few minutes later. "There is something about her. Everyone sees it," he said.

He was right. It was hard not to notice *all* the eyes that went to her, particularly male.

"Something wrong?" Frankie asked.

More than I could put into words. I crossed my arms as I leaned on a nearby post, watching them, watching her.

"No lead on what she is yet?" he asked.

"No idea, but I've got this feeling that she could turn our lives upside down if she wanted. There's a lot we don't know about her, and I think it's going to shock everyone when we finally find out."

"Heiko certainly thought she was valuable." Frankie didn't speak for a few seconds and then his hands went through his hair. "The reports of a heavy trail of vampire scent nearby is a bit concerning."

"I know. We're going to have to switch our attention from the eight and go after Heiko. He's not going to let this lie. He's going to come for us." He was going to come for *her*. Even if we weren't meant to be together, I'd at least set her free without a psychopath on her tail.

"It's going to be hard. He might expect it."

"We either wait for him to hit us or we hit him first. It's an either/or situation. I prefer to have the time and place under my control."

Yelling a few feet away caught my attention. Charlie, the perpetual pain in the ass, was starting something with Jobo, who had zero tolerance for his bullshit.

"Is Charlie still insisting Jobo insulted him a week ago?" I asked, not up on all the latest gossip. The two were getting closer to shifting and coming to blows. For as often as Charlie got his ass kicked, his memory was awfully short.

"Probably. Who can keep track of what that nut thinks?" Frankie asked.

"Even if Jobo did insult him, Charlie probably deserved it. How many times is he going to get his ass handed to him before he finally stops picking fights?" A glimmer of golden highlights caught my eye as River headed toward them. "Does that girl not have a lick of sense?"

"What? Ooh," Frankie said, spotting River walking over with the clear intention of injecting herself in between two shifters about to brawl, as if she were their kindergarten teacher.

"I'll be back. I have to go *save* her from *saving* them."

"Stop it!" she yelled as she moved in between the two men. "There's other ways to resolve your issues."

Did she not notice that she was the only one interfering? That maybe everyone watching knew something she didn't? With all the growling going on, it was hard to even hear her talking.

"Now calm down," she said. "We can talk this out."

Instead of talking, they circled her, as if she were a piece of furniture or a small boulder in their way.

She was so intent on her peace mission that she didn't notice me. She yelped when an arm wrapped around her and she was swung off her feet.

"Are you absolutely insane?" I asked, toting her away from the brawl.

"What are you doing? You can't let them fight," she said, trying to squirm out of my grasp.

"That's exactly what I'm going to do," I said, continuing to walk with her in my arm. "What did you think *you* were going to do, other than get ripped to shreds?"

"Stop them, like the only rational person here, obviously."

"They won't kill each other. Jobo will give Charlie a good scar, which he deserves because he's been starting shit again. Charlie will be a little humbler and hopefully a little less annoying afterward. Tomorrow they'll be fine. *You* wouldn't have been. Don't do that again."

"I can walk, by the way." Every set of eyes that landed on us seemed to make her angrier.

I dropped her to the ground a minute later.

"Oh, wonderful. The great Dante has deemed I'm allowed to use my feet again."

"Have you learned nothing from the past few years? The past year? This world is not a kind place, and it's only getting worse. Don't get involved in situations you can't handle."

She was trying to look around me, looking for a way to dodge me, and then gave up.

"Fine. Be a monster and let your people rip each other apart," she said.

"Without me, you'd be sitting in some vampire dungeon or hauled away by Heiko. I might be a monster, but sometimes that's what it takes to survive."

"I have more civilized things to do than get a lesson in survival from you," she said, turning and heading back to the library.

I walked back to the clearing where Charlie and Jobo had shifted and were going at it. I didn't particularly care to watch the fight. There were more important things to do, but someone had to make sure River didn't come back.

Gus walked over as Jobo was about to take some of Charlie's hide off him.

"Got that little girlie of yours settled?" he asked,

laughing again, as if this situation was an endless amusement to him.

"She's not my *girlie*." Although I couldn't fault him for the way it looked lately.

"You sure? She lives with you. From the looks I've seen pass between you two, there's more there than cohabitating." He whistled.

"Are you sitting up nights listening to the Hen Pack again?"

Gus laughed as if I hadn't just implied he was an old, gossiping hinny. "The Hen Pack, the kids, they're all gossiping, and I listen to every bit of it. How else do you think this old man entertains himself?"

"I don't have the time or energy to get involved with her, or care what people are saying about us." It would be even better if it wasn't repeated to me whenever he could grab my ear.

"Anyone who isn't blind sees the heat the two of you throw off when you're anywhere near each other. Everything else will fall into place."

"Gus, human mates have a hard enough time fitting into a pack, and she's not even that." I hated the fact I'd been thinking about the difficulties human mates faced. It certainly hadn't been on my list of deep thoughts until River showed up.

The crowd groaned as Charlie took a hard left, wobbling but not going down.

"You can convince yourself that it's nothing but a dead end, but I've seen harder situations smoothed out," Gus said.

I was already losing interest, looking back toward the library. Macky was running toward me with a book under one arm and frantically waving the other.

"I'm needed," I said, glad to have an excuse to leave Gus and the others to watch the end of the fight.

I met Macky halfway.

"I think I know what she is." He opened up his book and flipped to a bookmark about a third of the way through. "Look at this." He stabbed the page. "It's called a Luck Charmer."

"What is that? Like a leprechaun or something?" I'd never heard the term in my life, and I thought I'd encountered almost everything at this point.

"According to this author, they can shift a person, or persons', luck to good or bad. 'They can be recognized by their unusual eyes, sweet scent, erratic heartbeat, and strange, iridescent blood. Luck Charmers were rumored to have sat beside Attila the Hun and Caesar, changing the fate of many battles and possibly even wars. Although they're rumored to have been gifted with exceptional longevity, the heavy cost of their magic usually caused an early death. There are no known Luck Charmers left in existence. The race has been extinct for decades, if it ever truly existed at all.'

"The author says they're extinct, but this fits River to a tee," he said, not sounding very convinced. "I marked a couple other pages that might be useful as well."

If this were true... If she could change the course of wars... Of course she'd never tell a soul. How could she? If this ever got out, she'd be wanted for the rest of her life. There would be no place to hide, nowhere safe. I didn't even trust my pack with information like this.

"Give me the book and tell no one."

"Never," he said. "Because if I did..." He shook his head, smart enough to grasp the ramifications as well.

"Exactly." I took the book, hoping I didn't know what River actually was, praying it was a mistake.

CHAPTER 33

R *iver*

Dante was sitting at the kitchen table. The last time he'd been sitting there, waiting, he tried to take my blood with a syringe. That hadn't gone very well, so it looked like he was changing tactics. The needle was gone, and a book was in its place.

It was the same book Macky had carried out with him this afternoon. There'd been something weird about the way Macky acted when he walked out with it. Now I was afraid it had something to do with me.

There was no need for an invitation to sit this time. I met my fate with as much grace as I could. Dante watched my every movement, as if he assumed I was going to take off. It was too late for that, and I knew it.

The sound of the chair scraping against the floor was unnaturally loud in the heavy silence. He flipped open the book to where it had been bookmarked and slid it across the table toward me. It lay there in between us for a few very long seconds.

"No interest in glancing at it?" Dante asked, leaning back in his chair as if he already had all the answers.

I was caught. Maybe not red-handed, but Dante wasn't an idiot, and neither was Macky. They knew.

"If you'd like." I pulled it forward, scanning the page. It would've been naive to think details of my race weren't written down somewhere. It wasn't as if no one ever knew of us. Still, to see the details in print made it hard not to twitch.

I glanced at the cover before shutting the book. I leaned back and met his stare as if I had nothing to hide, refusing to go down without a last-ditch attempt.

"This Chaplin fellow seems to know a lot, but these Luck Charmers he's discussing are extinct." My mouth was dry and my heart felt like I was on speed, but my expression was as serene as a lake on a breezeless day.

"There's no use denying it, especially since I can test it with a drop of your blood," he said, as calm as I was pretending to be.

And it kept getting worse. He knew if he took fire to a drop of my blood, it would elicit a rainbow mist. I was done. There was nowhere left to hide, no lie left to tell. It was over. The only thing left to find out was how much honor he truly had. How ambitious was he, and what was he willing to do to achieve his goals?

I nodded, silently admitting the truth. I ran my fingers over the wood grain of the table as I forced myself to have a conversation I'd been dreading my entire life. "Left to our own devices, we don't use our powers. We let the energy glide over us, but we don't direct it. We don't want to. It has a steep cost. That's one thing that author got right." I looked up at Dante, hoping he'd sense my sincerity. "Let me go and I will move on from here. You'll never hear of me again. I would never act against this pack. I have no reason to, and all it would do is hasten my death."

I wouldn't act against him, but that didn't mean he wouldn't use me until I was so spent that I died an early death, like so many others of my kind. Pushed to achieve his ends, battle after battle, until there was nothing left to give. A normal life had never been in the cards for me, but somehow I'd always held out hope for something more than doing others' bidding until I died.

"I won't use you," he said, answering the question that mattered most but leaving the rest of my fate unsaid.

"You're not going to let me go, are you?" I asked. He hadn't been willing to release me before. This would surely make it worse.

"No. Not until I'm sure it's safe. I can't afford to let someone like Heiko get to you." There was remorse in his tone, his eyes, and even if it shouldn't matter, it did.

I ran a hand through my hair, trying to come to grips with a future that was murky at best and sometimes like trying to see through pea soup. "Will it ever be safe?"

"I don't know, but I'll try to make it so. Other than Macky, no one knows what you are, and they won't. You have my word that I won't use you, and I *will* let you go when I can. And what you are, that doesn't leave us. I give you my word as alpha of this pack."

"What about your war?" I asked, sure there was a clause in this somewhere.

"That's not the way I want to win." The conviction in his tone left little doubt.

I'd never met anyone like him in my life. Here I was, in his house, the key to winning his war, and he wouldn't use me? Take advantage of an unimaginable opportunity? It wasn't as if I hadn't seen him in action, watched him walk from a raid, covered in his enemy's blood. He had a killer instinct.

"Okay." It was utterly inadequate for the advantage he was willing to give up to protect me.

Unable to sit still, I got up and fussed in the kitchen, wiping things that were already clean.

He got up and grabbed a drink.

I wrapped my arms around myself as if I were cold and sat in front of the fire, waiting for him to ask something else. He had to have more questions.

He stood, leaning on the counter in the kitchen, giving me space.

After all he'd discovered today, he really wasn't going to push for every detail? He was willing to let it go? Let the rest of my secrets stay buried? The longer the silence stretched on, the more I felt myself watching him, finding myself not as averse to talking. Almost wanting to after all this time.

"Ask," I said.

He studied me for a moment. "You're sure?"

I'd already had his full attention, but now it was more intense.

"You said you'd keep my secret, so yes, *ask*." I would be begging him to ask a question soon. "There are a lot of things I don't know. I don't have all the answers, but I'll try."

He walked over slowly and settled into the chair, as if afraid to crowd me.

"How does it work?" he asked, resting his chin on his fist. His expression reminded me a bit of Macky's perpetual curiosity.

"Everything in the universe has a flow. Sometimes it drives positive things to a person, and sometimes negative. I can change that flow. I can turn a person's luck from bad to good, or vice versa." I tilted my head back and lifted my hands. The air all around me lit with currents of sparkling light, blueish white and dark gray, swirling about. "People can't see this normally, but it's how it looks to me all of the time."

"You see that around people?" he asked, mesmerized by the swirling light.

"Around them, in the air, around places." I put my hands down, the light fading. "There used to be more of us, before we were captured and used until we died. I don't know anyone else of my kind." That was the truth. I didn't know any more of my kind, but I knew there were others. I'd felt them. They could probably feel me. But I'd protect their existence to the end, just as I'd hope they would mine. Hopefully they were still free.

"Why did you stay in that dungeon for so long? Couldn't you do something to get out?"

I pulled my knees up to my chest, wrapping my arms around them. "I can make a person, or a group, miserable, but it's hard to use my abilities for my own benefit. The drain it causes shortly after... The stronger the sway, the harder and faster it hits. It's not a good getaway plan if you can't stay awake to actually get away."

He tilted his head slightly. "The day you slept like you were dead, you'd used your abilities?"

"Yes." I'd told him to ask, but this wasn't the questioning I'd expected. There were a lot of things about my kind that remained unknown, even to me, but there was one thing that had been drilled into me from before I could walk: don't inflict harm unless you absolutely have to. It was the number one rule of our kind. What you shifted, the energy you redirected, always had a cost.

"What Carly and Amber said was true? It was you that night at the gathering?" He leaned forward, as if he couldn't quite believe I'd done that. They'd been blaming it on me, but no one believed them until now.

"Yes." I stared straight at him, waiting for a judgment that didn't seem to come, or at least he hid it well. He didn't look any more annoyed than a second ago.

"Why? That was before you fell into the hole, and their pokes never seemed to bother you much," he said, the corners of his eyes deepening, as if he didn't believe they had the ability to provoke me.

I was coming clean, right? Might as well try to stick to that as long as I could. If he found my reasons petty, then so be it.

"They weren't getting to me. I spent nearly a year in a vampire dungeon. It had nothing to do with what they did to me."

"What was it then that made you do it?"

I leaned my chin on my knee, rethinking my whole *ask me, ask me* bit from a few moments ago, knowing how petty I was about to sound.

"It was Gus' birthday cake, the one Henrietta made." He'd probably lecture me for going after them over a cake. He could say whatever he chose. I wouldn't hesitate to do it again. If that made me petty, too bad.

"That's why it tasted so bad? They did it?" He rubbed the back of his neck.

"I think they salted her sugar." I still had a hard time thinking about that night without getting irate and wanting to do worse.

"Now that I could see pissing you off." Instead of looking annoyed, he laughed.

I cleared my throat, trying to figure out how he'd read me so well. The man baffled me sometimes, and always when least expected. I guessed he wouldn't be a good alpha if he wasn't a good judge of character.

When he finally stopped laughing, he said, "So when you shift luck to different degrees, it…" He lifted his hand.

"There's a price. I'll eventually weaken and die. I'm not sure how long that will take, as I've heard some last longer, but that's the end game." For someone who wasn't paying the price, he seemed a little sensitive about spelling it out.

He nodded, leaning back in his chair. "And your parents have passed?"

"My father was taken before I was born, and my mother was taken when I was four. I was raised by a family friend who hid me, so the knowledge of my kind was limited. They told me what they could and that was about it. It's not much more than what I've told you, mostly that I shouldn't do anything unless I want to die young." I laughed, even though nothing about it was funny.

He didn't share my gallows humor. "Don't do it again. They aren't worth it." He was intent, waiting for a reply or commitment, the atmosphere growing heavy.

Too bad I couldn't make that promise. "I'll try."

He shook his head but smiled, as if he knew me too well to be surprised by that. "How did you end up in a vampire's basement?"

"Like I said, there was a family friend, a woman named Heidi, who took me in after they got to my mother. She disappeared one day. Several people saw her die from a vampire attack, and a neighbor came and told me. He knew I didn't go out much or talk to many people. He thought I'd gotten caught disobeying some minor rules and was lying low. Humans don't tend to notice my odd scent, and even if they do, they think it's some candy-apple body wash or perfume.

"His name was Chopin, and he offered to let me stay with him for a bit. I'd done pretty well laying low at his place for a few months when it was Chopin's birthday. I just wanted to do something nice to thank him. So I took the little money I had from selling some knitted goods for a little money. I was going to use it to get ingredients to make a cake. I went to a store that didn't usually have other races than human, and I walked right past a vampire on my way in. That was it. One sniff and they knew something was off. I got thrown into the basement, and that was the end of it."

"Why haven't you tried to reach out to this person since you've been here? Or have you?"

"It wasn't like we were together or anything more than friends. I didn't want to put him in a spot where he felt he had to try to save me, returning his kindness by getting him in a mess."

Dante stood up, and I figured he was going to walk into the bedroom, having heard enough from me tonight. Instead, he grabbed his phone off the table and tossed it on the couch beside me.

"Call him. Talk as long as you want. I still can't let you leave knowing Heiko is out there, but as long as Chopin is willing to keep quiet about where you are and understands the situation, he can come here and visit. No one will touch him."

I picked up the phone, holding it in my hands as if it were priceless. "Really?"

"Yes."

We looked at each other, and it was almost as if I were looking at someone I'd never met, or hadn't really seen. Dante might not be the best of men, but he was turning out to be far from the worst of them. I might have called him a monster, and maybe he was, but I was starting to think he might not be my enemy.

"Make your call. There's a charger in the drawer if you need it." He walked out of the room.

CHAPTER 34

D*ante*

It all made sense. That kind of secret shouldn't be told. It wouldn't set you free. It would cage you for the rest of your life. Last night's information had kept me awake for hours. I should let her go. Find a place far away, somewhere she had a chance to get on with her life. A place where there weren't as many shifters and vampires and no one would know she was different.

She smiled at me when she walked into the kitchen. That was definitely something new.

"Things went well?" I asked, having heard her on the phone for a while last night.

"Very well." She grabbed a cup of coffee. "Did you mean what you said about my friend visiting?"

"I don't say things I don't mean." She had her hair in a messy ponytail that somehow made her look more adorable as she sipped her coffee.

"Because he wants to come as soon as possible." She sucked in her lower lip, looking at me like I might say "gotcha" or something.

"Does he need help getting here?" With all the rules in place, sometimes it was hard for humans to get around these days.

"He said he can get here. He's pretty resourceful." She smiled again, and I was starting to see the dangers in our getting along. "Gotta go get dressed for the library."

* * *

Jobo was leaning over a map, pointing. "We trailed the scent back to here, where we know the smaller crew surveilling this place is holding up. Some of them left this morning, and our people are following them now in a northeasterly direction."

"Any sightings of Heiko?" I asked, looking at all the marked spots.

"No, not yet, but someone caught his scent around this location." Jobo tapped a spot on the map.

Frankie stepped into the doorway of the planning room in the East Building, his hair standing on end. "Dante, got a minute?"

I walked out into the hall, and he shut the door.

"What's wrong?" I asked.

"Chopin is here. River's *friend*? The one you told us to expect in a few weeks or so."

"Already? How did he get here so quickly? Was he on foot? Most humans don't have access to a car." Unless he was tied into some other race and getting extra bennies, which didn't sit well at all.

"That might be because he's *not* human." Frankie's hands were in his hair. "He's a *shifter*! He's one of us."

I wouldn't insult Frankie, or anyone in my pack for that matter, by asking if he were sure. A shifter *knew* another shifter. It was impossible not to. I also couldn't lose it the way I wanted, either. Frankie was already on edge. I didn't need him walking out of here and getting everyone else riled, but nothing about this sat well.

"Do we know his pack? Did you ask?"

"He was very noncommittal. I think he's a lone wolf." Lone wolf was the name given to a werewolf that didn't have a pack, either by choice or a deficiency in personality when they couldn't get along in a pack setting. Either way, it didn't bode well for River's friend.

"Where is he now?" I asked, already heading out of the building.

"We're holding him at the gatehouse. Do you think she knows?" Frankie asked.

"She didn't mention it."

No way she knew, but Frankie was already protective of her. If he found out this guy had conned River in some way, it wouldn't help to keep the peace. It was bad enough I was ready to rip this Chopin apart. I couldn't have half my guards losing it on him.

A couple of my guards were lingering outside the gatehouse when I got there.

"I've got this," I said as I neared. They backed away slowly. Frankie joined their group, all of them staring at Chopin.

Chopin was leaning on the desk inside, watching me as intently as I was him. Dark sandy hair on the longish side, he was lean for a shifter and fairly average looking. It was clear how he passed as a human, at least to another human.

My inclination was to rip his jugular out right then and there. The only thing that stayed my hand was River's face this morning when she told me he was coming to visit. If he disappeared, she'd be worried. He'd have to make at least one appearance, but after that, all bets were off. He better answer my questions correctly or he'd be leaving here tonight, never to be seen again.

"We need to talk," I said.

"I couldn't agree more."

He spoke with more arrogance than expected. It made me like him even less, if that were possible.

"Follow me."

Chopin drew attention as we walked, every shifter instantly recognizing him as one of our kind who they didn't know. I walked all the way to the back of the campus, to a wooded area not often used.

I turned on him. "What kind of fucked-up game are you playing?"

"What game I'm playing? I'm not the one holding an innocent hostage." Again he spoke with more bravado than he could back up.

"You better watch your tone or you won't be seeing her or anyone else ever again." I took a step toward him, making it clear he wouldn't have too many opportunities to answer my next question correctly. "Why didn't you tell her what you were?"

His shoulders dropped a smidge and he looked out at the trees, a flash of pain on his face. "Because I was afraid it would scare her away and she'd have no one."

He was in luck. He'd hit upon the only answer that didn't make me angrier.

"How did you come to know her in the first place? Why were you running in human circles?" Nothing about this guy's story was adding up to something innocent.

"I had a falling-out with my pack. I needed somewhere to live, and it was easier to pass as human than tell a bunch of humans their neighbor was a shifter, as I'm sure you can imagine."

So he *was* a lone wolf. I'd never trusted a shifter who couldn't fit into a pack, and I certainly didn't feel good about this one. Still, my read was that he was being honest, but not with the right person.

"You need to come clean with her," I said, my tone making it clear this wasn't a request but a demand.

"And you need to let her leave," he said.

Maybe I didn't *totally* hate the kid. He was at least fighting for her against someone he knew could rip him apart.

But he had lied. I wouldn't broach what she was, but he knew she was different. Had to. No. I fucking hated him.

"The only reason you're not dead right now is I don't want to upset her. This is the way it's going to go down: you're going to see her, and you *are* going to come clean. After that, I'll see what she wants done with you."

He nodded, looking like he'd agree to anything just to see her. My flesh was itching, and I wanted to rip his head off his shoulders. He was lucky I didn't have the heart to kill him yet.

I called the library. "Tell River her guest is here. We'll meet her at the cabin."

I walked away, giving him my back, praying he'd take the opportunity to pull something so I could kill him with a clean conscience.

River was waiting for us at the cabin, her face lighting up as she saw Chopin walk in behind me. That light in her eyes, for a man who'd been lying to her, made me want to go into a dark rage. It would end tonight.

"You're making lasagna," Chopin said, smiling wide. I'd never tasted River's cooking, other than what she'd helped prep for the cafeteria. Another level of rage burned.

"Of course I did! It's your favorite," she said, walking over and practically jumping into his arms for a hug.

The rage went atomic. My skin itched. I was a ticking bomb. I backed toward the door, knowing I was on borrowed time.

"I'm going to leave you two alone. I know you have a lot to talk about."

I left the house but didn't go far, digging out my phone. "River is in the house with that shifter. I need eyes on him at all times."

"You got it," Frankie said.

CHAPTER 35

R*iver*

"Come on, I'll make us some tea, and we can sit in the living room and catch up while the lasagna bakes," I said.

Chopin's smile stiffened, which was so unlike him. I'd gotten a raw deal, but who knew what life had dealt him while I was gone? He looked healthy enough, but there was a sadness lurking in his eyes. He'd seemed happy last night when we talked on the phone, but now... Did he not want to say anything? Wanted to let me unload, holding back his own nightmarish experience?

"How have you been? Everything been okay? You didn't say much last night." I handed him a cup of tea and led him over to the couch.

He settled into the chair, the way Dante would when he was trying to keep his distance.

He put the tea down without taking a sip. "I need to tell you something that's long overdue. And I want to explain why I kept it to myself before I tell you what it is, because you might get upset."

If he didn't want to upset me, he was doing a lousy job. "You've done a lot for me. I'm sure it's not that bad. Even if it were, I'd forgive you anything after the risks you've taken." I'd been on the brink of homelessness and certain death when he opened his home to me. He'd barely known me but took me in as if I were family. He'd never blinked an eye at the extra expenses. He'd never come onto me either, even as I suspected he'd had a crush. There was nothing I wouldn't forgive him.

"Let me get this out before you exonerate me. I need to." He ran his hand over his jaw, not looking at me.

I nodded, waiting. As each second ticked by, my apprehension grew like a dead weight settling heavier on my chest. It didn't matter what he said. He was the person who'd let me share his roof, his food, kept me alive. These weren't the actions of a bad person.

He cleared his throat. "When I offered you a place to stay, I didn't want to scare you off by overloading you with details that didn't have any bearing on the situation. I was worried you'd fear accepting my offer if you knew certain things."

I opened my mouth but stopped short when he raised his hand.

He sat forward, rubbing his hands together. "Then after you were moved in, I was afraid you'd leave if I did come clean." He switched his focus solely to me. Anxiety filling his eyes, sharpening the lines of his body. "But I always planned on telling you everything at some point."

"Whatever it is, tell me. It can't be that bad," I said softly.

He took another moment, looking down again, before he said, "I'm a shifter."

All the air felt like it was knocked out of me.

"A shifter?" I leaned back in my seat, staring at him as if I'd never seen him before.

Maybe it was because I'd spent so much time with shifters these last weeks that suddenly it was like a veil had been lifted. His build, although not as large as some, still had more musculature than a lot of humans. Then there was the way he moved, so gracefully. The way his sense of smell had always seemed better than mine. His strength.

All the little details I hadn't paid attention to popped out at me now. I wondered how I'd never seen them before. It was as obvious as the nose on my face, but I'd been blind. He'd said he was human and I accepted that as gospel.

"Like Dante."

His eyes hardened before he looked away. "Yes, like Dante."

My brain couldn't seem to filter through most of my emotions because it was too busy being stunned. Details of his actions in the past, the ones I'd used to confirm what a good person he was, were layered over this new information, and suddenly didn't seem quite so noble and clean-cut. Like when he walked in the house winded and said that he thought he'd been followed. Followed by whom? He'd been part of the upper echelon. He'd been one of the predators.

Part of me wanted to run away from him. But more than that, a burning rage demanded answers.

"All those times you acted afraid?" I sat back, hands fisted on my lap, trying to contain all the feelings growing inside of me.

He slumped back. "It's what would've been normal. I wasn't trying to deceive you, but I didn't want you to think I was different."

"You thought putting on a charade was better? You treated me like a fool who couldn't handle the truth, someone you had to manage." Who was this person? He wasn't who I'd imagined, that was for certain.

He leaned toward me. "It wasn't meant to be a lie. I was trying to help you feel comfortable so you didn't leave."

I jerked away from his outstretched hand. "By lying?"

His nostrils flared slightly, triggering more unfortunate realizations. Every single shifter in this place sensed something different in me because of my scent.

Every. Single. One.

"Did you take me in because you knew I was different?" I'd never told him what I was, but I hadn't had the heart to *lie* to him. Before he let me into his home, I'd made sure he realized I might be a liability. I'd told him all I could. Even after I shared as much as I could to protect him, he hadn't returned the trust by sharing what *he* was.

"That had nothing to do with it." He shook his head so adamantly that it struck me as overly defensive.

"But you knew before I said a word." My accusation left a bitter taste in my mouth.

"Yes. It's obvious."

"And it had nothing to do with it?" I asked. "Please, if I meant anything to you, just tell me now."

"Maybe there was a curiosity that I'd stumbled across someone who might be more than met the eye, who might, I don't know…"

"Be of use to you somehow?" I asked, holding back the disgust that was growing.

"If I did, it was only in the beginning."

All the nights we'd stayed awake talking, his acting as if he was as scared as me. I'd cooked and cleaned, tried to do whatever I could to repay him for taking such a risk for me, but he'd never been in danger. He'd been eyeing me as a possible asset. Or, at best, I'd been nothing more than a pet to him, or an unpaid housekeeper? Even humans were paid to clean house.

Only minutes ago, I'd told him it didn't matter what he said. That wasn't turning out to be true.

"What about your family? The ones that died? Did you make that up too?" I asked, already fearing in my gut what he was going to say.

He didn't answer. That said it all.

He reached out to touch me again, and I jerked my arm away. He froze. It was a knee-jerk reaction but still how I felt. In that second, we both knew things were very different between us, maybe permanently.

"River, please...don't look at me like that."

"I'm not trying to hurt you, but I need some time to come to grips with this."

"I'm not any different than anyone else here, and you seem to be fine with *them*." Now he was hurling harsh accusations at *me*.

Them. How could he not see the difference?

"No one here pretended to be anything other than what they are. You..." My entire time with him had been an act, written and directed by him.

"You still haven't told me how you got caught," he said. "Why did you go to that store?"

He knew his time was limited, that he should ask all his questions now because he'd be asked to leave soon. He was right. The only reason he was still here was because of my loyalty for what he had done, twisted or not.

"We'd run out of some things. I was tired of asking you to get everything." I hadn't told him about the cake last night, not wanting to hurt him. I didn't tell him today for the same reason, despite how his confession had hurt me.

He bent forward, burying his head in his hands. Was this an act too? How could I trust anything he said or did?

"Do you hate me?" he asked, sounding genuinely gutted.

Did I? The betrayal was too fresh, my feelings too jumbled toward him to label. It might not be hatred, but it wasn't good.

"Even if things were different than I thought, you still helped me when no one else would. I'll never forget that."

"You're talking like I won't see you again," he said, finding the strength to look up.

"I need some time. For now, I think maybe you should go." I stood.

He got to his feet, moving to block me. "What are you going to do? Stay here? Be his prisoner?"

Was I? Dante said he wouldn't let me leave until it was safe, so technically I was. But I didn't feel like it anymore. This place was starting to feel like home.

"Right now, I need time. I think it would be a good idea if you left in the morning," I said, trying to remain calm. Chopin might've been faking distress before, but his desperation in this moment felt real.

"Do you have something going on with this man? Clearly he didn't move you into his house for no reason."

"That's none of your business." I moved around the other side of the couch so I could get to the door, and caught a glimpse of Frankie through the window. He was standing by the bushes, watching very intently. I gave a slight nod.

Frankie didn't budge from his spot.

I opened the door, feeling more confident now that I knew there were eyes on us. "I think it's a good idea if you leave now."

Chopin didn't move at first, as if he didn't quite believe this was it.

I waited silently. I wasn't the needy homeless girl that he could play games with.

He walked to the door, pausing near me. "Please call me after you take some time."

I nodded but doubted I would. The person I'd bonded with didn't exist. What we bonded over had been a lie.

I opened the door wider. He dropped his head and left.

I walked out to the porch and took a seat in one of the rockers as soon as he was out of sight.

Frankie walked over a few minutes later and settled into the rocker next to me. We rocked in silence for a few minutes, Frankie clearly sensing the turmoil.

"I wasn't trying to spy on you," he said after a few minutes.

"You were following orders. It's fine. I get it." I wrapped my arms around myself, feeling chilled.

"I was following orders, but not to watch you. Dante—and to be truthful, I—wanted to keep an eye on that guy. You obviously didn't know what he was or you would've mentioned it. No one wants to see you get hurt."

I stopped rocking, not minding the company as much now. "Oh…"

"Some of us might be getting used to having you around, even if you are turning out to be a lot of trouble." He laughed.

"I know. I've got a little baggage," I said, laughing at his teasing. He almost felt like a brother.

It was exactly what I needed.

CHAPTER 36

D*ante*

I'd run for miles. It had barely calmed my inner beast enough to stay human, but I couldn't seem to stay away any longer. Chopin was standing in the distance, leaning on a tree, waiting for me. Jobo was off farther in the distance, making a walking gesture with his fingers.

Good. It was the only thing that stopped me from dragging Chopin out of here by force. Anyone who lied that gravely about who they were deserved to be run out of here like a dog.

He'd be getting a nice little warning of what would happen if he ever set foot in this place again. I didn't want him walking out with a black eye everyone could see, but a few punches in his gut would work well.

"She knows," Chopin said as I neared.

"Good."

He bent forward, his hands covering his face, looking worse than if I *had* beaten him.

"I didn't mean to hurt her," he said.

He kept shaking his head, as if he wished he could take it all back. The desire to punch him grew weaker. The man was already broken.

"You love her," I said.

"Once you get to know her, it's impossible not to. It's not what she looks like or that there's something different about her. I've never met anyone with a purer heart." He looked at me as if he were cursing me. "You'll see."

River had a draw for sure, but I wouldn't lose my heart that easily. I couldn't. I wasn't a lone wolf but an alpha with a pack to worry about.

"What are you planning to do?" I asked, torn between wanting him gone and pitying the pathetic creature he'd become in the span of a day.

"She wants me to go, so I'm going. But if I find out that she's harmed—in any way—I will come back and I will hurt you," he said, finally showing a glimpse of strength coming back.

It was the first thing out of Chopin's mouth that made me respect him at all. My urge to punch him faded a little more.

"That's fine, but the lady wants you gone, so I suggest you leave now."

He stood there for a moment, as if he'd received a death sentence. Then he walked past me, toward the gate, without another glance. Jobo followed him as I headed toward the cabin.

Frankie was lingering outside as I approached.

"How'd it go?" I asked.

He kicked a stone on the ground. "I think she feels

pretty fucking betrayed," he said, sounding like he wanted to go beat the shit out of Chopin as much as I did.

"It's okay. We got her."

He nodded.

River was sitting on the couch, staring at nothing, when I walked in. She didn't hear me as I entered, and instead of a cup of tea beside her, there was a glass and a bottle of whiskey. I was nearly standing on top of her before she looked up.

"I saw Chopin leaving."

She shrugged. "You obviously knew."

I nodded, suddenly hoping she wouldn't ask me. But she would. She was too smart to not.

"Did you force him to tell me?"

I nodded.

"Yeah. That's what I figured."

She stared off into nothing again. Betrayal, even unintended, stung. I'd felt the burn too many times not to spot it in someone else.

"I've got to go catch up on a few things," I said, turning to leave and give her space.

"Right now? It's pretty late, and I've got a whole tray of lasagna."

Her big, bright eyes were practically begging me to stay, and I could see the need in them. This wasn't a smart move. I needed to get out of here. I couldn't be the person she wanted me to be. I was more monster than man, and as cold as they came when the situation was needed.

"I've got some planning to do. Something that needs handling in the next day or so," I said, taking a step toward the door.

"Yeah, sure," she said, smiling and yet looking like she'd just been betrayed again. She stared at the fire, with a look that said she was utterly alone in this world.

I should leave.

I didn't. I made the stupidest decision of my life.

"It can wait," I said. I should be hightailing it out of there, but something about her had always called to me, and now, seeing her like this, I couldn't seem to do it.

"Care to join me?" she asked, waving the bottle of whiskey at me.

"I'm good, thanks."

"Are you sure? It's a very good bottle." She smirked, because of course I was familiar with it, having bought it. "Here, you can even have the glass if you want. I probably need the bottle."

She poured a couple fingers of whiskey before holding the glass out to me. After I accepted the offering, she saluted me with the bottle and then took a swig. And then another.

I took a sip before putting it down, coming to terms with what had to be done, the very real probability that she needed to discuss her feelings.

"You don't seem...*fine*." I'd never willingly dug into someone else's feelings in my life. I didn't like acknowledging my own. The way she was staring at me, as if I were an alien, wasn't helping matters.

"I thought you might want to talk. But if you don't, that's good too."

She still wasn't talking, but her eyes were on me as she took another swig.

"I don't think talking is going to help," she finally said, then took yet another shot from the bottle before setting it on the table.

There was a need in her eyes, a want, but what she was looking for, I didn't have to give. She was a virgin. Nothing about this was casual to her, and I wasn't in a place to give anything to anyone.

"What you're thinking about isn't what you want," I said.

"You don't know what I want. Don't worry. I'm not expecting anything from you." She licked her lips, staring at mine, waiting to see if I'd reject her or take the invitation.

She might believe she wasn't expecting anything from me if we did this, but I couldn't see a way out of hurting her. Nevertheless, I couldn't bring myself to leave her. In fact, I was barely able to keep myself from grabbing her and taking her invitation, no matter where it led.

She leaned forward slightly. "I'm done waiting for the right man. I'll find him when it's the right time."

It was bullshit. She didn't believe what she was saying at all. All my reasons for this being wrong didn't matter because the mention of an imaginary Mr. Right in the future obliterated any sane thoughts. The only thing left in the wake was *mine*.

* * *

River

Dante, who hated to talk, was offering to discuss my *feelings*. Maybe it was the grilled cheese he'd made me, or how he'd watched after me when I crashed from pushing bad luck on the hateful duo, but what I wanted now had nothing to do with talking. I wanted him, which wasn't logical, sane, or smart, and I didn't care. There wouldn't be any future here, and I didn't care about that either. Right now, all I *needed* was his hands on me.

He had been sitting there, looking as if he were frozen while I spoke, and then it was like something clicked. He reached forward and dragged me onto his lap, his hands on my waist as I straddled him.

He wrapped his arm around my back, curving me toward him. This time wouldn't end with a few kisses, not with the heat building between us. His lips met mine, greedy and taking. I wasn't holding back anything, and neither was he. We were like two people devouring each other. My shirt was gone, and so was his, and I didn't even recall it happening. He stood with me in his arms, walking us to the bedroom.

I wrapped my arms around his shoulders, weaving my hands into his hair, knowing something had to be said before we continued. "There's one thing. The actual act might feel a little different."

He stopped walking. "Why? Is something going to happen?"

"It might feel more intense." Something that might feel like a tinge of pleasure with another woman might feel like an exploding orgasm with me, if he cared that was. For someone who wasn't a Luck Charmer, the intensity might be a complete shock to the system.

"I think I can handle it," he said with a smile, continuing to the bed.

He thought I was delusional, but he'd been warned. He had no idea, and neither did I. I'd only heard stories secondhand, from people who hadn't actually experienced it either.

He carried me to the bed and then stopped, suddenly seeming as if he had his own concerns. His hands framed my face and his shoulders tensed.

"For human females, it can hurt the first time," he said.

He was trying to go slow, for me. He was worried about hurting me. He didn't get it, didn't see how every time he was kind to me, it shredded any resolve to stay away from him. There was nothing he could say that was going to stop this.

"That's not the case for my kind," I said. At least, I hoped not. That information might also be unreliable.

I touched my lips to his, letting him know how ready I was. He didn't hold back, deepening our kiss.

He tugged off my pants, then his own. I'd seen his penis before, but now, engorged and large, knowing what we were about to do, I tensed. Was I as large as a human female? Or shifter female? Was this going to work?

My fears didn't last as he moved his fingers lower, dipping into me. I no longer worried about being too small or big or anything, as a surge of need washed it all away.

I touched him everywhere, loving the satin hardness of his flesh, the feel of his skin rubbing against mine. I lost myself as his lips traced the lines of my body, from the curve of my breast to the intake of my waist. All thoughts blurred as we came together.

When he entered me, everything I'd been told seemed utterly inadequate to describe the feeling of bliss that spread through my body. It was as if discovering your soul had been ripped apart because you'd just found the missing piece. Together, it was as if our life forces weaved their way around their other, finally complete. All the feelings between us mixed, heightening everything by the power of ten.

He broke our kiss, looking into my eyes, startled. He cared. He had to if he felt even a fraction of what I was feeling.

I lifted my head, catching his lips with mine, not daring to think about anything beyond this moment. For the first time in my life, I felt like I utterly belonged with someone, and I wanted to relish the feeling. I wrapped my arms tight around his shoulders, pulling him into me as the feeling continued to build.

Every stroke of him inside me, every touch of his hand on my skin, the trail of his mouth across my breast, wound the chaos that had taken over my body tighter and tighter. I felt like I was going to break into a million pieces. One last push and we both arched in an explosion of release that had me screaming and Dante growling out a curse.

Dante's arms gave out and he dropped on top of me, flattening me back onto the bed. He rested his forehead against mine for half a heartbeat before rolling off and onto his back.

A few minutes later, he turned his head and stared at me as if seeing me for the first time. "Was that what you were expecting?"

"Sort of." My weak response didn't begin to cover what had just taken place.

What just happened? I'd known I was attracted to him, that I'd even started to care for him, but how did we keep connecting like this every time we touched? It shouldn't be this intense between us.

Did this mean my feelings were deeper than I realized? No. They couldn't be. I wouldn't let them be, because that would be emotional suicide.

I went to get out of bed, but he grabbed my arm, pulling me back down beside him.

"Where are you going? I thought women liked to cuddle."

It would be so easy to settle in next to him if it was a normal situation, or a real relationship. It wasn't, so I tugged my arm gently from his hold.

"I think it's better this way." I had to leave so neither of us forgot exactly what this situation was. So *I* didn't forget.

"Why is that?" he asked, staring at me as I got to my feet.

"Like you said, it's not permanent." I tried to keep my tone light.

He sat up in bed, his expression losing its playfulness. "I didn't say that to hurt you, but I didn't want to lie, either. This can't go anywhere, and we both know that."

I wasn't an idiot, or not usually if you didn't count tonight. I definitely wasn't delusional. There was no future for us. But I didn't need to hear him say it. Knowing it was enough.

"Never thought it would." I went to leave.

"There's something else," he said.

"What?" My question was sharper than intended. He needed to stop delaying my exit. I needed out of the room.

His eyes, the ones that had held so much heat before, seemed to close off as I watched. He moved to sit on the edge of the bed, gripping the edges, his forearms tensed.

"You might be able to leave soon. I'm handling some things that will make it easier for you to be safe."

My shoulder hit the wall, my body looking for something to keep it upright. "You mean Heiko?"

"Yes."

"He's ancient. That's going to make him stronger than an average vampire. Are you sure it's a good idea?" I suppressed the tremble that wanted to shoot through my body.

"I've taken out worse."

His arrogant confidence did little to calm my anxiety. What if I didn't want to leave? How did I broach that when I'd told him I didn't need anything from him? That I knew there was no future here? Even though his emotions had been strong enough to feel the strange connection Luck

255

Charmers formed, that didn't mean he cared anywhere enough to try to make something of this situation.

"Okay, then." I hoped my neutral reply wouldn't betray my thoughts.

"I thought that would make you happy." He was watching me as intently as ever.

"It does. Of course it does." I tried for a more upbeat tone and tossed in a smile for good measure.

I turned and headed out the door before he discovered that leaving with his blessings smarted more than I'd ever admit.

CHAPTER 37

R *iver*

I woke the next morning, wishing I'd stayed in bed with Dante. What if that had been the only night I'd get with him? I'd been so quick to leave, and now I rued the hours lost.

No one was in the kitchen. I drank my coffee alone. It tasted more bitter than usual, or maybe that was me. How much time did I have left here? Why was the idea of leaving him hurting me so badly that I'd rather chop off one of my limbs than endure it? What had happened to me? Had I fallen for him? It felt like it.

I finished my coffee and headed toward the library, intent on not thinking of him at all. I'd spend some of my ample free time there looking at maps, focusing on where I'd be heading next. Much wiser than worrying about him, thinking of leaving here.

I looked up at the sky and saw the sun peeking out of

the clouds and then hiding behind another. Even the sun was refusing to help me out my mood today.

I took another step, and a glimmer of something dark drew my attention skyward again. To the northeast, a dark cloud stood out, one no one else could see. It glimmered with flecks of obsidian as it moved, marking its unusualness. I'd only seen the likes if it a handful of times in my life, and they always preceded a disaster. Because it wasn't really a cloud. It was a wave of bad luck, swarming above.

I took a deep breath, calming myself with the thought it was moving away from here. Whatever bad was going to happen, it had nothing to do with me, this place, or these people.

Macky was sitting at the table, smiling up at me, maps laid out in front of him, as I walked in. It was as if the universe was pointing me in the right direction—find somewhere new, focus on somewhere away from here. I was about to start a new life, have a clean break. That was a good thing, and the only place I should be directing my energy.

"Are you done with those?" I asked. "I'd like to take a glance at them when you are finished."

He got up from his seat and waved me toward it. "All yours. You can even take my seat. I had to make some copies for Dante, but he's got them, so I'm done."

I didn't sit. I couldn't. "I didn't realize he was taking a trip. Somewhere close?"

"Not that far. About a half a day northeast of here."

I leaned forward, resting my palms on the table in front of me. Suddenly it was hard to breathe.

Oh no. Not Dante. No, no, no.

"You okay?" Macky asked.

I straightened and crossed my arms so he could see my hands shaking. "I'm fine. I just forgot something. Do you know where Henrietta is? Or Frankie?" I was heading toward the door before he spoke.

"Frankie left with Dante this morning, but Henrietta is probably over helping them organize the new building they're planning by the front of the campus." He followed me, looking as if he thought I was about to fall over.

"Thanks. I'm sorry to leave you, but I really need to go talk to her."

"Yeah, sure. If you need anything, let me know." He waved, standing there watching me go.

I broke into a run, not caring who saw me or what they thought. I didn't stop until I found Henrietta in the front of where they were planning on breaking ground, talking to one of the construction crew.

I ran right up to her, startling them both.

"Henrietta, can we talk for a minute? It's important." I was breathless, but not just from the run.

"Of course. What's wrong?" she asked.

I grabbed her arm, tugging her far away from anyone who could overhear.

"Dante's in trouble, maybe Frankie too, and anyone who went with them today."

She patted my arm. "You scared me there for a minute. I'm sure everything will be fine. Dante's gone on many raids and missions. He's very cautious."

I grabbed her shoulders. "It won't be this time. Has Dante said anything to you about my origins? What I am?" He'd told me the only other person who knew was Macky, but this was his aunt. He trusted her.

"No. Why?" Her brows dropped.

"I'm going to take you into my confidence and beg that you never betray what I'm about to say. I'm a Luck Charmer."

I waited for something to click. I had a feeling I'd be waiting a long time.

"I don't know what that is," she said.

"You don't have to. I can explain it to you on the way, but you have to get a car and we need to follow them. Now." I loosened my grip, realizing my fingers were digging into her.

"Can't we just call him and tell him something's wrong?"

She didn't get it. We didn't have time to talk. I couldn't help them unless I was there. And how did I warn them when I didn't know what was wrong?

"He'll never believe it, and even if he did, he might not let me help him. Their luck is shifting as we speak. I don't know what's coming, but there's something. I can feel it. I need to get close to where they are or I'm afraid more than one of them will die tonight."

"I don't know. This sounds…" She shook her head.

"Out of everyone in this place, you saw me for who I was before anyone else. You knew I didn't want to hurt anyone. Please believe me now—we have to go. I'm begging you." My hands were still on her shoulders, and I wasn't going to let go unless she said yes or I was dragged off her. "Please, he might die."

I was on the verge of hysterics and probably looked it. I loved him. I loved Dante, and he might die, and there might be nothing I could do.

"Henrietta, we have to go!" Tears were now flowing down my cheeks.

"Okay! I'll do it. If you're that sure, we'll go now."

I didn't know if it was my desperation or determination that got her moving, but she kicked into gear.

We both ran toward her cabin, where she grabbed keys off her counter and the blanket off the couch. "Easier to get out if they don't see you. We aren't going to want to deal with questions."

I got onto the floor of her truck, and she threw the blanket over me. A few minutes later, we were driving out of the gates.

"We're good," she said.

I got up off the floor and into the seat, looking at the gates behind us.

"What is it you're going to do when we get there?" she asked. "How is it that you think you can help when you don't know what's going to happen?"

She was looking at me like she'd smuggled out a psych ward inmate and was now appeasing me to keep me calm.

"It's hard to explain, or put into words, but I can save them. I know I can. After I do it, I'm going to go into a deep sleep for a while. You might not be able to wake me for a day, or maybe a few days. I might look bad, but I'll be okay. You just need to let me sleep and I'll come out of it." And if I didn't? At least I'd saved people I cared for, perhaps even loved. It wasn't the worst way to die.

It made me wonder if *all* of my people had died being forced to help others. Had some of them willingly given their lives to save people worth saving? Because if you could save the ones you loved, how did you not try?

"This is going to make you sick?" Henrietta asked.

"Not sick, but it takes a toll." *Draining my life force* would be a more accurate description, but she didn't need to know that.

"How high will the price be?" she asked.

"There's a price for everything in life, and this one I'm willing to pay. I'll wake up. If I don't do this, some of them won't make it." I looked off in the distance, seeing the dark cloud that seemed to get darker by the minute.

"How long will you be sleeping before I should get worried?" she asked.

"I'm not sure. I've never done anything as big as what I might need to, but I'm young. I'll come out of it." I should. I hoped I would.

"I don't like the sound of that." Henrietta's brows nearly knitted together.

"Like I said, I'll be fine. If I don't do this, they *won't* be. Do you know where you're going?" I asked, keeping my eye on the cloud ahead of us.

"Yes. I don't like the fighting aspects, but I helped lay out the plans for today. I know exactly where to go."

I believed it. Henrietta was tough and strong, but kind too. She wouldn't enjoy the blood sport. I leaned against the door, keeping my eye on the cloud that would dissipate after the disaster struck. As long as that cloud was there, it wasn't too late.

* * *

"What the fuck? Why did you bring her here?" Jobo asked, swinging around and staring at us as we walked into the abandoned building. There were radios and boxes with wiring. A computer and a little antenna-looking thing sat on a table by a window.

"Is this close enough?" Henrietta asked, ignoring Jobo.

"Can we get closer?" I walked through the room, right to the window, feeling the trail of energy but wishing it were stronger.

"Not unless you want to fuck up everything," Jobo said.

"He's right. We can't get closer without risking the mission," she said.

"What the fuck is going on?" Jobo asked.

"Jobo, trust me, this has to be done. You'll see," Henrietta said. If I had a few extra minutes, I would've hugged her. She was vouching for the psych ward patient like she believed me.

"Then this will have to work." It would cost me more, but there wasn't a choice. I looked out at the afternoon sky and could see the looming energy.

I might not know all the ways of my people, having lost them too young, but they'd passed down the essentials before they were taken. I could do this.

Jobo's handheld beeped.

"Don't tell him I'm here. I have enough to fix, and I can't have anything else go wrong," I said.

Jobo was looking at me, to Henrietta, and back. "Is this something to do with what you are?"

"Yes. Now I have to concentrate. There's no time left to talk or something bad might happen."

His device beeped again, and he looked at it like he'd forgotten how to answer.

"Go on like nothing is happening," Henrietta said.

He crossed the room, trying to get space from us as he answered. I forced his chatter out of my mind and began my silent chant, letting it build while watching the dark cloud move in the distance. The energy rose the way it always did, answering my call. At first it felt like a charge in the air, and my fingertips tingled. I continued chanting until it built around me, filling the room.

It continued to build, and build, until it felt like an inferno churning inside of me. Even as I thought I'd boil from the heat, I let it build more, knowing exactly what was at stake. Of all the stories that had been handed down, these waves of bad luck had stuck with me most, the retellings of the loss of life and the horrible events that always came. They weren't that common but I'd seen them before. This was darker and larger than any I'd ever seen.

Even when it felt as if I couldn't take the slightest bit more, I continued on. This moment needed everything I had.

Jobo dropped something in the distance. Henrietta took a few steps back, looking at me as if she'd never met me before. The power grew further, until it was slipping out of me and I had to direct it away, or it would take on a life of its own.

I stopped chanting and, with a deep breath, let it go. The windows of the building blew out around us like a bomb went off.

CHAPTER 38

D*ante*

"Jobo, everyone in place?" There was silence on the other end. Frankie, who was beside me, looked concerned. "Jobo?"

"Yeah, we're good. Everyone's in place," Jobo said.

"Why do you sound distracted?" We were about to raid a coven, led by one of the most powerful vampires we'd ever taken on, and it seemed like he was watching an action movie in the background.

"No, I'm good. Everything is good," he said, sounding a lot more present.

"Then start the countdown."

"Starting countdown. Over," he said.

We were huddled down, stationed around the sprawling ranch that we'd tracked Heiko back to. Frankie and I were off in the corner, and there were five more groups of four spaced around the perimeter.

I looked down at my watch, counting down the minutes. Before another minute passed, Heiko stepped out the door. He was followed by another vampire, and then another. They continued to come out.

Frankie froze. "Holy shit."

They'd known we were coming. Had been waiting for us. Vampires continued to pour out until there were more than two of them to each one of us.

It was too late to fall back. They knew we were here. I was going to lose a lot of men before today was over. This might've been the worst mistake of my life, but I wouldn't go down without a fight.

"What do we do?" Frankie asked.

"We do what we do best. We fight." It was too late for any other option. They'd expected us. The odds were on their side. There was no retreat. They'd chase us down and slaughter us.

If I was leading my people into a battle stacked against them, I'd draw first blood.

The countdown was a couple minutes away. "Don't follow until everyone else joins."

"Wait, what?" Frankie said. "You can't."

It might be a suicide mission, but I was going to take out as many vampires as possible before I died, hopefully one in particular. I might die in this battle, but I'd take Heiko with me. He would never touch River again.

"Stay back. That's an order."

I shifted and walked out of the forest, into the clearing. All eyes shot to me as I let out a roar that shook the trees.

No one moved, stunned by my appearance. I'd taken one step in their direction when a thundering noise exploded. A blast from behind them, from inside the ranch, ripped through the air. I dropped to the ground as the blast blew debris everywhere.

In a second, it was done. There was nothing but charred pieces of vampires all over, mixed with cement, glass, and the other remnants of the enormous house. We'd gone from annihilation to being handed a gift. The enemy was dead and we hadn't lifted a finger.

I got up and walked around the grounds, my pack coming out to join me. The house was leveled, the blast point looking like it had originated in the living room area, near the front of the house.

"What the hell happened?" Frankie asked, walking over, followed by more of my pack.

I pointed to the charred hole in the ground. "They were going to win this fight one way or another. If they miscalculated the numbers, they were going to blow us up." I looked around the place. "Let's do a quick sweep. I don't think we're going to get much, though, so let's be quick. The blast might have attracted attention."

I went back and fetched my phone, calling Jobo while grabbing my stashed clothing.

"Dante?" he answered.

"Yeah. It's over. Break everything down and get moving."

"Oh, good." His sigh was loud, as if he'd thought he would never hear from us again. "We saw the blast, and—"

"We? Who else is there?" I did a mental count, but everyone who was supposed to be here was.

"Uh, yeah, I had a couple last-minute visitors."

My blood pressure spiked and the urge to shift immediately kicked in. I somehow knew River was involved.

"Dante?" Henrietta's voice rang through the phone. "I'm here, along with River. We're leaving now and will meet you back at the cabin."

"Why the hell are..." I took a few deep breaths. "Put River on."

"She's fine, but she can't get on the phone right now. We should discuss this more when we get back."

I stood silently, trying not to crush the phone or shift and rip apart everything that was in a few-mile radius.

"Dante, everyone is good," she said, as if she could see how badly I was straining through the phone.

Henrietta wouldn't lie about this. If she said River was okay, I had to believe her.

"Leave immediately. I'll meet you at the cabin."

"We'll see you there," Henrietta said.

I walked into the cabin.

"How did it go?" Henrietta asked before I barely made it over the threshold.

"Where is she?" I asked, walking father into the cabin, Henrietta on my heels. I pushed open the door to River's bedroom, and then went to mine. She was lying on my bed unnaturally still.

"River?" I grabbed her ice-cold hand. The only thing that stopped me from letting my inner beast out and losing it was that I'd seen this before.

"She'll be better soon," Henrietta said, lingering by the door. The quiver in her voice said she was trying to convince herself as much as me.

"What happened?" I turned, nailing Henrietta with a stare. "How did she end up there?"

"Come in the other room and I'll explain. I'm not sure if all our talking disrupts what's going on with her or not," she said.

I followed her out, but my patience was about as strong as a thread holding back a lion.

She grabbed a bottle of scotch and two glasses from my

cabinet and took a seat at the kitchen table. I joined her but didn't sit. I could barely stay human, let alone recline in a chair.

She poured us each a glass, threw hers back, and started. "She came to me this morning. She explained what she was and said she had to go to where you were. See, she knew there was going to be a problem with your raid. She could feel something off. I have no idea how, but I guess she senses certain things."

"Then what?" I asked, as she refilled her glass and threw back another shot. Henrietta never drank like this. She barely drank at all.

I wanted to grab the bottle, smash it against the wall, and tell her to keep talking. But she was clearly rattled enough to need it, and I wasn't going to derail her.

"We went out there, close to where you were going to attack. After that, it gets murky." She poured a double this time. "I don't know exactly what happened. She was standing there by the window, looking out, and her lips were moving. The craziest feeling filled the room, this live energy buzzing all around. Honestly, it felt like I was standing next to a god. I got goosebumps as I watched her hair floating in the air around her, and then her feet even left the ground. She hovered as if she were weightless. You wouldn't believe it unless you saw it. Then, all of a sudden, there was a blast so strong that it blew the windows out. It was so strong that it knocked Jobo and me to the floor."

Her hand was shaking as she raised the glass again. "We saw the blast in the distance next. There's not much more to tell. I got to my feet and she was lying there, unconscious, but she'd told me that might happen and not to worry."

I walked back to the entrance of the hall so I could see

River. "For how long? How long will she be like this? Did she say?" My throat was raw.

"She didn't know. She said it would happen and that she'd get better. That she was young and could handle it." Henrietta leaned on the table, appearing older than she'd ever looked.

I thought that I'd killed my pack. I should be dead, and instead River was lying in a bed, appearing as if in a coma. It made me wish I had died. If she didn't come out of this...

"Are you sleeping with her?" Henrietta asked. "Because I'm telling you now, that girl is in love with you."

My heart seized and my gut clenched. If River did love me, it was working out for her almost worse than I'd feared.

I didn't answer Henrietta. I left the house, shifting before I hit the porch. For weeks I'd tried to keep my distance, knowing that a relationship between River and me was doomed to failure. Now I was positive it was, because I had probably killed her.

* * *

It was the next afternoon and she still hadn't stirred. I'd tried every trick I used last time and she wouldn't wake. Henrietta had forced me outside for a break, but I refused to leave the porch.

The last ten people who'd spotted me took one look in my direction and kept walking. Not Gus, though. He beelined over.

If I didn't like that old man so much, if he hadn't been so good to me through the years, I might've told him to fuck off. I wasn't in the mood to talk, not to anyone about anything.

"How you holding up?" he asked, taking a seat in one of

the rockers. I should get rid of them. People always assumed it meant company was welcome. It wasn't.

"Just thinking."

He nodded, rocking and making the wooden boards creak to the most annoying rhythm. It was almost as bad as the birds chirping and people talking as they walked by.

"Heard that little girlie of yours took to bed, but Henrietta said she'd be fine."

Henrietta probably said a lot more than that. Once Henrietta got going, she didn't like to leave out too many details, especially if it was Gus she was talking to.

"She's not *mine*."

"You keep saying that."

"Well, she's not. She'll be leaving soon enough." Even telling him that made it feel like I was gutting myself, but there was no other option. If she managed to pull through this time and stayed here, I'd end up killing her, whether I wanted to or not.

She was half dead right now because she'd wanted me to survive. She deserved a better life than what I'd end up giving her.

After all the things I'd done, she'd still hurt herself to protect me and my pack.

Gus sighed loud enough to let me know he wasn't altogether happy with where he assumed my thoughts were going. He got off the rocker with a last creak and walked down the wooden steps but didn't leave until he gave me one last unwanted piece of advice.

"Sometimes there doesn't seem to be a way, but that doesn't mean there isn't one. I can see where your head is, but I wouldn't make any rash decisions. That's all I'm saying."

I nodded. As much as he might *think* he knew, the only way to repay River was to let her go. I'd always thought shifters were the most loyal race on Earth, but that was before I met her. If she stayed, this would happen again and again. I'd end up being the death of her, and that was if she survived this time. I wouldn't let that loyalty be used against her, even if she was the one insisting on her own demise.

CHAPTER 39

R*iver*

I stretched the stiffness out of my arms, sitting up in Dante's bed. The last time this happened, I'd woken to Dante in a chair beside my bed. This time I was alone.

"You're awake! Oh thank God!" Henrietta rushed across the room, laying a hand on my forehead. "You feel warm again." She put both hands on my head, then my arms, as if she wanted to see if I was only partially thawed.

"Is everyone okay?" I asked, then grabbed the glass of water she had waiting and gulped it down. It felt like I hadn't had a drink in forever.

She sat down, taking my hand and smiling. "Not even a nick on any of them."

"How long was I out for?" It couldn't have been too short a time. I was dying of thirst.

"Three days."

Three? No wonder I felt like this.

"Don't worry. I told everyone you had the flu. Since we don't get that, nobody really knows what's normal. They didn't think anything of you disappearing or being half dead." She got to her feet, feeling my head again, as if I'd start to freeze at any moment. "Are you hungry? I'll make you something to eat. I have to go call Dante too. He wanted to know as soon as you woke."

The knot that had formed as soon as I didn't see him untangled in my stomach. He couldn't be that upset that I'd butted in. I had been out of it for three days; expecting him to sit around here for all that time would be insane. He had a pack to care for. It wasn't like he'd abandoned me. He'd had Henrietta watching over me.

"That would be great. I'm starving. I'm going to have a quick shower first." I got up, feeling stiffer than I had in a long time.

"Go ahead! Lunch will be waiting when you come out." She grabbed me in a tight hug that continued on for a good minute. "We owe you such a debt." She wasn't letting go, squeezing me so tight that my joints were making clicking noises.

"I'm just happy everyone is okay," I said, trying to get air past her squeezing arms.

By the time I came out of the shower, my hair lying damp on my sweater, there was a steaming plate of eggs on the table. Henrietta was gone, but Dante was waiting for me near the table.

"Hi," I said, feeling shy, like I didn't know how to speak. I'd been fighting with him for a month, and now, because I'd nearly lost it when I thought he was dying, my brain could barely form words.

"Hey." He eyed me up and down, as if some hidden injury might suddenly appear or one of my arms was going to spontaneously fall off. "How are you feeling?"

"Good. It's over. Everything's back to normal." Or mostly. I was well and alive. Life went on, even if he was looking at me like it wouldn't.

As we stood staring at each other in silence, it was clear something had shifted. He wasn't mad, but this wasn't how a happy man looked. This was the appearance of someone resigned to bad news. I took a seat at the table and toyed with the eggs, my appetite not what it had been a few minutes ago.

"What was the cost?" he asked, gripping the counter. The tendons in his arms strung so tight they looked like they might snap.

"Whatever it was, I paid it. It's done and over. There's no need to talk about it."

When I'd been in my rush to help, I hadn't thought about praise or gratitude. It hadn't entered my mind. But if I had thought about the possible reactions I'd get, this definitely wasn't what I'd have imagined. It was as if he had this anger or disappointment lingering under the surface, as if I'd done something horribly wrong instead of saving him.

"You're right. What's done is done. That's not why I wanted to talk to you." He hadn't moved from his spot. He was barely moving at all.

I thought he'd come to see if I was okay, but that delusion was clearing up fast. I'd saved him at a cost to my life and had a sinking feeling that repayment wouldn't be to my taste.

He was looking toward the windows as he said, "Heiko is dead. I'm letting you go. Frankie is going to make the arrangements."

As I feared, I'd saved his life and he was kicking me in the ass on my way out the door. Instead of being crushed, I felt fury fill my veins. Sorrow might come later, but the betrayal was too thick right now to elicit anything but cold rage.

"When?" I dropped my fork onto my plate.

"I think sooner is better."

"Because of what I did? Did you not like the way it was executed?" I asked, not even trying to cover my disgust. I'd given up some of my life for him, and this was what I got?

"It's for the best."

"Yes, I agree." I shoved the food away from me, getting up.

"I'm doing this for you." Grittiness broke the calm of his voice, as if his inner beast was trying to come to the surface.

"Yes, you're very good at dictating what I should be doing." I turned to leave, afraid of what I might do or say if I didn't. He wanted me gone? I'd been trying to go for a month. He didn't need to tell me twice.

"You're upset right now, but it's for the best," he said. I wasn't sure who he was trying to convince.

"Yes, of course. You know it all, don't you? You think everything is your choice? Well, guess what—there's a whole universe just waiting to fuck you up. So you go ahead and think you can control it all, and I'll go on living in reality."

I went to my room and shut the door before he could say anything else. The door to the house sounded seconds later. I didn't waste any time shoving stuff in my bag. Screw him. I didn't need his help. I'd leave on my own. I'd rather walk out of these gates than take anything else from him.

There was a knock at my door.

"River?" Henrietta asked.

I wiped my face with my sleeve before saying, "Come in."

"You didn't eat your... Are you okay?" She looked at the bag I was packing. "What's going on? I saw Dante leaving, and he didn't look good either."

My hands froze on the bag as I sat on the floor next to it. "Dante very politely kicked me out." Saying the words made my chest tight and my eyes burn. It was nearly as bad as hearing them.

"He said you had to leave?" she asked.

"Yes. He offered me arrangements, but I don't want them." I took a deep breath, and then another, before forcing myself into action again. I grabbed the warmest wool socks I had and pulled out the hiking boots Henrietta had given me.

She followed me around the room, looking like she wanted to grab the items out of my hands and put them back. "He's scared. He doesn't want this. He was devastated when he got back and you were sick."

"So torn up he could barely wait to give me the boot." I shoved some more socks in my bag.

"Just stay. He's not going to force you to leave. Things will get better. I know it. He's afraid you'll keep risking yourself for the pack until there's nothing left of you."

She looked like she was ready to fight to the death to get me to stay. But she wasn't the person I needed to step up and fight for me. That person was telling me to leave.

I sat on the ground again, beside my bag and boots. "I *can't*. You don't understand." I took another deep breath, shaking as I did, before looking up at her. I didn't bother trying to hide the tears that were falling down my face. "I love him. I don't know how it happened. I don't want to, but I do. So you see, that's why I can't stay. He's been pushing me away from the minute I got here. I don't want to fight for someone who won't fight for me. He wants me gone? Then I'm ready to leave."

She dropped onto the ground beside me and wrapped an arm around my slumped shoulders. "Then let me help you leave like I offered you a while ago. Let me know you got away safely in case this place is still being watched. Let me do this for you if for no other reason than you saved so many people I care about."

I nodded, afraid if I said another word I'd break down so badly that I'd lie on the floor crying for hours. I needed time to regroup, but first I had to get out of here.

* * *

Dante

River should have the cabin to herself while she was still here. It would only make it more difficult if we both stayed there until she left. There were plenty of other places I could crash. It was better if she left hating me. It might hurt now, but it would be easier for her to move on.

Frankie was walking from the cabin as I neared the area.

"Did you talk to her?" Frankie would handle the logistics. He'd make sure every detail, from how she got there, to where she'd go, was lined up as safe as possible. I'd told him to push her to get as far away from here as possible. Maybe she would want to go somewhere in Europe. There were countries there that had almost no species that would pick up on her unusual traits. Maybe I should make that one of the requirements. This was too important not to be involved in. Her being safe was the only thing about this situation that felt right.

"I went to find out where she wanted to go, like you asked, but she wasn't there. Was coming to find you to see if she was crashing somewhere else."

She'd left the cabin on her own, not that I blamed her.

"She's probably with Henrietta." I stared off in that direction, having a hard time suppressing the urge to go there now. The idea of River leaving here, not having a final few moments with her, made me want to rip something apart. Plus, this might be too important for Frankie to handle at all. I should be the one to see her off.

"Does she really need to go?" Frankie asked. "Almost no one wants her to leave. Everyone feels like she's part of the pack."

Of course they did. How could they not want to keep her around? And they didn't even know what she'd sacrificed for them, and for me.

"It's better for her."

"Because of what she is? Jobo didn't tell me much, but I put the pieces together and know she saved our asses somehow. That thing didn't just blow like that. Something, somehow, shifted." He looked at me as if I didn't fully understand her value. He had no idea.

"That's why she has to go," I said.

He shoved his hands in his pockets. "That sucks, but I get it." He kicked the ground and then looked around for a few moments, as if dreading what was to come. "I'll head over there now."

He turned in that direction.

"No. I'll talk to her." The betrayal I saw on her face had been haunting me all day. I couldn't let her leave without talking to her one last time. She'd realize this was for the best. She was too logical not to.

"Yeah, okay."

I left Frankie and headed toward Henrietta's place. I was about to let myself in when she opened the door, her mouth in a straight line, her eyes accusing. She stepped back, letting me in and then crossing her arms.

"Is she here?" I asked. It would make sense River would rather stay at Henrietta's, even if she was sleeping on the couch.

"You had to push her away, didn't you? What's wrong? You like this one too much?" Henrietta shoved me. My aunt had never hit me before in my life—she hated violence—but she looked like she was on the verge of shifting and brawling with me.

I breathed in deeply, determined to get my answers without her help. River's scent wasn't here. I walked in farther, taking a deeper breath and still not picking up her unique smell.

I spun toward Henrietta. "She's not at the cabin and she's not here. Where is she? I know you know."

"She left today. She told me what happened and didn't want to stay another night." She scratched at her arms, flinching as if she was using all her strength to suppress her inner beast.

River had left. I'd pushed too hard. I'd forced her from the only safety for miles and miles. The thought she was out there alone felt like someone was fileting my insides. What the fuck had I done?

"Where? Do you know where?" I crossed the room, ready to shake the details out of my aunt.

"Why does it matter to you? You don't care, right?" She shrugged, never one to be bulldozed.

I'd never wanted to kill my aunt until this moment. I still wouldn't, but the urge was there.

"This isn't the time to hold out. She's out there, with no one to help her. What if she was followed? Even though Heiko is dead, you know the vampires watch us. This isn't the time for lectures."

"She wasn't tracked. I drove her and dropped her off," she said, walking into her kitchen.

I followed her. "Where?"

"Why would I tell you?" she said. "So you can drag her back until she goes somewhere you deem okay? You don't get to do that. When you push someone away, they're gone. That's how life works." She was straightening her kitchen while I was ready to climb the walls.

"You don't understand. I can't let her stay. It'll cost her too much."

She spun, putting her hands on her hips. "It's *her* choice. *Hers*. Not yours."

"I won't do that to her, but I can't just let her leave and not know she's okay."

"Why?" She shoved me again. "Tell me why!" she yelled.

"I love her. There. Are you happy? Will you tell me now?" I was nearly screaming back, at my wits' end with her.

"Then why make her leave?"

Did she not understand anything? She was acting like I wanted River gone when the idea was ripping me apart. I couldn't think of anything but her, where she'd go, how she'd be.

"Because if she stays, it'll kill her. Do you want that? Don't you get it? I'd die for her."

I braced my hands on her counter, dropping my head, feeling rawer than I thought possible.

My aunt moved closer, resting her hand on my shoulder. "She's at our safe house a few towns over on the border of Elm Reservation. She's got keys to the car there, and I gave her a stack of cash."

"Thank you."

"What are you going to do?" she asked.

"I don't know. Make sure she's safe? Whatever I can."

CHAPTER 40

R *iver*

I settled into the small house that would serve as my home for the night. Henrietta had insisted on leaving me with a stack of cash and the keys to the car outside. The destination for tomorrow was unclear, but I also had maps to help me decide. Maybe I'd just drive in the direction of the strange feeling of my people that tugged on me, growing stronger and stronger. I didn't know who was near, but when I gave Henrietta a direction, that was how I'd chosen.

A flash of warmth shot through me again, like it had before, but it was stronger this time, the strongest it had ever been. What did that mean? How close were they? What I would give to have one of my kind. I'd ignored them when I was younger, not wanting to hear all the things that they'd wanted to teach me, and now all I did was crave a snippet of that information. Maybe their pull felt stronger tonight because after being with the pack, the loneliness was even starker. My psyche was clinging to some connection, hoping that there were people out there that I belonged with.

Maybe I'd keep heading in that direction. There was nowhere else pressing to go and nothing but time on my hands. My future was wide open, which should've made me happy. It might in time, once I could get *him* out of my mind.

I went to the window of the small house, pulling back the drapes. Instead of seeing one of my kind, I saw Dante striding up the drive.

I swung open the door, letting it slam against the wall, and walked out onto the stoop. I squared my shoulders, ready for whatever he might throw at me.

"Why are you here? You wanted me to leave; I left. If it's about me using this place, don't worry. I'll be gone in the morning."

"I didn't come here for that." Instead of harshness, there was relief as his gaze ran the length of me.

"What, then? You want to talk? I'm not interested in any more of your discussions."

I'd already replayed his asking me to leave. How many ways did he need to say it? Was he here to get a last kick in? Until the last shred of pride I had was lying shriveled up in the gutter, along with my common sense?

"Where do you plan on going?" he asked, walking closer but stopping as I backed up.

"It doesn't matter. I'm asking you to leave me be." He didn't have the right to ask me anything.

"I'll help you go wherever it is you want."

"You aren't getting it. I don't want help from you." Something faltered in his gaze. Of all the things I could've said, I'd hit on something that might have hurt. Maybe he did care—a little, anyway.

"River, I can't leave you here alone. I know what can happen."

"You mean like I could get held hostage somewhere? That sort of thing?" This conversation wasn't helping anything. I'd give myself a few seconds more to look at him, breathe in his scent, before I walked back inside and shut the door. I'd exit with as much dignity as I could summon, as if this wasn't taking me apart a little piece at a time. If I'd known how bad it would hurt to leave, I would've escaped way back when Henrietta first offered to help me.

"I know you don't understand, but I was trying to do the right thing. Maybe I handled it wrong, but my intentions were good. I don't want to hurt you, of all people." He walked toward me, as if he couldn't stop himself.

"Why? We're nothing. It doesn't matter what you do." I took another step back, knowing I shouldn't be talking to him. The more he said, the more hurt it would bring.

"That's not true, and we both know it."

I wanted to cry almost as much as I had right before I left. This time I couldn't. If I showed weakness, I was done. He'd given me a harsh reminder of what I was worth on several occasions. I'd gotten soft, for the first time in a while, and I wasn't going to let it happen again.

"If you're here to tell me how you want me now, it's not going to work. You've spent too much time and energy reminding me and everyone else that I wasn't part of the pack to change my mind," I said. I walked into the house, grabbing the door but still hesitating.

He was on the stoop, holding the door open so I couldn't shut him out yet. "I'm not trying to convince you to come back. I still think leaving is the best thing for you, but not because any part of me wants you to go." He took another step, slowly closing the gap between us.

I should walk away, refuse to hear him, but the pain coursing through me was reflected in his eyes.

"I never should've kept you to begin with. Even then, it was for me. I couldn't seem to let you go," he said. "I wanted you from the second I saw you. But I'm in a war. There's already a target on my back. They'll follow me, and if you're with me, you as well. Knowing what you are, what might happen if you stay, what's already happened..." He gripped the edge of the door, as if trying to keep himself from touching me. "You let yourself be used by me."

"I wasn't used. I did it willingly and would make the same choice again." And again, until it took everything from me.

He leaned slowly toward me until his shirt nearly brushed mine.

I couldn't step away from what I saw in his eyes.

He cupped my face. "That's why you have to leave. You have to let me help you get somewhere safe. I can't watch someone I love die because of me."

I tilted my head back, not able to tear my eyes from his. "I can't let someone I love die if I can stop it."

"I'd give you forever if I had it to give."

I leaned into him. "Then give me tonight."

He pulled me into the house and closed the door, wrapping his arms around me,

"When this ends, I'll find you," he said.

"Will it ever end?" I curled my arms around his neck, knowing this would be the last time I'd see him. I'd leave on my own in the morning.

"I'll kill every vampire there is if I have to." Dante smoothed a hand through my hair, pulling me closer.

It would never happen. This war between them might span more decades than either of us lived. I'd have to grow old being satisfied that I'd loved with all my heart.

"I don't want you to wait for me, though," he said. "If you meet a good man, a nice, quiet one who doesn't get himself into trouble, if you could actually love such a boring creature, I want you to try to be happy."

I forced a laugh as I held back tears. "And if for some reason you stumble upon some horribly wicked girl you think you could be with, then you should do the same." Those words felt like razor blades slicing me as I spoke, but it was true. Thinking of him alone was more painful. I wanted to imagine him being happy and fulfilled.

I jerked upright and froze. With everything going on, with my emotions so scattered in every direction, the feeling I'd pushed to the side had somehow snuck up on me.

"What's wrong?" Dante asked.

"There's someone coming," I said, pulling away.

"Who? I don't hear anyone."

"One of my people. I can feel them."

"How would they find you here?"

"We can feel each other, but it's not an exact science. It's this weird thing that's hard to explain," I said, scrambling back to the door.

"Would others of your kind seek you out?" he asked, following me.

"I was thinking of seeking them out if that means anything." I moved to the window, and he pulled me back.

"It might be a trap," he said, moving to the window. "Well, whoever you felt, they're here. And there's something weird about them."

I pushed him out of the way to get a look for myself.

A woman appeared on the stoop. Her coloring was totally different than mine, her hair almost black and eyes nearly silver, but I knew exactly what he meant. Her eyes had a glow that dominated her face. There was a dewiness to her skin that reminded me of myself and the family I'd lost.

"Hang on, don't go charging out the door. There might be others waiting," Dante said, scanning the yard in front of the cabin and down the drive, past the approaching stranger.

I swung the door open anyway. I didn't need anyone to tell me that she was here in good faith.

"Hello," she said. "I'm Rowan." She looked at Dante, who was looming behind me, for a split second. If he scared her at all, she didn't show it.

"I'm River. Come in," I said, opening the door wide and bumping my back into Dante so he was forced to give her space.

She walked in, barely sparing the place a glance. "You look healthy." She sounded relieved. "I could feel you growing weaker for a while. There was a little slip when I lost your signal, and I got scared. Were you ill?"

"I used my gift to save friends and loved ones"––I darted a glance at Dante––"but it was my choice. I'm fine now." I didn't want this stranger placing blame anywhere but where it belonged. Me.

"Then this is a good place?" she said, looking at the house and Dante. "When I first started sensing you, you felt at a greater distance, but here you are." She spun, looking at the house as if this was home.

"I was farther away. I only came here yesterday." I remembered the first time I'd sensed another of my kind while working in the kitchen back at the pack head-quarters.

"So you left the good place? The safe place?" she asked, squinting. "Why did you leave? Why wouldn't you stay? This is not good. Not good at all. You *have* to go back.

More of us are coming. I could feel them growing as I traveled."

"What do you mean more are coming?"

She grabbed my hands, smiling. "Yes. We have to go back to the safe place. We need to be there when they arrive to welcome them. We don't have any time to waste and must leave now."

"But I..."

Rowan was so set, her focus on what had to be done so strong, that it was hard to tell her the safe place she'd been heading for wasn't a possibility.

Dante stepped closer. "She can't go back there. I don't want her to be hurt or die doing what she did again to save me. There's conflict coming. I'm sorry, but it's not the place for your kind to be safe."

She shook her head. "But there are more coming. She'll be fine. That's why we need to go there." She glared at him as if he were an idiot. I wasn't sure I'd ever seen someone speak to him like that, other than me.

He stared at her, obviously not sure what to do.

"What do you mean, *I'll be fine?*" I asked.

"Did no one ever teach you about your people? How did this happen?" She frowned, moving closer to me and ignoring Dante, who seemed to annoy her. "Numbers shield us. We were meant to live in clans. Our energy feeds off one another. It wasn't until we were pulled apart by greedy rulers that we began to die off." She gave Dante a pointed stare as she said, "And I don't want to go anywhere else. There's nowhere safe for us. Word is spreading of our kind again. If you have found a place where we can be safe, then we have to go to the good place or we'll die."

Dante stepped closer. "You're saying that the more of your kind who come, the safer she'll be? That it'll make her stronger? That if she uses her gift to save me and my pack, it won't deplete her?"

"That's exactly what I'm saying. We're meant to live in a clan. We have to live in clans in order to have the life we're supposed to live. Having a community of our kind will strengthen us. Now we need to go."

"If you're saying that having her kind around will strengthen her, then every one of you are welcome." Dante smiled as though he'd received the best gift in the world.

"That's wonderful!" She threw back her head and laughed in a lilting tone. "With the ones on the move here now, hopefully there will be enough of us that we can be whole and healthy."

"Wait here," Dante said to Rowan. "Do not leave."

Dante was looking at her like her life depended on being in that same spot when he came back. He grabbed my hand, tugging me after him into the bedroom.

"Are you positive you really want me to stay? Even if it means taking in more Luck Charmers and whatever grief that might entail?" I wouldn't survive if he changed his mind in a few days, or a few weeks.

He lifted me, and I wrapped my arms around his neck.

"It took me a while to realize how much I wanted you, loved you, and I made some very bad choices along the way. But there is no way I'm letting you leave now. I'll take all the luck I can get, good, bad, blond, brunette, whatever shows up, as long as it means I get to keep you with me. I'll never let you go."

His lips collided with mine, and I swore, in that moment, I'd never let go.

EPILOGUE

R *iver*

"You really want to stay here? You don't want to move to one of the larger houses?" Dante asked, his fingers weaved in mine where they laid on his chest.

We'd only officially been with each other a week, and we'd already fallen into a routine of lying on the couch in front of the fire every night after dinner. There wasn't a spot that existed that was better than this.

I looked around the place, the wood walls, the homey chair I liked to read in, the kitchen table we ate breakfast at. Nope. This place was perfect, and he wasn't getting me out of here unless it burned to ashes.

"No. It took me long enough to be allowed to stay. I'm not leaving," I said.

He squeezed my side. "We might at some point, depending on how things go. If it can even happen for us. I'm not sure if a shifter and a Luck Charmer can conceive but you never know. Unless that's something you don't want?"

Babies? I'd never been secure enough to imagine having babies.

"You'd want that?" I asked, feeling out the idea, wondering what it would be like to have little Dantes running around.

"I want as much of you as I can get, and if there's a way to make more of you, I want that too."

He kissed my head. He did that a lot now.

"And if it's not be possible, are you going to be okay with that?"

"If it isn't, there's other ways to do it, if that's what we want. The only deal breaker for me is you trying to leave. Everything else is a bonus." He ran his hand through my hair, toying with a lock.

A loud banging sounded on the porch, and we both turned our gazes in that direction.

"Although even if we don't have kids, we might still need more room," Dante said. "Especially if the rest of them have this need to be close to you like this one does."

Rowan did seem to have a thing for togetherness, but Dante couldn't understand what it was like not having your people and then discovering them. He'd always had people.

Rowan had moved into my bedroom the night she arrived, and I'd moved into Dante's. Sending her off to stay with someone else after the journey she'd taken to get here wasn't something I was ready to do. Even though we were strangers, there was a connection from being among the few left of our race.

"You don't understand. It's like being a loner and then discovering you had a pack all this time. As more come, she'll want to move out...eventually."

"Yeah, or they'll all want to move in here with you." Dante's chest rumbled under my cheek, and I lifted my head.

"She's not going to want to be with us forever. She'll get bored." She would eventually want to have a place of her own anyway. I mean, *probably*.

"If you say so."

The door swung open and Rowan entered, trying to drag a tree in with her, tip first.

"Hey, guys! Look what I got!" Rowan was smiling down at her accomplishment as she battled to get the tree over the threshold.

Dante got up. "I'm guessing you want this inside?" he asked, without a hint of enthusiasm in his voice.

"Yes. It's a gift for you two. I thought it would look great next to the fireplace." She jumped up and moved to the spot. "Right here."

"But it's not even December yet. It might die before Christmas," I said.

"Oh, I didn't kill the tree. I had the guys help me dig up the roots. This way, after the holidays we can replant it. It's just a visitor, and then it will go back home to the forest."

I stuck my head out the door and saw the wrapped root ball. Guess she was serious about this plan.

Dante dragged it inside and propped the tree against the wall, where we all stared at it.

I didn't know all of Rowan's story, but she'd said enough for me to know it hadn't been easy. And yet here she was, recently transplanted, surrounded by strangers and happy for everything she received.

"I think this would be a great tradition. Every year we can get a new tree and then replant it," Rowan said, staring at the tree in awe, as if she'd never had one before, which she might not have.

Dante smiled. "Yeah, that sounds great." He snuck a look at me and raised his brows.

Yeah, maybe she *wasn't* leaving.

"I'll be back. Henrietta said she had some ornaments for me." Rowan was on the move again. The girl definitely didn't like standing still for long.

"So eventually we might need a bigger place," I said.

Dante tossed me over his shoulder and walked us into our room.

"What are you doing?" I asked, laughing because I already knew.

"Going to enjoy our privacy for all of the twenty minutes we get."

I loved this man, not only because he loved me, but because he loved me so much he was willing to take everything and everyone who came with me.

To be notified of new releases you can text **Augustine** *to 22828. Don't worry! I won't flood your email box. You're more likely to wonder if you signed up correctly. Two emails in one month is my record.*

Or, follow me on one of these platforms:
https://www.facebook.com/groups/223180598486878/
http://www.donnaaugustine.com
https://www.bookbub.com/authors/donna-augustine
https://twitter.com/DonnAugustine

ACKNOWLEDGMENTS

There are some people who have stuck with me, book after book. I don't think I'd have the confidence to publish without each of these people's stamp of approval. Donna Z., Lori H., Camillia J. and Ashleigh Macleod, I'm forever grateful!

A special thanks to Arran and Editing 720.

ALSO BY DONNA AUGUSTINE

Ollie Wit

A Step into the Dark

Walking in the Dark

Kissed by the Dark

The Keepers

The Keepers

Keepers and Killers

Shattered

Redemption

Karma

Karma

Jinxed

Fated

Dead Ink

The Wilds

The Wilds

The Hunt

The Dead

The Magic

Born Wild (Wilds Spinoff)

Wild One

Savage One

Made in the USA
Las Vegas, NV
26 February 2022

39817R00168